Project: Q-29

A Novel By:

David Robert Mohr

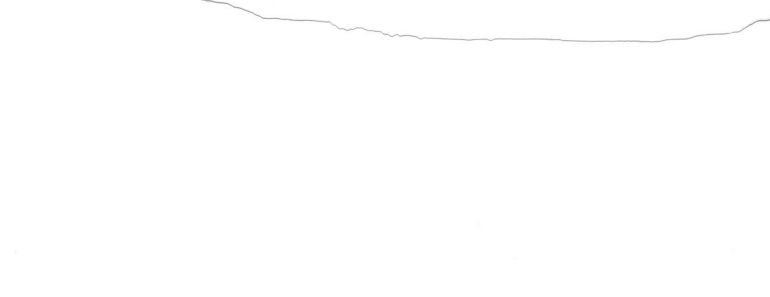

Dedicated to my son Micah.
I always wish you all the best!

<u>Chapter I</u>

"How long has it been here?" asks Sheriff Marshall Winston, a real gentleman who is aging gracefully.

Marshall has been with the force for some twenty-seven years. After his training, he became an officer in his small hometown of Lutts, Tennessee. He received much of his experience from the then well-seasoned sheriff of the county, and was determined to be as good as he was. Following in the footsteps of that sheriff, his father figure, Marshall left the small town and headed for the city. He saw many years of action, brutality and acts of inhuman cruelty so bizarre, he still shudders on occasion. Now in his mid-sixties, Marshall has returned to his hometown. Becoming sheriff meant a lot to him. He always kept in touch with the only 'father' he had ever known. In becoming sheriff of Wayne County, he felt he closed the circle. He was able to use the gift given to him. He came back to his roots, and now he will be able to pass along this "gift" to someone else. He can still remember the proud look on the face of his dear friend. That smile of approval, the thankfulness of knowing how he helped young Marshall. Never really knowing his own father, Marshall will never forget "Gypsy Bob", a man his real father would never be.

Marshall has just come from Gypsy Bob's grave, where he visits regularly. The thought of someone else possibly having lost a dear loved one, causes his crushed spirit to sink deeper into that lonely place within his soul. He knows the loss of a loved one. Now, as the year of 1998 comes to a close, he feels someone else is going to know that pain.

"'Bout three days," answers Mike.

Mike Toggle, a man in his forties with jet black hair and glasses to match. Right down to his pocket protector, the same one he had in high school, he is what everyone would call the typical "Geek." The kind of guy who was always picked on and who always ended up in a position of power - in this case Manager of a local Supermarket in Collinwood. The type of guy who always lets you know he is the boss, requiring you to put up with his stupid ideas or be fired. He is liked by few. Mike had called the sheriff to have a car towed.

"I don't want this car here taking up my valuable space where paying customers could be parking. I have a right to have this car removed you know. I'm manager of this store and it's my..."

"I get the picture, Mike. I don't need a complete dissertation about your history nor your legal rights," interrupts Marshall, in his soothing, yet authoritative, southern voice. "Let me call it in and see if there has been any reports about stolen vehicles and we'll see what we can do."

"I know what you can do, you can have it towed down to the impound..."

Marshall walks away while Mike is babbling and gets into his patrol car.

"...yard and keep it there..," Mike rambles on while following Marshall. "...until somebody claims........hey!"

Marshall rolls up his window to get some privacy.

"This is Sheriff Winston, Suzie you there?"

Marshall's patrol car is, as usual, immaculate. He keeps it clean. He says, "I've had enough dirt in my life from the city. I want everything spotless from now on!"

"This is Marshall. Suzie do you read me?"

Still no answer. When Suzie doesn't answer it usually means she is preoccupied; and unless one of the officers calls with a priority one call, she will not leave what she is doing to answer the radio.

Marshall decides to examine the car, and its surrounding area, for any clues while waiting for Suzie to finish up whatever she had gotten herself into.

"You know, that was not very nice of you, I was right in the middle of a sentence and you just cut me off," babbles Mike. "You're a public servant ya know and you're supposed to be nice to people.

You're supposed to help people and do what's necessary to keep the peace. That wasn't a very peaceable thing you did. You should..."

"You know Mike, a lot of people would be less hostile towards cops if I were to shoot you dead right now," Marshall butts in.

Mike "clams up" in shock.

"In fact, I'd probably get an award. I imagine most of the town's people would be downright grateful to me," Marshall continues. "People in this town have been getting more and more hostile ever since you moved in. My theory is this: 'If you no longer existed, this town would become the peaceful haven it once was.' So maybe you're right. Maybe I haven't been doin' my job. Hmmm, lesssee. You said I'm supposed to do what's necessary to keep the peace. Well in my humble opinion, this is very necessary."

Marshall slides his .357 magnum from its holster and points it at Mike's head. Gasping, Mike's face grows pasty and his eyes open as wide as saucers. With his mouth agape, his pearly white protruding teeth glistened in the sunlight. As Marshall cocks back the hammer of his gun, Mike starts screaming as loud as his squeaky, raspy voice will allow.

Marshall can't help but chuckle while shaking his head as Mike turns and runs toward the store. Putting his gun away, he notices a small yellow puddle of water where Mike had been standing. Again he laughs.

"Thanks Clint. You were right about the .357."

Looking around the car, nothing appears abnormal. Whomever was driving pulled in with no problems. They were even within the bright white lines, front tires right up against the curb...good driver who ever they are. Beautiful car, too: a bright, little red 1972 Corvette. The kind of car kids dream about, and thieves steal. The doors are locked so Marshall looks in through the windshield. The side windows are tinted so dark he can't see through them. The car looks normal. No obvious signs of a struggle nor foul play. Marshall presumes the car to have been stolen and left here to be picked up. Marshall's eyes slowly open wide as he cocks his head to one side.

"This don't make sense," he mumbles aloud, then dashes back to his patrol car. "Suzie," he shouts grabbing the radio's microphone, "9 1 1. This is Sheriff Winston. I need you now!"

Chapter II

"Oh my!" says Suzie jumping up from her task. Her eyes pop open, as if she has just been caught snooping through someone's desk. "I've got to get that, and now!"

Suzie is a sweet gal in her mid-twenties and full of life. The type of girl who doesn't really get much done at the office, but she's just so nice and kind and tries to be helpful, that you just can't let her go. Everybody likes Suzie. Everyone always has a kind word about her. The mere mention of her name brings a smile to the face of all who ever met her. With a soft smooth complexion and big beautiful eyes, she can soften the heart of even the wildest beast. If she was as devoted to any man as much as she is devoted to her pastries, she would never have any time to herself. Her normally bubbly voice turns to nervousness as she frantically tries to wipe the cookie dough from her hands to answer the radio.

"I'm coming! I'm coming! Oh! Hang on I'm coming!" she shouts to the radio, as she stumbles across the room.

"Suzie, get your hands out of the batter and answer me. This is important. And Suzie, you know I can't hear you." Marshall, like most everyone, knows

Suzie well.

"OH! I'm sorry sheriff. I was just in the middle of making your favorite chocolate peanut butter cookies. What's the problem?"

"Mmmmm," he says smacking his lips. "Can't wait! Hey Suzie, I need you to run a check on this plate for me. We've got a strange situation on our hands. I think we may have a really warped individual out here. It's still too soon to tell, but I already don't like what I see."

"Sure thing Marshall," she says licking her fingers and grabbing a pencil. "What's the number?"

"Baker five Charlie four seven nine."

"Baker five Charlie four seven nine. Got it. Is that a Tennessee plate?" asks Suzie.

"Sorry darlin', yeah it is. It's from Lawrence county. Oh and Suzie, wipe your hands CLEAN this time before you use the computer. Thank you darlin'. Rich, you out there?"

Morris Richard Laverton, deputy. He is Marshall's progeny and next in line to become sheriff of Wayne County. Richard, or Rich as he prefers to be called, has followed in Marshall's footsteps, though not to the degree in which Marshall followed "Gypsy Bob's." Richard stands at 6'2" with brown-blonde hair and a thick mustache that is always neatly groomed and never hangs over his upper lip. A thinking man by any right, but also a man of action. Having moved in from Chicago, he enjoys being able to help people and the community without having to have his life on the line as fiercely as it was when he was with the Chicago force. After being grazed by bullets, twice while on duty and three times when off, he decided to move his wife and three kids to greener pastures. His crystal blue eyes have finally begun to pale the scar from the bullet which almost took his life. Part of his eyebrow still missing, never to grow back.

"I'm here."

"I want you to come over here to the Supermarket and check something out. I've got a really bad feeling about what I see here, and I want your help."

"Whatcha got?"

"Well nothing concrete yet. I'll talk to ya when you get here, and bring that Slim-Jim of yours with ya too. I wanna get inside a car here."

"10-4 sheriff. I'll be there in around fifteen minutes."

Marshall starts with the mandatory paper work, looking up occasionally in thought, only to return to the clipboard to fill in more spaces. From the corner of his eye he is able to see Mike sneaking out of the store towards his car, which is conveniently parked in the closest space to the front door.

"What's the purpose of..," he thinks out loud, contemplating what he saw through the car's windshield. Shaking his head and biting his pen, he returns his thoughts to the paperwork in front of him. His silence is interrupted.

"Sheriff, this is Suzie. Do you read me?" Her voice more concerned than usual.

Around here the typical crimes are usually shop-lifting, domestic quarrels, friends getting drunk and out of hand - the usual small town stuff "stereo types" are made of. Suzie didn't like what she had to tell the sheriff.

"Go ahead Suzie." Marshall pauses for a brief moment. "You awright?" He notices the uneasiness in her voice.

"I'll be okay. I didn't mean to be so obvious," says Suzie, as she tries to regain her composure and recreate that "Professional" police dispatcher air about her. "I got a make on that plate."

"Okay Darlin', catch your breath and tell me whacha found," Marshall says in as soothing a voice as he can. Marshall is beginning to feel the concern of his first instincts. He is sure there is a murder on his hands, and from what he has seen so far, it is not going to stop after this one.

"The car belongs to Carey Warjill. The car has not been reported as stolen nor missing. I called Carey's house. His wife, Anastasia, answered. She is very worried. She had called the police to report her husband missing. She said he had been missing for three days. He left to go visit some friends and was supposed to be back in four to five hours. When he didn't come home that night, she figured him and his buddies got drunk and fell down somewhere and that he would be back the next day. He has not called, nor come home, and that is not like him, according to Carey's wife. Sheriff, do you think..,"

Suzie can no longer speak. She has been dispatching here for three years now and has never had to deal with anything like this.

"Calm down Suzie. We don't have enough evidence to think anything yet," is the sheriff's reply. "Hey, he might be just lost in the woods and probably still drunk."

"Okay sheriff. I've got Anastasia's phone number if you need it. I'll be right here if you need me. Thank you for trying." Suzie knows what Marshall is thinking. Though he is trying to comfort her, he is not a good liar. She knows he is thinking the worst.

A look of deep concern falls over Marshall's face mixed with a look of pity and sadness for Carey's widow. He knows in his gut that Carey is gone. Now it is just a matter of finding the body and the killer.

"Suzie, get me somebody from the lab. I want this car checked inside and out. Finger prints, hair samples, the works."

"10-4 Sheriff," is the only reply back over the radio. Suzie is scared.

Rich pulls into the lot and sees Mike, the store's manager, walking back towards the store. Mike is wearing a fresh change of clothes. Rich's car angles upward as he comes in the steep driveway.

"Excuse me!" yells Rich, "Where in the parking lot is Sheriff Marshall?"

The lot has filled up with shoppers and the other police vehicle is not easily seen.

"Yeah I'll tell you where he is. He's down five isles near the middle of the isle. I want that car outta there, it's in a good spot ya know." Mike banters on: "You know what that crazy sheriff did? I'll tell you what he did, he threatened to shoot me. He said he was going to shoot me dead. He's crazy you know. I think he should be locked up."

"Oh come now Mike. I think you must have misunderstood him."

"Misunderstood nothing! He pointed that gun right at my head!" Mike blurts in excitedly, "I don't think I mistanded, stooded, misunderstood...I...I didn't misunderstand him!!! He threatened me!!!"

"Let me assure you Mike. You must have misunderstood him. You see, Marshall isn't that type of person..."

"Yes he did, he threatened me," Mike interrupts.

"No, no. You misunderstood. Marshall doesn't

make threats. At least, not idle, threats," Rich says calmly as he releases the brake and drives slowly away; leaving Mike standing there with his hands on his knees and that same expression on his face as when Marshall had pulled the gun.

Reaching Marshall, Rich gets out of his car and gets the Slim-Jim. Walking over to Marshall and handing him the tool, Rich says with a smile and a slight laugh: "You really pull your gun on Mike?"

"Oh come on Rich. Would I do something like that?" retorts Marshall with the boyish grin of a teenager who is trying to get away with something.

"To anyone else, no," he says with a slight laugh. "I wouldn't be surprised if you cocked the hammer back and fired a shot passed his ears," smirks Rich with a note of jealousy in his voice. "I heard Suzie. Do you think we'll be looking for a body, or..," Rich stops abruptly. He remembers all the bodies he had to deal with back in Chicago. He definitely is not looking forward to finding another one. "Maybe he really is lost in the woods. If he got drunk enough, him and his buddies can be out there somewhere still." Rich is trying to convince himself. He wanted to leave this type of police work behind. That's why he came out here. "My God!" he is thinking. "Did it follow me here?"

"Sorry Rich. I believe we definitely have a murder here," says Marshall as he pops open the Corvette's lock. "I don't like the looks of this."

Rich moves to the front window to get a look inside.

"I don't see anything unusual in there."

"W-P-X-C-1-O-3 point 3 your only place for all your favorite...."

"The radio?" asks Rich with a puzzled, disturbed look on his face.

Unlocking the other door, Marshall tells Richard to take a look inside. Stooping down, Rich can see what Marshall had been eluding to, or so he thought. The ignition key is still on. The car was never turned off. It had run out of gas.

"I didn't notice the ignition switch from the front window. How did you see it?" questions Rich.

"I didn't. But that only convinces me more."

"Then what did you see? Everything looks normal. I do agree that something is awry, but a lot of people leave the car running and dash into the store. Especially if they're just going in for a six pack or something."

"Usually," says Marshall calmly and in a very concerned voice. "But when you run into the store and leave your car on, you usually put the car into park and you usually don't take the time to refasten your seat belts."

Richard's eyes flare, then grow bitter, then angry. He starts to slightly bite his lower lip.

"I imagine who ever we're dealing with thinks they're pretty smart. It's as if they're mocking us. Taunting us to try to find them," states Marshall.

"This is only the first instance," says Rich. "We can't be sure this is going to continue."

"You know better than that. How many times have you seen a missing body, in a situation like this and it ended up being the only one?"

"Howdy Marshall," says the sweet voice of Elaine, one of the cashiers. "What? Another car parked here? I see Mike finally called you guys to check it out."

Rich and Marshall look at each other then back at Elaine.

"I told him after the third one that this was kind of weird and to call ya'll. It seems that only a certain elite few are allowed to park here without something happening to their car, and it gettin' towed."

Elaine can hardly contain herself while talking to Marshall. Soft brown eyes all lit up. Eyelashes batting feverishly. It is easy to see, and she does make it obvious, she is very sweet on Marshall.

"Certain elite few?" questions Rich.

"I do believe I was talking to Mister Winston young man," Elaine replies. Elaine has the most beautiful, soft, and fake southern accent this town has ever heard. "Isn't that right Marshall?"

"Certain elite few, Elaine? What are you talking about?"

"Well I'm sure I could tell you everything, but you see these packages are just weighing me down, and with the sun and all, well, you know. If you'd like, I'm sure I could whip us up something for dinner and we could discuss it then. Give me a call and tell me what you decide. I'm in the book you know," she says as she turns with her packages which contain all of a loaf of bread, some toilet paper and some paper towels. She is very careful to drop her receipt as she leaves.

"The sun?" quips Rich, giving Marshall a coy, yet inquisitive look.

It has been unusually cool all day. The sun has been coming in and out of the clouds all morning though never staying out long enough to heat things up.

"Never mind her. I think we need to talk to Mike."

"Let me. He's too afraid of you right now. You'd probably make him so nervous he'd conveniently forget all the details."

"Yeah. You go ahead," Marshall agrees.

"Don't give up on us baby..," faintly emanates from the Corvette's radio.

"Hey, great song. I haven't heard this one in years!" exclaims Rich.

"Yes it is, but..," Marshall looks a little puzzled. "I figured that battery would have been worn down by now. Must be a strong battery."

"Well it's only been here for 3 days, and most of the first day it was probably running," says Rich. "The radio doesn't draw much power unless you have it up really loud. The battery is just about gone though, you can hear the radio starting to fade out."

"Whatever," Marshall says while walking over to his car as Rich walks into the store to talk with Mike.

Chapter III

"I don't know what you're talking about," says Mike. "This is the only car that has been here for three days. I haven't had any other cars towed, and even if I did I'm allowed to you know. I'm the manager of this store and I have the right to make sure my parking lot is not being taken advantage of by anyone."

"Calm down Mike," reassures Rich while motioning with his hand the way a performer tries to quiet an audience in the middle of an ovation. "Calm down. I'm not Marshall. I'm not gonna pull a gun on you, and unlike him, I fully understand your rights. You see, I respect your position as a Manager. That's why I came straight to you and not to 'YOUR' employees."

Rich is patronizing him, but Mike found someone who 'recognized his authority' and his ego is soaring. Richard realizes he can find out anything he wants from Mike, provided he continues to play the role of being Mike's subordinate.

"Well," says Mike in an abrupt, surprised, yet delighted tone. "Thank you. Thank you very much. If a few more people around here would realize that, and act the way they're supposed to, a lot more would get done around here."

"You know that better than I would. I have never been a manager. Some people aren't cut out to be one you know," Rich says.

Rich is laying it on thick. He has to. He wants this case solved and over with. He no longer wants to live the tumultuous life he removed his family from. Now here it is, showing its ugly face, again disrupting his peaceful haven.

"You have to realize, a lot o' folks are envious." Rich is now speaking in as simple a voice as he can. He is trying to make Mike feel bigger and more important than himself, the 'lowly man' in front of the manager.

"Yes well it's not really as easy as everyone thinks." Mike is feeling proud. "So you agree that I had every right to have those other cars towed, without calling you guys first?"

Mike's question, whether intentional or not, came out in the form of a test. Rich picks up on it quickly and isn't about to bring Mike back down to earth just yet.

"I mean, if, there were any other cars?" continues Mike.

Obviously there were others. Richard knows he can start calling around to all the tow yards looking for cars that were picked up from this store and when they were towed; but that will take too long, especially when the cretin on the other end of the desk has ALL the answers.

"I told you Mike," begins Rich, "I'm not a manager and I've never been one. How would I know those kind of things from a manager's point of view?"

"Well that's true. I guess you wouldn't know about these higher functions of a manager," Mike answers arrogantly. "You've probably never been to management classes either. Sorry, I didn't mean to put you on the spot like that," Mike says, talking down to Rich. "I should have phrased my question differently. I meant to ask: 'It wouldn't have been wrong for me to have those cars towed from a legal, or police point of view, now would it?'"

"Mike I ain't no lawyer," starts Rich.

"Yes I know that. Being a manager I'm trained to pick up on these things," he interrupts.

"Like I was saying," Richard continues speaking in the same sympathetic manner he started with, while using all his power to control his emotions and keep himself from exploding all over Mike. "I don't know what any fancy lawyer would have to say but from a Police point of view, as you are probably very familiar with, you did nothing wrong. You were, as you pointed out, completely within your rights as the manager of this establishment, to exercise your authority to have those non-customer's cars removed." Rich pauses a moment. "'Bout how long was each car sitting there before you had it towed?"

"It varied. Some were sitting there a couple days, some four days. One car I was very, very patient with and I let it stay there five days before calling Al's to come and get it. That's were all the cars are, at Al's. Al is a good friend of mine, so I give him all the business I can. He really appreciates me and respects me too."

"Well that was mighty kind of you in both respects."

Rich had him going and doesn't want him to stop. He has to get him talking again, but he must keep Mike feeling like he is in control of the conversation. "THINK! MAN! THINK!", Rich thinks to himself. He has never been at a loss for words in a situation like this before, why now? Rich takes a deep breath and realizes that he has lost his composure because of Mike's haughty attitude. Calming himself down, he comes up with a thought.

"Five days huh? That really was kind of you. It's almost as if they were using your parking lot like a storage yard."

Rich is almost holding his breath. Did that do it? Will that get Mike talking again? Will Mike notice his uneasiness?

"Yeah, five days, and I still received flak from all the cashiers about having it towed."

Rich breathes a sigh of relief to himself as Mike continues.

"I'm sure you can imagine the talk that went around about me after that. I heard the gossip, I heard the murmurings."

Rich has to say something to keep him going.

"I can't believe that, even after five days? That's ridiculous. I mean, five days in that same spot and they still gave you grief?"

"Yeah, even after five days in that same spot. Now that I think about it, every car I had towed was in that same spot. What a coincidence!" exclaims Mike. "What are the odds of something like that happening?" Mike laughs with a grunt and snort which resembles a donkey with asthma.

Feeling his blood boil at this, Rich gets up and voices a phony laugh. It is the kind of laugh you give to appease someone who told a really stupid joke. The kind of laugh you give just before you rip someone's head off verbally. Rich wants to. He wants to lay into Mike. This is no coincidence.

Needing to calm down, Rich goes to the water cooler in Mike's office and gets a drink. Without looking back at Mike, who is now amused with himself and still laughing, Rich presses on.

"All four of them? Wow! That really is a coincidence," Rich says with as much of a chuckle as he can muster.

"Oh no," snorts Mike as his laugh begins to subside. "There were, let's see...1, 2, 3, 4, 5, 6, 7, 8 and then this one, 9. Nine cars in all."

"And all parked in the same spot?"

"Yeah, can you believe it? I'll bet the odds of that happening are bigger than the odds of winning a lottery," Mike says shaking his head up and down; proud of his analytical observance. "I'll bet I could run a 'Guess How Many Cars Were Towed From This Spot' pool and no one would guess an answer that high!" He says snorting again.

Rich can take it no longer. He feels like he is going to explode, but still needs more information. He knows all the cars had been taken to Al's. He wants to know when.

"Yeah," he says, trying to be cordial. "When did you have the first one towed?"

"Huh?" Mikes says in his usual, abrupt, shocked way.

Rich knows he has just stepped over the line and took control of the conversation. "Big mistake!" he thinks to himself. "I have to fix this or I'll get nothing else out of this moron."

"Yeah ya know records of this sort of thing. I may not be a manager but I know that every good manager always keeps records, records of everything. Hey, I even once knew a manager so efficient," 'pathetic' Rich thinks to himself, "that he would even keep records of when each employee went to the bathroom," Rich says humbly.

Rich can hardly believe himself. He can't

believe this refuse is coming out of his own mouth. He comforts himself with the thought of catching whoever the criminal is. If he can get this one off the streets, this peaceful little town will once again become just that, a peaceful little town.

"Oh that!" Mike starts. "Of course I kept records on that. I have a file right here that has all the times and dates for each car. I even have the receipts from Al's, you know the place I told you I had them towed to. It's all right here. You see, I'm a good manager too." His voice becoming determined. "I keep all sorts of records, and it's a good thing too, 'cause you never know when you'll need them," Mike speaks while looking directly at Richard, his hands folded neatly on the desk.

"We down at the station would be very grateful if we could borrow them for..."

"Oh no!" Mike interrupts. "My records never leave this office. What happens if you lose them or they get held for evidence, then where will I be?"

Rich is losing it. "Maintain Rich, maintain," he keeps thinking. "You've got to stay calm."

"Well Mike, I'm sure a good manager like you has a copy machine."

"Of course I do," says Mike in a very condescending tone.

"Would you please make copies of everything in that file for me? It would sure help."

"Sure! I'd love to help, especially a person like you who respects my authority."

Mike begins looking through his file drawer. As he flips through the files, Richard is looking over his shoulder hoping to see anything which might be useful later on that Mike might not be so inclined to share.

"Cute," Rich thinks to himself as he sees a folder go by through Mikes fingers labeled: 'Employee Rest Room Use.' He knows now that anything he wants to know regarding any of Mike's employees will be somewhere in this office. Even if he has to get it without Mike's permission.

"Here it is," he says pulling it from the drawer. "Elsie would you come in here please," Mike says over the intercom. "That's my secretary. All good managers have secretaries."

In walks Elsie and the whole room stands still. Elsie is a very beautiful, symmetrically proportioned intelligent woman who should be working as a model; not for this guy.

"Elsie make copies of everything in this file for Mr. Laverton, then be sure to give it back to me personally," he orders her in a stern voice.

Having had enough of Mike, Richard knows it is time to take his leave, at least for the moment.

"Thank you Mike. I know that all real good managers always have a lot of work to do, so I won't take up any more of your very valuable time. I'll just wait outside with Elsie. This way I can follow your example of working hard and start reviewing some of this information while Elsie copies it," Rich says in excusing himself.

Rich feels an air of accomplishment come over him. He was able to maintain his composure. He really wanted to hit Mike, but he didn't. He paved the way for another visit if needed.

"Of course, of course, I have so much work to do here, exactly. Well okay, but be sure not to mess up the order it's in, it's arranged by date and I want it kept that way. And Elsie don't forget to give that file back to me when you're done. Put it in my hand only. Only me. Got it?"

Elsie rolls her eyes as she turns and walks out of Mike's office.

"How did you do it?" Elsie says after they leave Mike's office and close the door.

"I don't know," Rich says while shaking his head. "I don't know."

On their way to the copy machine, Rich decides to take a walk to the front of the store.

"I'll be right back," he says as he moves past her.

Rich is looking for any clues he can find, and thought maybe there is some significant relationship between the parking space and the store front. Maybe there is some good vantage point. As he walks the length of the store from the inside, he finds nothing. Most of the time he isn't even able to see the space because of other cars, trees and signs in the window.

"Why only that spot?" he thinks aloud to himself. "It is a good spot, but definitely not the greatest spot. It surely isn't a good enough parking place to kill someone over and certainly not a good enough place to kill several people for," he continues thinking as he continues to stare out the window.

"Here you go Rich," Elsie startles him as she hands him the copies.

"Oh. Thank you. Thanks a lot."

"Is there something that should concern us?" she asks coyly.

"We're not sure, yet. We don't have much to go on."

"If you need anything, ANYTHING, from Mike's office, I can make copies for you. I know how hard it can be to work with him," she tells Rich in a direct, concise manner; letting him know that even if Mike was going to be uncooperative, she will help.

"'Preciate that. A lot!" Rich breathes another sigh of relief.

Flipping through the file on his way out, he is looking for some kind of common denominator. There isn't one to be found. The cars towed are as diversified as the cars currently in the lot.

"What is the connection?" he keeps thinking to himself.

Mike is clearly into keeping files. He even composed a list with columns and rows of each car, its color, year, make, model, tag, state and number of days it sat, before he had it towed. This made it easier for Rich. The only thing not on this list is the day of week and date the car was towed. He will have to look at the copies of Al's invoices for that. Rich starts looking down the list:

YR	Color	Make	Model	Tag	State	Parked
1.) 87	Blue	Plymouth	Wagon	GHB543	Tenn.	4-days
2.) 91	Blue	Toyota	Corolla	MINE	Tenn.	3-days
3.) 93	White	Ford	Pick-up	A3U 592	Tenn.	3-days
4.) 90	Green	Pontiac	Trans Am	SPEDEMN	Virg.	2-days
5.) 85	Tan	Ford	Mustang	X1R 875	Tenn.	5-days
6.) 91	Silver	Toyota	Corolla	B5G 153	Tenn.	3-days
7.) 72	Maroon	Honda	Accura	X6Y 105	Tenn.	3-days
8.) 89	Gray	Mazda	LX	T4Q 010	Geor.	2-days
9.) 72	Red	Chevy	Corvett	B5C 479	Tenn.	3-days

He then begins to match the cars with the tow date. The Plymouth was towed on July 1st, Friday, at 7:00 p.m. which means it was parked there on Monday, June 27. Rich decides to make his own columns and fill in the rest:

YR	Color	Make	Model	Tag	State	Parked	Day Parked	Day Towed
1.) 87	Blue	Plymouth	Wagon	GHB543	Tenn.	4-days	Mo-Jun 27	Fr-Jul 1
2.) 91	Blue	Toyota	Corolla	MINE	Tenn.	3-days	Mo-Jul 4	Th-Jul 7
3.) 93	White	Ford	Pick-up	A3U 592	Tenn.	3-days	Th-Jul 7	Su-Jul 10
4.) 90	Green	Pontiac	Trans Am	SPEDEMN	Virg.	2-days	Mo-Jul 11	We-Jul 13
5.) 85	Tan	Ford	Mustang	X1R 875	Tenn.	5-days	Mo-Jul 18	Sa-Jul 23
6.) 91	Silver	Toyota	Corolla	B5G 153	Tenn.	3-days	Sa-Jul 23	Tu-Jul 26
7.) 72	Maroon	Honda	Accura	X6Y 105	Tenn.	3-days	Fr-Jul 29	Mo-Aug 1
8.) 89	Gray	Mazda	LX	T4Q 010	Geor.	2-days	Tu-Aug 2	Th-Aug 4
9.) 72	Red	Chevy	Corvett	B5C 479	Tenn.	3-days	Fr-Aug 5	Th-Aug 4

Monday seems to be a favorite day. The only safe day appears to be Sunday. This store is open on Sunday, so the chances of the space remaining empty are pretty slim. It is a fairly good spot. Rich walks out with his copy of the file. Puzzled, he is hoping Marshall will be able to find something, anything, he is not seeing. Rich walks back to the 'Vette.

Chapter IV

"Whoop! (tsk) Dang nabbit!" says Pops angrily, spilling the finger print powder.

"Easy there, my friend. Just take your time. This car's not going anywhere 'till you're done with it."

"Sorry Marshall, but this DANG ARTHRITIS (humf)"

"Yeah, I know. I'm not that bad…" Marshall pauses slightly and Pops looks up. "Yet," he says with that boyish grin of his. "You just keep going. I'm gonna chat with Richard for a while. He's on his way back, and seeing the length of time he was in there, well, maybe he found something."

"You go right ahead. I shouldn't be too much longer. By the way, those hair samples I retrieved from here should be ready by tomorrow. If you want, you can call in and get the results," Pops tells Marshall without looking up.

Pops is brushing the dust he spilled but doing so, carefully. He figures, as long as the powder is down there, no sense just scooping it up. May as well let the powder do its job.

"Who knows what may show up," he thinks to himself. "Sometimes the obvious places aren't where the prints are."

Pops is a dear old man. He was supposed to retire fifteen years ago. Actually he did, but as they say: "You can't keep a good man down." At eighty years old, he still had the energy and vitality of a younger man. It was not uncommon to hear twenty five year old "boys" (as he would call them) say: "I hope I have that kind of energy when I'm that age." Of course, when Pops hears them say that, he would always reply: "My age? Why you don't even have my energy now at your age, you little snot! Go ahead and sit a few more years in front of that idiot box and see what kind of mush ya turn into!" Pops (back twenty years ago or so) loved watching the kids play sports in the park. Lately, there has been less and less of them. He blames the TV, and no one can change his mind. Pops is not what you would call "Old Fashioned" though. He even likes a lot of today's music. "I think Guns 'N Roses got a pretty good thing going, they just need to learn the English language. What'd I get, six good songs off their last two albums? All the rest of the songs, (humph) they clearly couldn't find any adjectives and verbs other than that same old cuss word! Ruin an otherwise great song," he would say. All the young people love him. He never tries to step on "their world." He always tries to give it a chance and tries to understand it, before drawing any conclusions. Even when he does disagree with them, he would talk it out and try to explain things. He has helped many young people get their lives on the right track. He would help them, without them even realizing they were being helped. He was by every definition of the word, and described by everybody, as: "Cool."

"Well this is strange," he says as he continues dusting for prints.

"Find out anything Rich?" asks Marshall as Rich is approaching.

"Yeah. This is car number 9."

"NINE?" exclaims Marshall.

"Yes sir, nine."

"He waited this long to call us?"

"Yeah. He felt it was his right as a manager to just have them towed, without having to get the police involved."

"What a complete moron. Nine cars hang around his parking lot and he just tows 'em," says Marshall gesturing with his hands stretched out to include the entire parking lot. "Somebody's been using this lot for, whatever, and he finally calls us. Didn't he think it was kinda strange for NINE cars to have to be towed from his lot?" he asks in disbelief.

"Actually, he did think it was a strange coincidence. Especially, and you better get a grip on yourself for this."

Marshall looks sharply at Rich.

"Especially since every car was parked in this same spot," Rich says in as sincere a voice as he can. He wants to keep Marshall calm.

"I'll kill him!"

Rich grabs Marshall's arm as he starts toward the store.

"Hold it Marshall.   Come on now, we have work to do," says Rich.

"NINE cars have to be towed from this same spot and he finally calls us!" Marshall says very angrily.   "What was going through his mind? Did he think that people just loved this spot as a good dumping ground for their cars or what?"

"Marshall calm down. I spoke with him and was able to get somewhere. If we go in there now all fired up, it will only hinder us." Rich is trying hard to calm him down.

"Oh you're right," Marshall says with indifference. "Whacha get?"

"Believe it or not, Mike kept a file on it. I have a list of all the cars and the dates they were towed." Rich hands the list to Marshall. "I cross referenced the tow date to the vehicle and figured out the date the car was parked here, then added that to the list."

"No similarities," says Marshall.

"None that I could find. I was hoping I just

missed something and you would spot it."

Marshall is leafing through the folder.

"I'm going to give this stuff to Suzie and have her find out what she can. I figure we can at least find out if any of the cars have been reported stolen. I imagine, though, we are just going to come up with a bunch of missing person's reports."

"Sad to say it, but I think you're right," Marshall says in agreement.

"Maybe we'll find a common thread there."

"Tell that idiot inside to send for a tow truck on your way out," Marshall says with disgust as Rich turns to leave. "We'll be done with this by the time it gets here."

"You got it, sheriff."

Marshall turns and walks over to the passenger's side of the car. Pops is still leaning in on the driver's side dusting. Marshall crouches down to look inside.

"You finding any...What in the world...? I've never seen print dust do that. That's not normal!"

"Nope."

The print dust is most assuredly acting in a peculiar fashion. It is sticking to the finger prints and sweat residue left by whoever was last in the car, but it is doing so in a most unusual way. If you've ever played with a magnet and steel shavings, you would understand, for that is how the dust looks. It looks like steel shavings on a piece of paper that someone has just pulled along with a magnet.

"Is there some fan on, or vent open, causing that?" asks Marshall.

"Nope. The only breeze blowin' through here is the cross wind from these two doors being opened, and that should have made it point towards your door or mine."

The dust is pointing towards the center console of the car. Still, Pops is able to get a set of prints. He only found one set of prints in the car and from his findings, there had been only one person in it. He will have to take the prints back to the lab to analyze them more and also go to Carey's house for a sample of his prints to make sure they match.

"Love that smell," says Pops.

"The print dust?" Marshall asks in amazement.

"No, no, not the print dust, that fresh smell like just before a rain."

Marshall sticks his head in the car.

"Hmm. I wonder why that smell would be in here?" he says, taking a deep sniff.

"It's possible this guy was running a portable

copier or portable laser computer printer before he disappeared. Those machines cause the air to become ionized and smell fresh. He may even have one of those portable air cleaners. Did you see anything like that when you got here?" Pops asks.

"No Pops. You were the only one to go into the car. I just opened it up and glanced around. I didn't want to add any prints to the car or chance rubbing some off."

Pops looks up at Marshall.

"That might be your first connection. If you didn't find any of that type of equipment, you might have some kind of computer thief on your hands."

"Yeah, I was thinking that. We'll have to see what Suzie and Rich come up with from that list. Hey, the tow truck should be here pretty soon, do you want to do anymore with this one, or is it okay to have it towed?"

"Take it away," answers Pops in a disgruntled tone. "I can't see how I'm going to find anything else on this car. Everything is clean and virtually untouched. It's almost like whoever was in here got out and disappeared, then someone robbed their car."

"I was thinking something along those lines too," Marshall answers back. "I was entertaining the possibility of this actually being two unrelated crimes. The first being the disappearance of Carey, the second being his car getting robbed and the crook decided to be smart and lock everything up."

"It's possible. It's possible they could be related also," counters Pops.

"What do ya mean?"

"Since the keys are here, the thieves could have waited 'till he got out of his car, abducted him, then came back for his stuff and left the car running."

Marshall nods in agreement.

"If that's the case," continues Pops, "we've got someone who likes to play games. I think I'd better take a good look at those other cars. Where are they?"

"I don't know, I didn't get the tow yard from Rich. He's probably still on the road, so you can call him."

"Right," says Pops. "I'm done here. I'm gonna call it a night and get started again in the morning. I'll get in touch with Richard then." Pops is packing up his stuff. "I'll let you know what I come up with. I'm going to drop these prints off at the lab on my way home and have someone over there check 'em out," he says walking to his car. Pops pauses for a moment and then turns back around. "Marshall," he calls out. "You be careful," he says as Marshall turns toward him.

Pops has an uneasiness about him. He doesn't like what the print dust did. He has never seen anything like it before, and it bothers him.

"I will Pops," Marshall answers sincerely. "I

will and thanks."

"Good night Marshall."

"Good night Pops."

As Pops drives off, Marshall can't help but think about everything they all have found so far. None of it seems to fit. There are possibilities in their theories, but not enough to make a case; not even enough to make a solid line of thought.

A truck from Al's Towing arrived and took the car. Marshall questioned the driver a little, but didn't press him too much. "I don't know anything, I just tow 'em," was the only response he got. Al's has a history of making deals with store owners unscrupulously towing cars and this worker is probably afraid of getting involved or connected with Al's less than honorable business practices. Marshall decided not to press the issue. He could do so at another time.

Wanting to isolate the problem, Marshall puts up traffic cones and "Police Line Do Not Cross" tape around the space. Until he can make some sense out of this, or at least set up an around the clock watch, he wants to keep this spot open.

"I imagine Mike's gonna have a fit about this," he says aloud to himself while constructing the barrier.

Chapter V

"Bye babe," Jeff says while hugging his wife. "I'm gonna miss you so much." He gives her a tight squeeze.

"I'm gonna miss you too," she says as they continue to embrace.

Jeff and Virginia Colt are saying more than their usual morning good-byes. Jeff is late for work, but still doesn't want to leave. Virginia is going to Atlanta, Georgia to see Jeff's mother. They had planned to take this trip together, but Jeff had to cancel his vacation because of a special project at work which he cannot let sit for the three week vacation they had planned. Not knowing when he will finally be able to go, they decided Virginia will take the trip without him. It is a long drive from Bridgeport, Washington to Atlanta, Georgia.

"Promise me you'll be careful while I'm gone."

"Me be careful? You're the one who needs to be careful," counters Jeff. "You're the one driving clear across the country with a little baby, not me."

"Yeah I know, but I worry about you." Her

eyes looking softer than Jeff has ever seen. "I love you."

"I love you too, and very much." Jeff can't help but embrace her one more time. "I wish so much to be going with you."

"Me too," she says nearly crying.

"Oh babe. Don't cry. It's only going to be three weeks. I promise we'll be back together then," Jeff is very reassuring. He wants her at her best, emotionally, for the long drive. He wants to be sure she is going to be able to keep her mind on the road. "You make sure you stop as soon as you get tired," he states firmly. "I don't want my baby falling asleep at the wheel. After all, you've got three lives in your hands."

"Three?"

"Three. Yours, the babies and mine, 'cause I won't be able to live without you." They pull each other even closer, which is nearly impossible as they are already pressed up against each other. "I put everything into the car for you. I stacked as much as possible into the trunk, so you won't feel cramped in the car."

"Did you put the camera in the car? I wasn't able to find it this morning."

"Yeah, it's under the driver's seat."

They stand staring at each other. It seems like

forever, like it will never end, yet, at the same time, it feels like only a fleeting moment.

"I'd better get going," Jeff says. "And you'd better get going to, if you want to miss all that traffic. If you leave now, by the time you go through Seattle, you should miss most of that traffic through the city."

"Oh!" she says rushing into his arms again. "You still didn't promise me you'll be careful!"

"Don't worry babe, I will be. I promise I'll be careful." Jeff is again very reassuring to her. "But I noticed that you never promised me that YOU will be careful."

"Errr, you weren't supposed to notice that."

They both twitter.

"Well I did."

"Okay. I'll be careful."

They give each other one last kiss and Jeff heads out the door. She is standing in the doorway, watching her husband leave. They wave at each other. As he is pulling away, she can hear the baby's cry.

"There you are my little poo-poo!" she begins playing with the baby.

Virginia is very good with kids. In fact, she is very good with people. Virginia is shy to the extent that she needs to get to know someone before she can be herself and open up. After that, she is fine. Virginia always looks for the good in people and is always trying to find a reason "why" they may have done something wrong. She can't accept that some people are just "bad." A beautiful young woman who, in every sense of the word, is also a lady. Her skin is white and very smooth. She has a beautiful feminine softness about her which radiates from within. Her hair, brown with blonde highlights, is long and full. Her big brown eyes are so warm and inviting, you can get lost in them. She is self-conscience about her appearance, and has a very low self-esteem do to her rough childhood. Her make-up, which she always wore though never needed, has to be perfect.

"Oh! You've got a smelly diaper. Yes you do. You do, you do."

Micah is amused and smiling. As she changes him and gets him ready for the trip, they laugh and giggle and smile at each other. Micah, not talking just yet, makes his cooing and gurgling noises. Jeff loves to stand back and watch the two of them play. It brings joy to his heart.

"We're going to see grandma!" she says gleefully, then she starts nibbling his neck. Micah lets out a joyful scream and tries to run away. He loves it when his mom chases him.

Having finished dressing and feeding herself and the baby, they head out. She makes sure, as she always does, that all the doors are locked. She buckles Micah into his car seat. Standing with her head in her folded arms, which are resting on the roof of the car, she is staring in the direction her husband has just gone - the opposite way she will be traveling.

"Ohhhh, I wish he was going with me," she says softly; her brown eyes welling up. She stands staring for another moment. Shaking it off, she closes Micah's door and walks around to her side of the car and gets in. After checking her make-up, she readjusts the mirror and they're off. Pulling away from the curb, she turns on the radio.

"Please....don't take the girl..."

"Oh! I love this song," she says singing along.

With the sun just coming up in front of them, they begin their long journey east.

"You're late, man, what's wrong with you? You know we've got to keep this thing going," says Arthur, one of Jeff's coworkers, in a stern, angry tone. "I've been covering for you all morning and I don't appreciate having to make up excuses for you. You're not the only one on this project, and I expect you here on time."

This is the first time Jeff has been late in over two years and Arthur is not in any position to come down on Jeff. He is neither superior nor subordinate to Jeff. They are both equal in their position of employ.

Jeff is an athletic person who stands a modest 5'11." "Just the right height," according to his wife. He has a rock hard stomach and biceps to match, yet, he isn't big like a body builder. He is the kind of strong and has the kind of muscle, that is for work and not for show. Jeff will give you the shirt off his back if you need it. If you are an unappreciative person, or one who tries to take advantage of others, you'll get nothing - even if you need it. He is a very fair man and believes in being nice to others. Jeff always has a song in his heart, and one coming out his mouth to match. He isn't one to cause trouble, but at the same time, he will not stand idly by and be stepped on. He will put up with a lot, but when he had enough, you knew it.

"I don't like looking bad, and when one of us isn't here for the project, it makes us all look bad. I'm going places in this company, and I don't need you screwing it up for me," Arthur is speaking angrily, almost yelling, but doing so in a whisper.

"Jeff," comes a voice from across the hall. "There you are. Good."

"Yes sir, Mister Calvitch sir, here he is. I was able to find him for you. Like I said, he's here, and has been all morning."

Arthur is a real butt kisser. Jeff, and Mr. David

Calvitch for that matter, hate the way Arthur tries to suck up.

"Good morning sir," replies Jeff.

"Yes it's a good morning all right. The "whole" team is here, as we have been all morning," interrupts Arthur. "I've been keeping an eye on the whole group for you sir. We've all been doing our part."

"You're here early, Jeff. I wasn't expecting you 'till about noon. This is good, though. You'll be able to make the meeting you were going to miss. Now you'll be able to hear everything first hand."

Arthur's face drops as Mr. David Calvitch continues.

"I know how tough it was to leave your wife for work when she's going on a trip. Did she get off okay?"

"Yeah, I imagine so. I left before her, but I packed the car before I left. I was going to come in later, but I knew if I didn't get out of there, I wouldn't have let her go. Then I'd have missed a day of work, and she would not have left until tomorrow."

"And then it would have started all over again, right?" Mr. Calvitch says with a smile. "I know how that goes." Mr. David Calvitch is also a family man, married for thirty five years. "I still have trouble getting out of the house in the morning. I wish I could just take her to work with me," he says gazing longingly into the air.

"Yeah, then nothing would get done," laughs Jeff.

"You are right about that, young man. You are right about that."

Patting Jeff on the back, he leads them both to the next room.

"Say Arthur, if you're going to lie about someone be sure you check with them first. He's been lying about you all morning, Jeff. And for crying out loud, Arthur, don't use the bathroom excuse more than twice in an hour," David says, as he turns back toward Jeff. "This guy is a pathetic liar," he states.

"Yes sir, sorry sir," Arthur says in a cowardly voice, as he runs to catch up with them. "Could I get you some coffee for the meeting Mr. Calvitch, sir?"

"I hate butt kissers, don't you?" David says to Jeff, then, without missing a beat, turns to Arthur and says: "Sure, light with no sugar." As he turns back to Jeff he continues: "But I will take advantage of them whenever possible. If they want to be that way, it's their own fault." David calls back to Arthur: "And be quick about it. The meeting is going to start in five minutes, whether you're there or not."

They go into the meeting room. It is very quiet except for the sound from the air filter/ionizer located in the back corner of the room and the occasional rustle of paper from the room's sole inhabitant. Since this is the only person of the ten expected, the meeting obviously will not be starting in five minutes. David knows that. He just really enjoys putting a scare into Arthur. David himself is always a good 15-20 minutes early for his meetings. This gives him time to make sure everything is set up and prepared. He likes being prepared.

"Ahhhhhh," he says after taking a deep breath. Love the way those things make the air smell." He takes another deep breath. "Ahhh. Wonderful, just wonderful. Don't you think?"

"Now how long is this thing going to be here?"

Marshall knows that voice and really doesn't need to hear it this early in the morning.

"Great! Just what I needed to start my day," he mutters. "Good morning, Mike, and how are you this fine morning?" asks Marshall.

It is a fine morning, weather wise. The sun is shining and glistening off the dew. There is a still, a calm if you will, in the air. Everything feels right with the world. It is quiet. The stream of cars has not yet become its normal steady flow. You can actually hear yourself think, so to speak. This is short lived, as Mike's shrill voice cuts through the silence.

"I'd be doing better if all this wasn't here," he says motioning to the traffic cones and police tape. "This is not good at all for business, ya know." Mike is starting to get edgy.

"I know Mike, and I'm sorry," Marshall says while thinking: 'Did I say that?' "I was going to check with you first, to let you know about it, but it got late and you were busy, and well, I just thought I would discuss it with you this morning when I saw you."

Marshall had gotten a good night's sleep, and thought long and hard about what Rich said the night before. He knows Rich is right, he just doesn't want to have to play silly games. Marshall also wants more information and figures he can catch more flies with honey than vinegar.

"Oh," Mike is still puzzled. "So what's going on? I have a right to know, you know."

"Of course, of course, Mike. Here's what we've got so far," Marshall says as he stands up and dusts off his hands. He had been down checking the ground for anything he might find which would help with this case. Marshall begins, "All the cars that park in this spot have had their owners, or at least their drivers, not return to their cars...."

"Oh, not every car that parks here," Mike interrupts.

"Excuse me?"

Marshall expected to hear that from Mike, but wants him to expound on his statement. He wants a concrete answer. Was it every car that parked in this spot or not?

"Not every car. You said 'All the cars that parked in this spot', it was not every car."

"Would you expand on that a little for me?"

"What's there to expand? Some cars would park here, buy some groceries, then leave. It has only been nine cars so far that haven't left this spot. That's why I didn't call you 'till now, because it was not every car that parked in this spot."

They both stare at each other. Marshall shakes his head.

"There has to be a connection," he says.

"So how long is this spot going to be blocked off?" questions Mike, as if his mind had been completely wiped clean of everything just said.

"Look, later today sometime. I want to set up a surveillance team before just letting it lay open," Marshall answers in a disgusted tone. "I may want to ask you a few more questions later on, so please, make yourself available."

"Well, I'm a very busy man, so if I have time and can fit you in, I'll answer any more questions you have." The arrogance coming through in his voice.

"You'd better make yourself available mister, because as of right now you're a suspect of at least one missing person. Even if you're found clean you can still be held liable by the families of these people simply because of your negligence to call the police after the first instance. Now I'm trying to be patient with you, so don't push it. You can find yourself in a heap of trouble real quick if you don't watch it, so keep your nose clean. I'm tired of your attitude mister and I'm not going to put up with it. Got it?" Marshall says in an extremely stern voice. "Go on. You can leave if you want. I'm not holding you. YET."

Mike leaves Marshall and walks back to the store.

"Good morning, Mr. Toggle." Elsie had just arrived and was going inside as Mike approached.

"Good morning, Mrs. Harris - You can call me Mike," he says passing her.

Elsie stands there with a surprised look on her face. "Okay," she thinks. "This is kind of different." She notices two more patrol cars drive into the lot as she follows Mike into the store.

Chapter VI

A conversation "free for all" has been going on for several minutes as the last of the employees arrive. Mr. David Calvitch, President, CEO, founder and owner of the company, allows the talking to continue for a few minutes more. He always gives everyone time to get comfortable and relax before he starts any meeting. He feels this is important. In his days, he has attended strict, rigid meetings. The atmosphere would be tense from the start and remain so for most of the meeting; preventing everyone from getting comfortable enough to share their ideas. He found his approach best: Let everyone get comfortable with each other then, once the meeting started, the relaxed atmosphere would allow everyone to feel at ease and unafraid to share their ideas. Standing up, he begins.

"Ladies and gentlemen, may I have your attention please?" Mr. Calvitch has such a warm, humble, air about him, people just want to stop what they are doing and listen to him. "First, I'd like to say, thank you all for being here. I especially want to thank Jeff whose wife left for a three week visit to his mother's today. I don't know about the rest of you, but frankly, I didn't expect to see hide-nor-hair of him today, if you...know what I mean," he says with a sly, yet coy laugh.

"Ohhhhs" and "ahhhhs" and typical jeering emerge from the rest in attendance.

"I'm not suggesting anything," says David. "I just know how much you care about your wife. That's all I was getting at."

"Uh-huh, yeah sure," is heard from several of the attendees.

"I would also like to give a special thanks to Jill Hillson," David says as he turns towards Jill. "Thank you Jill, I do appreciate your being here. Jill left her son, Bobbie, isn't it?"

Jill nods yes.

"Yes Bobbie. Jill had to leave him home alone with the flu to be here, so if you have any questions for her, you'd better get them in quickly after this meeting." Again turning to Jill he continues, "Jill WILL be going home after this meeting to take care of Bobbie. Won't you Jill?"

"Well, I have a bunch of stuff..."

"Won't you Jill?" David interrupts, nodding his head up and down.

"I've got that..."

"Won't you Jill?" he interrupts again, nodding his head in a more pronounced manner.

"Uh. Yes. Yes I will be leaving directly after

this meeting," Jill says, shaking her head in unison with David.

"Thank you, Jill."

"Hey! I just remembered. My kid is sick too!" shouts a voice from in back.

"Charlie, you don't have any kids."

"I could borrow some."

"Maybe he should borrow a wife first," retorts another voice from in back that causes a burst of laughter from all to ensue.

"Sit down, Charlie," says David with a smirk, shaking his head and rolling his eyes. "Okay. Let's get down to business."

The meeting proceeds as normal business meetings do. The usual financial questions, status reports, and the like. The question of upgrading the computer system, the cost, the benefits, the drawbacks. The problem with the lab equipment being old and in need of repair. The current status of each of the projects currently in progress. Then, a touchy question about the project Jeff is involved with is aired.

"Regarding the subjects for Q-29," Jeff questions, "when will we be able to begin?"

Arthur's eyes widen. The whole room becomes perfectly still and very, very quiet. No one moves, nor raises their head. Everyone is just looking down waiting; waiting for someone, anyone, to say something.

"You've been putting me off for a little over a month on this one. I really think I deserve either an explanation, or a reason. You said you would have them. About three weeks ago you said you got a few. I'm being pushed for this project, so much so, that I had to send my wife clear across the country alone, yet still, I know nothing. Do you have them or not? We've gone just about as far as we can go with this thing until we get them."

The room continues quiet.

"Well," begins David. "I guess we do owe you at least something."

"Pops! You out here?" yells Marshall.

It's about two o'clock in the afternoon. Marshall went to Al's to check on Pops' progress.

"Over here in the blue wagon."

Pops is probing through the Plymouth. It was the first car to be towed, and the last he had to examine. He obtained a copy of the list of cars from Rich, and decided to work it from the most recent, to the oldest.

"Never in all my days," he says aloud. "Never in all my days." He then shouts over to Marshall,

"Take a look at those other cars. Notice anything about the finger print dust?"

"Same as the 'Vette, 'cept for the blue Corolla and this one," he says after examining the cars.

"Look real close at the Corolla and this one. I think you'll change your mind."

Kneeling down close, he can see the same pattern as was in the Corvette, but with less intensity. The force causing the dust to react the way it did is losing its affect with time.

"I figure, another couple o' days and this one would have been completely clean. Whatever was causing this has already dissipated, so much so, that I can't tell how many people were in this car, nor the Corolla for that matter."

"Did Suzie and Rich come up with anything?" Marshall questions slowly.

"Didn't talk to 'em yet. I got a copy of this list on the way home last night, and haven't called in to either of them yet. Here," he says handing his list to Marshall. "I've marked down the number of people I was able to find in each of the cars, 'cept of course for these last two."

"What's this number for the Trans-Am? You've got two numbers listed."

"I think there were two in that one from the dust marks, but there appears to be one body with three legs. Means either someone was sittin' in someone's lap, or somebody was holding something about the thickness of a leg."

"Three in the Pick-up, two, maybe three in the Trans-Am, one in the Mustang, two in the silver Corolla, three in the Honda, one in the Mazda and one in the 'Vette. Thirteen, maybe fourteen people."

"That's not even counting the ones from these other two cars," Pops adds. "We still have to find them."

"I think we've been looking in the wrong direction," Marshall says with strong conviction. "I think we've been looking in all the wrong places."

"What 'er you talking about?"

"We've been looking, scouring, this town and its back woods for missing persons. We've had six calls about missing persons within the last month or so, and we've been looking everywhere but here. I swear, I'm gonna kill him."

"Kill who?"

"Oh, that Toggle!" Marshall says with disgust. "He's been towing cars for over a month, and finally calls us. Those people haven't been just disappearing, they've been being kidnapped, and that moron has conveniently covered over any tracks the abductors left by towing their cars and not saying a word."

Marshall is pacing.

"Do you think Mike's in on this?" Pops asks with a look of surprise on his face.

"No, not Mike. He's just a stupid pawn who happens to be doing the bidding for someone he never met." Marshall takes a deep breath. "Have you found anything else we can go on?"

"Yes, but it may not help much, plus, I have to check it out at the lab to be sure of my findings."

"Whatcha get?" asks Marshall hopefully.

"Like I said, I can't be positive 'till I check it out at the lab."

"I understand."

"There are no similar prints across all the cars. Every set of prints I find in each car are in only that car. The other thing you already know about. All the dust seems to be pointing to the center of the car."

"Were the keys in every car?"

"Yup."

"Were the seat belts still fastened?"

"Yes."

"What we've got here, is someone who likes to play games."

"I would keep that parking spot free for a

while, if I were you."

"Thanks Pop, I am. I put two officers in place to make sure Mike doesn't pull the tape and cones down. I wanted to see what you found before I let anyone park there. Do you need any help with your stuff?"

"Nah, I'll be all right. Thanks, though."

"Let me know what you find." Marshall turns and walks to his car. Grabbing the radios hand piece, Marshall again tries to reach base. "Suzie, you there?"

There is no answer but knowing Suzie, he is sure she is not baking cookies. She would not be with something like this going on. He will try again later.

"Oh, Marshall," Pops says, coming up towards his car. "Something I forgot to tell you."

"Yeah?"

"Remember that smell in the 'Vette? The fresh air smell I was talking about?"

"Yes, why?"

"It was in the Mazda, the Honda and very faintly, in the silver Toyota. I predict it was in the other cars as well, but dissipated. I don't know if, or how, that will help, but I thought I ought to let you know."

"Thanks Pops. It's something else to keep an

eye out for. The more similarities and connections we find, the better."

"I'm going to go finish up. I'll call you from the lab with my findings."

Pops heads back to the cars to finish collecting his instruments. Marshall decides to drive back to the Super Market to take a look at the surrounding areas. If someone was abducting these people, they would need an easily accessible place to hide their vehicle. After all, forcing, or even carrying, bodies into a car in plain sight would generate too much publicity.

Chapter VII

"No ma'am, we haven't found him yet. I'm sorry," says Rich.

Richard has the unpleasant task of research and follow-up, that also includes the dispensing of unpleasant information. He and Suzie found the missing person's cases and matched them to the addresses the cars are registered to. Suzie is trying to get in touch with the owners of the Trans-Am and the Mazda that are registered in other states. She is also calling the local police in those states for any further information they might be able to offer. Richard had just come from the house the pick-up truck is registered to. He was there for a long time, trying to comfort the lady of the house. The woman's husband, son and daughter went off to go fishing for the day and never returned. Rich called for a female officer to come and sit with her for she was hysterical and Rich could not, rather, would not, leave her alone. He thought that telling her they found the car would inspire hope into her grieving heart. It had just the opposite effect. Now standing at this next house, facing the lady who lives there, he has to ask if he can search for finger prints to help identify the occupants of the vehicle. He hates to ask, fearing the outcome will be the same as the last home, but he has to.

"We did find his Mustang, Ma'am, and we're wondering..."

"Yes?" is the tearful response.

"Well, we were able to get finger prints from the Mustang and wanted to match them to your husbands, to make sure they are his. Since he has no criminal record, we don't have any prints of him on file." Richard pauses briefly. "Do you think you may have anything around which he might have touched before he left?" Rich is trying to be sincere and supportive.

"Yes. I think I do. Please come in."

She shows Richard to a sewing machine.

"He fixed this just before he left. I didn't use it the day he left, and have been too upset to use it since."

"Thank you, ma'am, thank you," he says as he reaches for her hand to give it a warm squeeze. "He's gonna be all right. We'll find him," he reassures her. "I'm going out to my car for some equipment. Is it okay for me to just come right back in here?"

She nods.

Rich lifts several good prints from the sewing machine. He labels them, then files them into his brief case. In one way he is hoping the prints matched and in another way, he is hoping they do not. A female officer, whom he had called when he went back for his equipment, has just arrived.

"Thank you, ma'am. I'm sorry to have disturbed you. Be assured, this is going to be a great help in finding your husband."

"Thank you," she says with all the strength she can muster. She doesn't want to cry, at least, NOT NOW, not in front of Rich.

After greeting the female officer, Rich tips his hat and turns to leave. The woman closes the door behind him, then falls to the sofa, weeping. The female officer sits with her, rubbing her shoulder, trying to comfort her and give her hope.

The curtain in the window is jostled then the door flies open. There stands a middle-aged man with wide eyes and a hopeful expression on his face.

"Did ya find 'em?" he asks excitedly. "Are they all right? Please say you found them. Tell me they're coming home soon." His hopeful appearance is quickly fading away to fear and sadness. "Tell me ya found them," he again pleads.

This rigid looking man is slowly breaking down. When meeting this man for the first time, you would think he is incapable of expression. To see the suffering in his heart come out through his eyes, his face, his stature and his entire being, is more than Rich, or anyone, can bear. Biting the inside of his upper lip, Rich lowers his head.

"No," he says while shaking his head. "We haven't found them yet."

Rich doesn't feel the time is right to ask for the prints, so he is trying to discern the most appropriate moment to do so. Thinking of his own wife and daughter, what he really wants is nothing other than to bring this man's family back.

"Nothing? Anything?" he asks almost crying.

"I'm sorry," says Rich. "We haven't been able to locate any of them."

The man begins to cry openly, putting his hands over his face.

"We did find your car."

"What? You found her car?" he says with a glimmer of hope in his eyes. "You found her car?" he sighs. "You found her car."

"Yes, we did. It had been towed from the Supermarket."

"You found her car," he sighs again, as if everything is now right with the entire universe. "That means there's still hope."

"Yes, yes. There is still hope," Rich interjects quickly. Thinking to himself: "I should ask him now, while he's feeling hopeful." He looks up at the man. "I hope I'm not being too forward, but I was wondering, is there anything around the house I would be able to get finger prints of them from?"

"Why?" The man is taken aback.

"Like I said, we found her car. We pulled three different sets of prints from it, and we want to make sure the prints are only of your wife and two daughters," answers Rich calmly.

"What would that do?"

"Well, it would tell us that no other person was in or around the car and tell us that she wasn't accosted in any way."

"Oh, I'm sure we can find something," he says darting off towards the other rooms. "Follow me."

There are several items in the house for Rich to get prints from, including the girls toys, the mothers computer, door knobs, etc. Rich is able to lift several good sets of prints of each of the three who were in the Honda. Filing the prints into his brief case, he is ready to leave.

"Wait, you can get more from this stuff here," the man offers optimistically.

"Thank you, but I'm sure we have enough."

"Are you sure? What if something happens to those? What if more than one of you guys needs a set? You could have several cops looking at 'em."

"I have plenty here for that, and we can always

make copies at the lab."

"Oh, okay."

"Thank you, sir," Rich says excusing himself. "This will prove most helpful to us."

"No, thank you. Thank you for not giving up." He is smiling hopefully, again. "Bye now," he says, walking Rich to the porch.

"I wish I could have left all the others this way," he thinks aloud.

It is dark now, so Rich decides to head home and call it a night. He will pick up again in the morning. Coming to a crossroads, though, he decides to go to the right instead of heading home. He wants to drop off the prints he lifted at the lab before going home. This will allow the technicians at the lab to get started on them as soon as they get in, instead of having to wait for him to get there. It is about ninety minutes out of his way, but he feels it will be worth it.

As he enters the driveway, the lab is dark; just a few parking lot lights on. He knows no one is there. He decides to leave the prints in the lock box outside. As he opens the outside door of the box, Pops is staring at him from the inside.

"Whoa!"

"Hey!"

In an obvious, awkward way, they are both

startled.

"What are you doing here so late?" asks Pops.

"I wanted to drop off some prints for you guys for in the morning. What about you? What are you still doing here?"

"I wanted to finish sifting through the prints I got from the tow yard. Hey, why don't you come in for a minute. I'll show you what I've got."

Pops has been here alone for a while and feels he can use some company.

They each close their half of the lock box and Rich heads over to the door. A bright light emerges from the lab as the door opens and Rich goes inside.

"I didn't think anyone was here because it is so dark outside."

"Oh, that. Those windows you see on the outside have been closed up for several years now. We needed to be able to create our own environment so we blocked off those windows. As you can see, we did a pretty good job of it. Now we can create day or night at our will," Pops explains.

"Here's the prints from the homes of those in the Honda, the Mustang, and the Pick-up truck," he hands three files to Pops. "I was able to get some really good prints and several of them. I don't think you'll have too much trouble matching them up."

"Thank you." Pops takes the prints and sets them on top of a small stack of other folders. "Suzie got prints for the out of state and out of county cars. I've only compared one set of prints so far but they do match. I checked all the prints from all the cars and my initial findings were right."

"None of the prints crossed cars?"

"Bingo! None of the prints from any of the cars matched any prints from any of the other cars. The only people in those vehicles were the original people in the vehicles," Pops states conclusively.

"Now it's a matter of who was in those cars," Rich states.

"Like I said, I did one cross check already. The prints in the 'Vette, match the prints of the owner of the 'Vette. I get a strong feeling we're gonna find the same thing with all the rest." Pops begins cross checking the prints. "Why don't you go on home. I'll let you know what I find."

Rich takes his leave and sets out for home. The road is narrow and lined, very thickly, with trees. With only his headlights to guide him, Rich feels his eyelids getting heavy. Glancing to the side, he sees light flickering through the trees.

"There's no houses out here," he thinks as he parks his patrol car at the side of the road. He walks through the trees toward the light.

"HELP ME! HELP ME!"

Rich hears the voice of a young girl screaming.

"KEEP QUIET!" a man's voice scolds back as several cracks of a whip come searing through the woods.

"AHHHHHHHHH!" the young girl screams.

"WHAT'S A MATTER WITH YOU? STOP IT! STOP IT!" a second man yells out.

"I CAN'T! I CAN'T!" a young man's voice bellows.

"YOU'D BETTER!" the first man calls out sternly as the searing crack of the whip again pierces the night.

Startled and scared, Rich crouches down low and continues on.

"Anybody out there?" he calls over his portable radio. "ANYBODY OUT THERE, I NEED HELP!" he says as forcefully and as quietly as he can.

"Rich is that you?" a familiar voice responds over the radio.

"Yes, yes, I've got trouble out here about 45 miles east of the lab."

"I'm on my way, what can you tell me?"

Rich indicated what he heard and gave approximate directions into the woods from the point of his car. Then he proceeds in cautiously, waiting for backups.

"HELLLLP MEEEE!" the young girl screams.

"Good-night boo-boo."

Virginia is putting Micah down in the crib she got from the hotel office. She had been driving all day and finally had to stop for some rest. Double checking that she locked and bolted the door, she calls home. The phone rings a couple of times.

"Be there, please be there," she says into the phone longingly.

The other end answers and she hears the familiar child's laughter, that of Micah, then her own voice says 'Leave a message after the tone.' Beeeep.

"Shoot. Hi honey. I just wanted to call to say hi and let you know I've stopped for the night. I guess you're working late... Well, I'm going to get some sleep now, but I'll call you again tomorrow. Bye honey, I love you..."

Jeff is frantically trying to get into the door and to the phone.

"I'll talk to you later."

Darting across the room he grabs at the phone.

"Hello, hello!" An annoying dial tone is all he hears. "Man, just missed her," he says as he puts down the receiver with disgust.

He had heard his wife's almost singing speech from behind the locked door leading to the garage. Fumbling in his excitement, he didn't get to the phone in time.

"Shoot!" he grumbles.

He plays the message again, just to hear her voice. While doing so, the phone begins to ring.

"HELLO!" he answers excitedly, before it completes its first ring.

"And a great big hello back to you."

"Oh, it's you."

"Well gee Jeff, I'm glad to talk to you too."

"Sorry David. I just missed a call from Virginia, and was hoping this was her calling to leave another message."

"Ah, yes. Miss the young gal already, do you? I know how you feel."

David Calvitch is, sincerely, a family man.

"Yeah. I do."

"Well, you'll be seeing her before you know it.

Three weeks is not very long you know."

"Yeah, right."

"Nah, I didn't believe it after I said it either," says David. "Anyway, I called to let you know that we'll have the subjects ready for you tomorrow, or at least a few of them."

"Great!"

"As they volunteer, and go through our screening process, we'll make them available."

"Screening process?"

"Like I told you at the meeting, we have to run background checks on them, hygiene checks, make sure they're in top physical form for this. I guess you can say, we're whipping them into shape for you."

"What about the governmental restrictions you told me about today?"

"That's been taken care of. All the proper paper work has been filled out, distributed, signed, sealed and delivered. We're all set."

"Thanks, Dave. That puts my mind at ease. I'd hate to think we were doing this without the proper authorization."

"Don't you worry. I take good care of my Tec's," David says in a very reassuring voice. "I'd better let you go, it's getting late. See you in the morning."

"Yes sir, see you in the morning, and thanks again."

"No problem. Good night, Jeff."

Jeff hangs up the phone relieved. His concerns about this project being laid to rest, he cand now continue without the tense pressure and frustrations it has brought. It seemed unusual to have gotten approval so quickly for this type of project, but knowing David, Jeff figured he had been working on the approval for several months. Jeff wasn't sure how he was going to handle this, emotionally speaking. He never worked with these kind of specimens before.

"As long as David got the okay, I'm sure everything will go smoothly. I just hope I can handle it," he thinks aloud as he makes his way upstairs to the shower.

After showering, Jeff hears a female voice coming from down stairs as he towels off.

"Hey, you had better take care of my honey bunny while I'm gone."

Jeff's eyes pop open.

"Virg!" he yells as he begins running down the stairs while still toweling off.

"Bye babe, I'll call tomorrow."

"HELLO! HELLO!" Jeff shouts, snatching up the phone. "Shoot! Missed her again."

Jeff is not having any success in connecting with Virginia.

Laying back on the bed in her hotel room, Virginia breathes a heavy sigh and awaits room service. Not wanting to wake the baby, she had ordered in.

"Room service!" mixed with knocking, calls a voice from outside, the door.

"Just leave it there thank you."

"Okay. Have a good night."

Looking through the peep hole, Virginia sees no one outside and opens the door to get her food. As she does, a man stares at her from across the parking lot. She notices him as she picks up her food. He starts walking toward her. Virginia gasps as her eyes widen with fear.

"HELLLLP MEEEEE! PLEASE HELP ME!"

Rich continues into the woods, pistol out and cocked. His eyes open and alert, he can feel his heart pounding. He knoww he should wait for backup but he can't just sit by and do nothing. He proceeds further; face sweating as he approaches a clearing. While keeping concealed, he positions himself to where he has a good view of what is going on. There they are.

"I can't believe this," Richard thinks aloud.

He is staring at a disgusting, yet strange, sight. He has never witnessed a scene quite like this one in all his days on the force, including when he was in Chicago.

"This is Marshall. What's going on?"

"Rich called in for backups. He's about thirty miles outside of town on Highway 56, about forty five miles from the lab."

"Backups? For what?" Marshall speeks in a direct tone, into his home based radio.

"He caught sight of light coming from the woods and decided to check it out. He heard screaming, yelling and the sound of a whip. He said the voices sounded like two men, plus one younger man and a young girl. He thinks it may have something to do with the missing persons."

"10-4, Smitty. Do you need me out there?"

"Negative sir. I think we can handle it. I've got several other deputies headed that way now. I just called to fill you in."

"10-4."

"If we need you, we'll call on this channel. Smitty out."

Marshall lies back into bed. His facial expression exposes him to be deep in thought. With his hands folded together over his chest, he clears his mind of this case - at least for now. Closing his eyes Marshall drifts off to sleep. He didn't bother to take off his boots because he knows he can get called in at any time and have to leave quickly. Having been an officer for a long time, he knows enough to get some rest whenever the opportunity presents itself.

Chapter VIII

"Ginya? Is that you?"

"Buddy?" questions a surprised, frightened Virginia.

"Virginia. Virginia Colt! Well I'll be a monkey's uncle."

"Buddy SeBlue," she says relieved. "How long has it been?"

"Too long darlin'," Buddy answers walking towards her. "How's that old man of yours?"

"Jeff's doing great! He's gonna be sore he missed you. How come you haven't called or stopped in or anything? I know you get up our way at least once a year."

"Sorry 'bout that. I changed my route and actually haven't been up that way for three years." He gives her a big hug. "Jeff's not with you?"

"No," she says sadly. "He's on some special project and had to cancel his vacation."

"You're here alone?" he asks astonished.

"Yes."

"Jeff allowed that?" Buddy is taken aback.

Jeff has always hated to let Virginia go away without him but hates even more for her to go away alone and Buddy knows that. He's known Jeff a long time.

"He didn't want to, but his mom is sick and I have to go see her."

"I hate to see you eat alone...," he begins to say looking down at her food.

"Oh that's okay," she interrupts. "I don't mind. I actually like it."

"Uh-huh, and cats love water. Listen, you didn't let me finish. This is Buddy you're talking to."

Buddy has known Jeff and Virginia for many years. He knows Virginia does not like to eat alone, but he also knows she is too polite to impose herself upon anyone.

"As I was saying, would you like the company of me and my wife for dinner?" he declares with an ear to ear smile of shear tranquility.

"You got married? That's great!" she exclaims. "When? Who is she? Do I know her? What's her name?"

"Slow down, slow down. Come on over and

meet her, she's in the truck."

"I can't, my son is sleeping."

"Jeff, a father? I can't imagine."

"He's very good with Micah," she says defensively.

"Oh, I don't doubt it. Shoot, he's a child himself. I just never would have imagined it. At least not for another five years or so. Hey let me go get the little woman. I'd sure love for you to meet her."

"Great, bring her over."

"I'm pulling that car carrier over there. The blue one."

Buddy is what you would call a great big teddy bear; another one of life's jewels. After meeting his wife, Virginia is happy to see he found a matching gem. They all enjoyed a couple of hours together, eating, talking and just goofing off.

"Excuse me," Virginia says with a cute girlish smile as she gets up. "I've got to use the potty."

"Bud, I was thinking," says Buddy's wife, Mary, after Virginia had left the room. "We've got three open spots on the rig, and there's plenty of room in the cab and sleeper for her and the baby. Do you think we could offer her a lift? It might take some of the pressure from the drive off her."

"Put her car on the rig?"

"Yes. I mean she has to go all the way to Georgia and we're going to Missouri. I'm sure she would appreciate having some company for at least part of that long ride."

"That's a great idea. Now why didn't I think of that? Anyway, I'll go put her car on the rig now, if she says okay, and we'll be off first thing in the morning."

Virginia is thrilled. She had not been looking forward to making this drive herself. They loaded her car onto the rig, said their good-nights and headed off to their rooms. Virginia lays back into bed; now feeling calm and peaceful. She smiles to herself and breathes a sigh of relief. She was very uncomfortable about having to make this drive alone in the first place. Now she wouldn't have to, at least not the whole thing.

Richard knows he has to act. There is no time to lose. He assesses the situation, runs across the clearing, takes aim and fires!

BAP! BAP! BAP!

Down it goes, releasing the young girl from its grasp. Turning, he sees the marks of the whip on the ground. Looking up, he sees a man bleeding and trapped under a pickup truck. Fire is crawling towards the truck. A young man comes rushing up over a hill with a damaged bucket, containing water. His leg and side are bleeding.

FOOSH!

To his side, fire flashes up. The fire surrounding them reaches a jug of alcohol. The young man throws the water near the truck and dashes off for more. Rich sees why. The fire is nearing the gas tank and the bed of the overturned truck. There are dozens of whiskey bottles littered about, several of which are broken.

"THIS SIDE, BOBBY! THIS SIDE! HURRY"

A voice beckons from the opposite side of the truck. There lay another man, pinned between the truck and a tree and encircled by liquor bottles. Rich runs and grabs a broken tree limb and jams it under the truck where the first man is trapped. Scared, the man looks at Rich from underneath the truck, then begins helping Rich lift the truck off his legs. Lifting the back of the truck, the man frantically pulls himself out, using his arms. The moving of the truck causes more alcohol to spill and catch fire. The young man returns with water, douses some flames and runs back for more.

FOOM! FOOM! FOOSH! FOOM!

"Get away from this clearing!" Rich yells to the now freed man.

"I've got to get my brother."

"The only way you can help in your condition is to drag yourself away from here."

The man reluctantly agrees and pulls himself along the ground crawling on his elbows; dragging his legs behind. The pain in his legs is excruciating.

Running around to the other side of the truck, Rich sees the other man. He props himself against another tree and tries to move the truck. It barely budges. The young man comes running back and stops abruptly, almost spilling the water he has retrieved. He doesn't see anyone.

"Over here!" yells Rich as he catches sight him.

Bobby runs around to the other side of the truck and drenches the ground near Richard and the trapped man.

"Come over here and help me push this thing," states Rich in a pleading yet direct manner.

The young man quickly moves into position, following Rich's lead. Both of them push and rock the truck back just enough to break free the trapped man. Holding the truck in place, the now freed man immediately falls to the ground with an agonizing scream, landing under the truck. Rich and the young man stare at each other in horror. If they let go, the truck would come down on top of the man. If they stayed, they would all die from the fire. Still, the now freed man lay unconscious. Rich is trying to reach for a branch or limb which he could use to prop the truck, or one which he could use to move the man, but it isn't going to happen. Everything is just out of reach.

FOOM!

Another small explosion. The fire is getting closer.

"Poppa?"

"That's my sister," says Bobby. "Over here! Come quick, we need your help!" he yells back.

She comes running over, frightened, crying and in a lot of pain. If Rich had waited a few seconds more, she would have been crushed. The Boa Constrictor which held her had just gotten hold of her when Rich came running in. The man under the truck had been whipping at it trying to draw it to him away from the young girl.

"AHHH!" she screeches a short abrupt scream when she reaches Rich and the two others. The bloody mess laying there traumatizes her. She turns to the side, falls to her knees and vomits. She begins to weep.

"Ya gots to help us sis!" the young man shouts; his muscles aching. "We gotta get poppa out from under this truck. Help us, please!"

"Please," says Rich. "All you have to do is pull him away a little." With sweat running down his face, again he pleads: "Please."

FOOM! FOOM! FOOM!

The young girl slowly gets up and turns to them. She comes close and puts her hand on her father. She pulls at his shirt collar and tries to move him. He hardly budges.

"He's too heavy!" she screams, "I can't move him! I CAN'T MOVE HIM!" She begins crying again, "I can't move him! I can't move him." She continues listlessly trying to pull him out from under the truck.

BOOOM!   several bottles of alcohol ignite simultaneously.

"AHHHHHH!" she screams.

"Calm down," Rich yells. "Calm down," he then says in a soft tone, trembling from the weight of the truck.

The young girl looks up to him with longing eyes, as if to say, 'help me.' Rich looks down and around, then down again. He sees the man is wearing a belt.

"Unbuckle his belt and put it around his arm then give me the other end."

The girl unbuckles the belt and is able to pull it out from under her father. She begins putting it around his left arm when Rich stops her.

"No, no. Put it around his right arm."

Rich only wants to roll the man out of the way so they can let the truck come to rest back on the ground. She hands him the belt and Rich pulls the man up rolling him back just enough to be out of the way, except for his legs.

"Move his legs," he yells straining.

The young girl pulls her father's legs out from the path of the truck.

"Now let the truck down easy," Rich says to Bobby.

They let it down easy, to a point, but then it drops. They thought it was already all the way down but it was not. It was slightly held up by the cargo in the back. Several bottles that were under the bed of the overturned vehicle are crushed, causing alcohol to come flowing out in all directions. Rich grabs the unconscious man and puts him over his shoulder.

"Come on!" he shouts.

They run out around the front of the truck. Fire is blazing out of control at the back off it. Rich knows they have to get out of there, and fast. Once that truck goes up, the whole forest, and their lives, would be at risk.

"This is Rich, anybody out there?" he calls into his radio.

"Go ahead Rich, we're almost there. I'm approaching your car now."

"We got an overturned truck, booze spilled all over, a big fire and several injured people."

"10-4."

Smitty calls for a fire truck as he, and several other officers, approach Rich's car. They all grab the fire extinguishers from their cars and hasten into the woods. They meet up with Rich, who is carrying one man; Bobby, who is helping the second; and the young girl. Some officers offer assistance to Rich and the injured as the rest continue on in, fire extinguishers pumping.

They are able to contain the fire and put it out, but decide to wait for the fire department before moving the pick-up truck. They gather at their vehicles to wait for the fire and emergency trucks to arrive, as well as assess the situation. In the midst of consulting and consoling each other they heard the noise:

BOOOOOM!

A near deafening explosion blasts out through the trees. Shooting up into the air is a ball of fire with two burning tires attached. A small smoldering fire had still been burning under the bed of the overturned truck.

"There goes the dynamite," Bobby says, looking upward.

"Rich, you go home and get some rest, we'll take it from here," says Smitty as he calls in for another ambulance and more fire trucks. "We'll sort the rest of this out, and give you a report in the morning."

The officers scurry about, grabbing whatever equipment they can find to contain some of the fires.

The landing debris is causing several smaller fires to erupt. These are the ones the officers would concentrate on until the fire department arrives.

As he is driving home, Rich decides to leave his radio tuned to the secondary channel. He is tired, very tired, and somewhat disappointed. He knows this is not at all related to the missing persons. This was a family of "shiners" whose operation got out of control. They were, no doubt, driving too fast through the woods and flipped their truck. Where the Boa came from is anybody's guess. He figures it is probably a pet or a tactic to scare unwelcome visitors. Rich makes it home, and crashes into bed.

"We missed you for dinner tonight," says his wife in a very soft voice.

"I'm sorry. I was going to call, but found myself helping a family of moon-shiners. Fools almost killed themselves."

"Shhhhh. Forget about all that, and go to sleep. It's time to forget about today, and focus on sleep. You need it."

Rich's wife, Angela, is very creative and poetic. She doesn't like Rich being a cop, but has been able to bear it since they moved here to Collinwood. She is very understanding about his profession and, even though it upsets her, does her best to hide all her anxious feelings. She had been thoroughly worried when Rich was not home on time. She learned over the years not to show it. She learned

to cope with it and not bring it up for that would make
matters worse. Rich never talks about what happens at
work.   He doesn't want to make it any harder on
Angela than it already is.

Angela is a sweet woman, very petite. She is
5' 5" with deep red, shoulder length hair usually worn
up.   She is not what most people would call model
material although still very pretty. To Rich, she is the
most beautiful woman in the world. Rich knows her
from the inside.   He knows the pain his being an
officer causes her.   He tried to quit the force, but
couldn't. By being a cop, it gives him the authority to
do something about crime. Before he was a cop, and
even during the time he tried to stop being one,
whenever he would see crimes being committed he
knew he just had to do something. Now, it is in his
blood and there is no way out for him. Angela knows
this, and Angela loves her husband very much. His
dedication to his job spills over into their family life
and that makes Rich a very good and concerned father
and husband.

As the two lay in bed, Angela rubs his forehead
and brushes back his hair with her fingers.

"Would you like me to fix you something to
eat? I can re-heat dinner or fix you something else if
you'd like," she asks softly.

"No, no thank you. I'm not really hungry."

"Did you eat?"

"No. I just haven't been hungry."

That is Angela's cue to leave it alone. When he's not hungry, it almost always means he is thinking about a case. She wants him to eat something, the way all wives do, but she knows not to push it. At the same time, Rich knows she is only being concerned.

"Thank you though. I know I'm gonna be famished when I get up in the morning," Rich says caringly. He knows that will make her feel better; letting her know she will be able to feed him in the morning.

"Well then," she says, with a smile brewing. "You get some sleep. Just remember, tomorrow is another day." She briefly pauses. "Today will become yesterday when tomorrow has come," she says in a soft and soothing voice.

With that, Rich falls fast asleep.

Chapter IX

As the morning sun is peeking through the tall trees, Sheriff Marshall Winston drives into the Super Market parking lot. Caleb Danielson and Jason Harris, both three year officers, are there waiting for him.

At 6'2" and 200 pounds, Caleb is a young man who can take care of himself. A very athletic person who enjoys everything from Moto-cross racing to football to baseball, and everything in between. He loves to tease the girls, and his brown hair and soft, caring, brown eyes let him get away with it. He loves people and always tries to help. He can quickly make friends, and keep them. His command of the English language was enough to astound the most lettered scholar, yet, he seldom uses it. He found too many people couldn't understand a word he was saying, unless he would talk at their level. A very serious young man. Some say, too serious for his age.

Jason, his partner, who is two months younger than Caleb, has a different attitude about life. Jason loves to have his fun though he does know when to be serious and is able to be when necessary. He is very laid-back. His usually messy blonde hair complemented his green eyes. He too, is very popular with the ladies. You can always count on him to try and bring you up when you're feeling down. He is two and a half inches shorter than Caleb, but just as strong. Like Caleb, Jason spends his fair share of time at the gym.

They are both dressed in plain clothes and had driven their own private vehicles. As directed previously by Marshall, they parked in inconspicuous places which still afforded them high visibility to the parking space in question.

Caleb and Jason have been best friends since they were born. They did everything together, including becoming police officers. They are very competitive with each other and for each other. When on the same team they would not only try to outdo the other team but, at the same time, try to outdo each other. Knowing when and where to draw the line made them both very successful in all their endeavors.

"Hello, boys," Marshall says walking up to them, carrying a leather sack.

"Greetings and salutations, sir."

"DUDE!"

Stunned, Marshall and Caleb turn to Jason.

"And Dude right back at ya," says Marshall, smiling.

"Attired as we are, am I to presume you wish us to maintain an unsuspected surveillance, focusing on this area?" inquires Caleb.

"Yeah, I want the two of you to stake out this spot," Marshall smiles again.

"What's the situation, sheriff?" asks Jason.

"Missing persons." Marshall begins to explain the case. "Mike, the store manager, has towed nine cars from this spot. It appeared to him that they were abandoned here. Mike let them sit for a couple-a-few days, then had them towed. We checked the tags, found the registration addresses, then compared them to the current missing persons reports we have on file. They matched."

"Someone's been snagging folks, and leaving their cars?" queries Jason.

"Exactly."

"Are we watching just this spot or the whole lot?" asks Jason.

"It seems whomever it is, they only abduct people who park in this spot."

"Weird."

"Did you run any print checks on the vehicles?" questions Caleb.

"Yeah, yeah we did. All the prints in the car belong to only the people who were in the car, and so far, all the prints match the missing persons."

"So far?" asks Caleb.

"Pops is still cross checking the prints."

"I guess somebody really likes this spot," quips Jason in an air of disbelief.

"Were there any signs of applied force attached to any vehicles, or any signs of a struggle?" Caleb asks.

"No, no, none at all."

"Anything else we should be aware of?" Caleb wants to make sure he has all the facts, and as much information as possible.

"Yeah, like, any other weird stuff?" Jason adds.

"Yup. From what we have, it looks like the culprit waits for their victims to get out of their car, then he, or they, we don't know that yet, grabs them, takes their keys, starts their car, fastens their seat belts and locks all the doors, before leaving."

"Dude, that's an awful lot of trouble to go through just to grab someone," says Jason.

"Exactly. Whoever this is, they appear to be playing games."

"And from no other spot but this one?" inquires Caleb.

"This is the only spot. Mike was very specific about that. One of the cashiers also said the same thing."

"How do you want us to work this?" asks Caleb.

"I want both of you out here at all times as much as possible. If one of you has to leave, work it out with the other so that at least one of you is here all the time. I want you on different sides, to give you two different angles to view this spot. Keep an eye on each other. Here." He gives each of them a portable two-way radio as he pulls them from the sack he is carrying. "You can talk via these things. They're not on any regular police frequency, so they can't be monitored with a police radio scanner. I want both of you here when the store opens, and I don't want you to leave until it closes." Marshall's voice now takes on a more commanding tone. This is serious and he wants to make sure Caleb and Jason understand the importance of this assignment.

"Do you have any leads of any kind we should watch for?" asks Jason, now in a more serious tone.

"Nothing yet. All we have is a theory built around a bunch of possibly unrelated facts that have been present with each car."

"Winston! You out there?" booms a voice from the sheriff's car's police radio.

BAM! BAM! BAM! BAM!

"You ready in there?" Buddy calls out to Virginia as he knocks heavily on her door. "We gotta get movin'."

Virginia opens the door looking beautiful, but the expression on her face bemoans: "I want to go back to bed!" She had driven for a very long time, on Interstate 90 out of Washington, before stopping here in Garrison, Montana.

"I'm so glad you're driving," she says sleepily while yawning. "I don't think I'm awake enough yet."

"Me? I thought you were going to take first shift? Shoot, had I known I was gonna be driving, I'd 'av slept in another few hours."

Virginia stares at Buddy with a glare of disbelief.

"Me? Drive that big truck?" she says to him, pointing at the truck. "You have got to be nuts!"

With a small chuckle, Buddy looks back at her and smiles.

"You ready?"

"Yeah, just about. I'm all packed up."

Buddy goes in and gets her suitcase and overnight bag, while Virginia dresses the baby. Of course, she can't "just" dress him. With Virginia, she can't "just do" anything with Micah. All the usual fun and playing with him has to take place. It truly is a pleasure to watch her with the baby. Even Buddy, who wants to get going, found himself just standing in the doorway, watching the two of them. He can't help but smile.

"Hey Gin," he says softly. "We're all ready out here, so, whenever you're all set."

"Oh, okay. I'm sorry. I just love him so much," she says turning to Micah and continues: "Yes I do. I do, I do, I do."

Micah begins laughing and wiggling and putting his hands into his mother's face.

As they approach the truck, Micah who is trying hard to talk, in his inquisitive way asks: "Dis?" while pointing with his arm to the truck.

"That's a truck."

"Dis?"

"Yes, it's a truck. We're going to go bye-bye in the truck. It's going to take us to see Grandma." Virginia is so good with Micah.

"Dam ma, Dam ma."

Micah's eyes light up and open big and wide. He always gets excited when he is going to be able to see his grandmother.

It has been a month since Micah, Virginia and Jeff have seen her. Jeff had to move to Washington because of his job. They had decided his aging mother would not move with them because the move to Washington is only supposed to be temporary. It should last only a year, maybe a bit more. After that, Jeff is scheduled to move back to the Georgia offices.

"Wow! It's really high up here," Virginia says as she climbs into the truck. "You can see everything."

After securing Micah's car seat everyone gets settled and they start off.

"A hundred bottles of beer on the wall..," begins Buddy.

"Oh, please!" both Virginia and Mary say as they turn at the same time to Buddy.

The three of them start laughing. When everyone else laughs, Micah laughs too; excitedly.

"That's one happy kid," says Buddy.

"Thank you."

"I think he looks a lot like you," observes Mary.

"I dunno, I was thinking he looks more like Jeff," offers Buddy.

"About half the people who see us think he

looks like me and the other half thinks he looks like Jeff. When you see all three of us together, you can see both of us in Micah."

"Whoda you think he looks like?" asks Buddy.

Smiling, Virginia says: "I think he looks like Micah." She turns to the child and says: "I'm gonna get you, I'm gonna get you," as she tickles him.

"Good answer," says Mary. "I like that. He looks like Micah. I like that."

"Say good-bye to Garrison," Buddy begins. "Sioux Falls, South Dakota, Route 29, here we come."

Getting onto the highway, Interstate 90, Buddy asks Virginia to get him something to eat. He had gotten all of them some food from the hotel, before leaving.

"Once we get on the road, we don't stop for nothin' but diesel," Mary says while taking the food from Virginia. "And I mean nothin'!"

"What about going to the bathroom?"

"You'll get the hang of it after a while," offers Buddy as Mary points to a portable facility.

"Eeeeeewwwwwww!" says Virginia, looking as if she has just bitten into a lemon. "On second thought, I think I will drive," she chuckles.

"Okay, where were we?" Buddy asks while

taking a bite of a breakfast sandwich. "Oh yeah, ninety nine bottles of beer on the wall."

"Ahhhhhh!" shriek Virginia and Mary as they begin pelting him with crumpled up napkins. "Not that song! Please!!!" they laugh.

"Babe, you gonna get more sleep, or stay up for a while?" Buddy asks Mary.

"I'm awake now, so I'll stay up with you for maybe a couple of hours, then I'll take a nap."

"That's how we make good time," explains Buddy. "We keep each other company for a while, then one drives while one sleeps. When I get tired, she'll take over so I can get a couple hours sleep. Then I get back behind the wheel and drive a couple more hours. By that time, we're both ready to get out and walk around, get more fuel and something to eat. It works pretty good. Even when we're not sitting together talking, we're still together. I can reach back and hold her hand while she sleeps and vice versa. We may not always be awake with each other, but at least we're together."

Virginia agrees, shaking her head yes. She can't help but think about Jeff. This new project has been keeping him away from home for way too many hours each day. She really misses him. She knows it's only temporary, but still, she can't help to miss him and feel lonely at times.

"Hey Buddy, stop it! You're depressing poor Virginia." Mary reaches back and gives Virginia a hug. "Can't you see she misses her man?"

"Oh, sorry Gin. I didn't mean nothin' by it," he apologizes.

"No, it's okay. I do miss him. It seems like you two have the ideal situation."

"It is for me," says Mary. "I just love the fact that when my husband wakes up in the morning and goes off to work, he's still right here with me. And when I'm ready for bed, and he wants to keep working, I can fall asleep with no problem, because, while he's working, he's still right by my side. Holding my hand if necessary. He makes me very happy."

Buddy is almost blushing.

"That's so wonderful," Virginia answers with tears forming in her eyes. "Don't you miss living in a house sometimes, and that kind of stability?"

"Sometimes, yes, but I know how much this means to Buddy, and I know how much he cares for me, that I don't even think about it, or at least try not to. When I find myself longing for all that stuff, I think about all the other wives who have it, but who don't have their husbands with them almost twenty four hours a day. That makes it worthwhile to me."

"Love you baby," Buddy says, kissing the back of Mary's hand.

"Love you too."

"That's just wonderful." Virginia reaches over and gives both of them a group hug. "I'm so happy for you both." She squeezes them together.

"We've got what we call the Paul McCartney marriage," says Buddy.

"The what?"

"Yeah, you know. Paul and Linda McCartney. They both worked together, they traveled together, they sang together. They never had to be separated on a regular basis. They never had to spend several hours a day everyday away from each other," says Mary.

"If I remember correctly," continues Buddy, "Paul said, in an interview, that he and Linda had only been apart for maybe a total of two weeks, or something like that, during their entire marriage."

"Even when she wasn't playing or singing, she was always able to find some way to help with what Paul was doing and vis-a-vis. As you have probably figured out, we are big Beatles fans."

"Speaking of which," Buddy says while popping in a cassette. "How 'bout some."

"Something in the way she moves.....," begins to echo softly from the speakers.

Chapter X

"This is Winston. Whatcha got Pops?" Marshall answers the radio call.

"Exactly what we thought we were going to get."

"All the prints match all the missing persons," states Marshall.

"All the prints match all the missing persons."

A moment of silence passes as both men are in quiet contemplation.

"Don't you go messing with that Mike character. I know what you're thinking."

Marshall is thinking. He is thinking more seriously on the assumption that maybe Mike is involved after all. Maybe Mike called the cops to try to throw them off his trail.

"Marshall, let Rich or me handle any more questions to Mike. I don't think he'd last a minute in a room alone with you. I know you don't want to scare him off; then we'd have to hunt down a fugitive. At least for now, he's still available." Pops speaks with determination.

"Yeah.   You're   right," Marshall answers slowly and seriously. "I think it's a good idea to put a tail on him, though."

"Want me to take care of that for you?"

"Please. Thanks Pops. Let me know who you finally assign that to."

"Will do. Pops out."

Marshall walks back over to Caleb and Jason with a very serious look on his face. He is not happy. Whoever is doing this is going through a lot of trouble to keep from getting caught.

"Was that Pops?" asks Jason sincerely.

"Yeah. He confirmed that all the prints in the cars belong to only the people who were in the cars; and they all belong to the missing persons."

"It would appear then, that your theory is correct," says Caleb.

"Well somebody's playing games," states Jason.

"I don't like games," Marshall says with a sense of purpose.

"Daddy," she says shaking her father gently. "Daaadyyyyyy!" she persists as she continues shaking him. "DADDY!" she begins shaking him faster and harder.

"Errr raa raa raa," is the only reply from the slumbering figure in front of her.

"Daddy, you have to wake up! You've been sleeping all morning and I haven't gotten my good morning kiss yet!"

Richard slowly opens his eyes. Standing before him is one of the cutest little girls you will ever lay your eyes upon. Soft curly brown hair and bright blue eyes.

"I have to go out and play," she says as if she can't be late, "and then you'll go to work and I won't get my good morning kiss!" She stands there pouting in her pajamas, staring at her father.

Rich can't help but break a smile.

"I get my kiss now?" she says with a completely opposite expression. Her face brightened, with her head cocked to one side, a tight, closed lip smile from ear to ear and her eyes rolled back with her eyelashes batting.

"Come 'ere," Rich says, pulling his daughter in close and tight.

"Emmm wah," they give each other a big kiss.

"Uh-oh! You forgot to watch out for this!"

Rich quickly moves his hand down to her side and starts tickling her while making rapid barking sounds into her stomach.

"Ahhhh ha ha ha ha!" she's laughing and shrieking.

Rich gives her another big hug.

"So what's on your agenda for today?"

"I have to go over Lisa's house. We're gonna play dolls. She got a new bed for her baby dolly and we get to put it together."

"Wow! That's neat! Well, you go have fun, and I'll see you tonight when I get home."

"O.K. Daddy."

She turns and runs out of the room, only to double back and stick her head in the door.

"I love you, Daddy!"

"I love you to, Sandra."

Rich begins his morning ritual of shaving, showering and getting dressed.

"Emmmm."

He smells the fresh coffee brewing and bacon

cooking as he finishes dressing.

"Rich?"

"Yeah, I'm in here."

"Work called."

"Oh sheesh, already. It's too early for this."

"Well actually, it's just about 11:30."

"WHAT?"

"It's about 11:30."

"I'm late! I've got to hurry."

"Rich, you told them you probably wouldn't be in until 12:30 today. You have got over an hour and you're already dressed." Then she adds, "Slow down," with a chuckle in her voice.

"12:30? What are you talking about?"

"You're kidding right?"

"No...I'm...not. What are you talking about?"

"You must have forgot. You woke up at six o'clock this morning and called in, to let them know you wouldn't be in until 12:30 or so, then you rolled over and went back to sleep. I got up around nine o'clock and let you sleep. I was going to wake you up at eleven, but you got up yourself. Coffee?"

"Well, no, Sandra woke me up. She 'had' to go play and couldn't leave without her good morning kiss. Yes, please," he says, reaching for the freshly poured cup of coffee Angela is holding out to him. "I tell you, I don't remember calling the office this morning."

"You came in late last night. You were so tired and frazzled. You didn't sleep well all night either. You kept tossing and turning. After calling in to work, you slept good."

"I must 'av, 'cause I don't remember anything. So what did work want?"

"Smitty wants you to give him a call so he can fill you in on what happened last night."

"Did he say anything else?"

"Actually, Smitty didn't call, it was Suzie. She did say to tell you something about Smitty saying it's not related, whatever that means."

"I didn't think so. Thanks dear."

"You ready for breakfast?" she smiles.

"Emmmm you betcha. It smells great, and I'm starved."

"That's a good combination. Come on, I'll fix you a plate."

As the two of them head off to the dining

room, Rich can't help but think about everything that's happened these last two days.

"Next time you go to the super market," he starts.

"Yes?"

"Next time you go. Park only on the east side of the lot."

"The east side?"

"Yeah."

"Why?" It is only natural for her to be curious.

"Just please don't park on the west side, at least not for a while."

Angela sees the concern, mixed with fear, in his face. She wants to know more, but she knows it is best not to ask. She trusts Rich; if he says park on the east, park on the east she shall.

"Okay, dear. I will only park on the east side of the lot, until you tell me otherwise."

"Promise me," he says sternly.

Angela knows now this is something very, very serious.

"I promise, Rich. I will not park on the west side of the lot, only on the east side."

"Thank you." Now, after breathing a sigh of relief, Rich sits down to eat. "Thank you."

"Thanks Jason," Marshall says as Jason is removing the traffic cones and 'Police Line Do Not Cross' marking tape. "You have a good view of both the spot and the front door from where you're parked, right?"

"Affirmative," answers Caleb.

"Good, good. I want you to keep an eye on that front door as well as this spot. When someone gets out of their car, watch them until they get inside and keep an eye out for them when they come out. We don't know if they're being grabbed on their way in or on their way out."

"You say that as if you're not even sure they're being abducted."

"At this point, I'm not really sure of anything," Marshall answers Caleb. He turns back to Jason. "You can put that stuff in my trunk, if you would."

"No problem, sir."

"Thanks."

Marshall begins looking around the lot again. As Jason approaches, Marshall instructs him to keep an eye open for any suspicious looking cars, vans, trucks, whatever, that come into the lot.

"Caleb is going to keep an eye on the people as they leave their cars and walk into the store. I don't think you have a good enough vantage point from your spot, but help him if you can and remember to keep an eye out for anything or anyone looking suspicious."

"Yes sir, Marshall." Jason is being more serious now. He knows it is time to 'Fly Right' as Marshall would put it.

"All right then fellas. I'll be leaving you two for now. I've got another one of those radios in my car, so you can reach me if you need me. I've got some checking up to do." Marshall walks to his car and, as he gets in, he calls back to the officers, "Hey! You two boys be careful, okay?"

After they confirm they will be, and thank Marshall, he drives off.

On leaving the lot, Marshall takes note of Mike's car. He takes down the plate number, the color, the style, and any distinguishing marks he can find. Marshall wants to make sure he has this car well in mind; just in case. He decides to drive over to Mike's house and have a look around.

Once Marshall is gone, Caleb and Jason get into their respective places and began the tedious task of surveillance. It's not too long after Marshall's leaving that someone pulls in.

"Hey, we've got one. Look alive," Jason says over the radio to Caleb.

The car pulls in, windows down, radio blaring:

"It happened to me again, third time lucky..."

Whoever this is, they are not good at parking or they just don't care that they are not within the lines. They take up almost two parking spaces.

"At least they didn't bash the curb," Caleb thinks to himself as he shakes his head.

The driver shuts off the car and gets out. Caleb watches the young lady go into the store. She appears to be reading a very long shopping list that is dangling from her hand.

"Man, what station was that? I love that song," Jason mumbles while searching the dial.

"Third time lucky...," The song is ending and fading while the D.J. is talking all over the music, "W P X C Radio 1 0 3...."

"Shoot, missed it," Jason says frustrated as he smacks the steering wheel.

Jason turns off the radio. He isn't really in the

mood to listen to the radio, but had not heard that song in a long time and just wanted to hear it again. He also doesn't want to be distracted by the radio while on a stake out.

"Did you see that one?"

"No, why, was she cute?" questions Jason.

"A real knockout."

"Oh, man! I missed her. I want your spot. I'll trade ya."

"No way man. I like it here."

"Tell you what, we'll trade off after a few hours."

"I don't think so."

"Okay, each day, we'll change spots."

"No no no no no no no no. Marshall told me to watch them go in and out."

"Maaaaannnnnnnn!"

"I'm sure she was really, really cute..," booms a familiar voice out from the radios.

Surprised, Caleb's and Jason's eyes nearly spring from their sockets.

"...but let's keep this channel open for

professional use only. Okay, boys?" says Marshall.

There is no immediate answer from either of them. Slowly bringing their radios up to their mouths, they both answer: "Yes, Sir," back to Marshall. Their tone of voice is as if they are two small children who have just been scolded.

"Thank you boys, and, keep up the good work. By the way Caleb, what was she wearing?"

Caleb thinks this question is strange after what Marshall has just said. Hesitantly, he begins his reply.

"She was wearing short, white, terry cloth, short-shorts; brown sandals with white flowers on them; and an orange tank top and..."

"Oh man!" Jason says aloud in his car as he listens. "And I missed it."

"And what?" asks Marshall.

"Well she wasn't wearing a bra, sir," Caleb answers in a kind of mild, bashful voice.

"Thank you Caleb. Keep up the good work," Marshall replies.

"Sir?"

"Go ahead."

"What was that all about?"

"Just checking to see if you're doing your job."

"How's that?"

"If you were only able to give me her dimensions and nothing else, then you were not doing your job."

"Thank you, sir."   Caleb is sure glad he mentioned her sandals.

With the list she had, the boys calculated it would take her about two hours to get what she wanted. After two and a half hours, Jason went inside to see if he could find her.   When he returned unsuccessful, there was another vehicle parked in the spot. A Motorcycle. A really nice, well beat up, dirt bike.   Breaking his line of thought from the Motorcycle, he calls Caleb.

"Where'd the chick go?"

"She came out, loaded up her car and left. We can just about pack it up for today."

"Why?"

"The guy on this bike works here and doesn't get off 'till the place closes. He's not supposed to park this close to the building but decided if his manager can park in the first spot he should be able to park here. I guess he's rebelling."

"Cool."

"When he pulled in, I got out and talked to him for a while. I set up a race for the three of us next month, when he gets off from school. I wrote down his description and what he's wearing, in case we need it."

They both decide to stay until the lot thins out a bit before leaving. Tomorrow they will find less obvious parking spaces then the ones they are currently in.

Chapter XI

"Why are they all sedated?" Jeff asks. "How are we supposed to start, with them all doped up? I was told they would be alert."

"Look!" snaps Arthur, "You just finish calculating the doses and WE'LL worry about measuring the results."

"You won't be able to get accurate results with them doped up on, whatever. You're introducing another chemical into the equation. I have each dose configured for normal, stable, specimens. This changes everything."

"You can still proceed and then base the results on that."

"On what? How will I know what those results are going to be on subjects which have not been sedated?" Jeff is getting angry.

Arthur is trying to just push this project through. He doesn't necessarily want it to fail but knowing he will not obtain full credit for it, he does not necessarily want it to succeed.

"Well you can figure it in now or don't you know how to do your job?"

Arthur wants Jeff out of the picture. With Jeff gone he will be in a position to take over all the years of research Jeff has put into this project. Then he can take over the project and get all the credit. The greed in Arthur's heart is blocking his thinking. His dreams of millions in royalties is just that, a dream. There would be no royalties paid. All inventions and creations are the property of David Calvitch and his corporation. Nothing goes to those being paid to create and invent.

"Just add the new component in!" Arthur snaps.

"Would you mind being so kind as to tell me just what it was you used, or would you have me run skin and blood tests to find the chemicals myself?"

By now, Jeff is ready to have Arthur thrown off the project. If he was only in a position to do so, he would. Several times he asked David Calvitch to put Arthur onto another project, but David wouldn't. David would only say, "Well, let's just leave things the way they are and see what happens." For someone who didn't particularly like Arthur, David surely wasn't in any hurry to have him dismissed, nor put onto a different project.

"Where's the memo I sent you? I gave you a list of all the chemicals we are using, including which specimen got what." Arthur is getting sassy. It is like listening to a third grader.

"I never received a memo from you."

"I put it on your desk personally. I suppose I'm going to have to start hand delivering them to you, huh?"

Arthur turns his back to Jeff and begins shutting down his work station. The sound of circuits being tripped and electric motors winding down penetrates the tension between them. The panel in front of him slowly dims, until only one green indicator button is lit.

"What are you doing?" asks Jeff.

"What do you think I'm doing?" Arthur again snaps at Jeff. "I'm going to get you a copy of the memo. You know the list of chemicals you seem to think is so important to your testing. The list you can't seem to have kept your hands on, that I have to go get a copy of for you, which is going to delay our testing again!"

"Well thank you very much," Jeff says in a disgusted tone as Arthur walks past him.

"Yeah."

Jeff shakes his head in disgust and turns to his table. He and Arthur have been on edge with one another for a long time; almost as long as this project has been active. Arthur is quite clear in his determination to receive more than his fair share of the credit for this project. If successful, this project willl go down in history, along with the names of the project's inventors.

Jeff had wheeled a cart into this area containing several vials of varying colored liquids, along with several syringes. He is working on a new drug to be used for underwater exploration. The drug will counter and prevent the effects of atmospheric pressure. This drug, along with an implant of a special "Blood Valve" will prevent the bends. The research started years ago and has been one failure after another. Breathing air under pressure causes the body tissues to absorb nitrogen due to the increased pressure. When a diver begins to surface, thus reducing the amount of external pressure, the absorbed nitrogen must be slowly eliminated through respiration, if not, bubbles will form in the blood stream causing the bends. The theory is: 'If the nitrogen cab be vented from the body continually, while on the dive, the bends will be avoided and divers could surface at will, regardless of the depth and the amount of time they were underwater. They will not have to decompress at various depth intervals.' Not having to decompress will eliminate not only the dangers of surfacing too quickly but also all the boredom, extra required air, stress and dangers associated with timed decompression stops.

The "Blood Valve," which will be used to vent the Nitrogen, will have to be surgically implanted into a major artery and secured. It will serve the dual purpose of venting the nitrogen and supplying the serum to the blood. The serum will be used to counter the effects of the bends, allowing the diver to continue, without losing consciousness. The "Blood Valve" will hold the blood, allowing the bubbles in the blood to collect, then vent it off into the water. The valve will run on electro-mechanical energy. The actual valve, which will open and close to vent the nitrogen, will be done electrically. In case of battery failure, the electricity will be produced mechanically. The mechanical device contains a small turbine, which rotates with the divers movement, and is connected to a tiny generator, to supply electrical power to the unit. The Blood Valve will become known by its marketing name of: "The External Nitrogen Vent Kidney."

Jeff knows it is back to the lab for him, so he packs up his cart and begins wheeling it away. He stops to examine the specimens on his way out. Approaching the thick glass wall, Jeff looks in and nods with approval. Counting in his head, there must have been about fifteen of them. They are all locked up in cages. Jeff can see some of the other technicians. They are wearing what appears to be radiation suits. The suites are black, not the usual yellow. The head gear is also out of the norm. The helmets are all black, with black visors, the sides of which are sticking out, like small plant pots. There are two antennae coming out of the top. The suits are also not baggy, as in normal radiation suits. They are very well fitting.

"I wonder what that's supposed to be?" Jeff is thinking: "This does not seem right."

He continues looking around.

"Children?" he says softly. "How did he get approval for children?" Jeff utters aloud in an undertone. He shakes his head in doubt and disbelief with a puzzled look on his face.

SLAM! A door bursts open, startling Jeff.

"Get in there!" one of the technicians yells, while trying to force a woman into one of the cells.

"NO!" she screams. "You can't do this to us." She is struggling and fighting to get free.

The technicians fling her across the room into an open cell. She lands in the cell with a rumble that resembles several bags of potatoes all being tossed onto the floor. He slams the door shut. The woman, who looks as if she has been defeated, lays curled up on the floor weeping.

"Please...," she pleads while she cries. "Please..."

Her cage door bursts open again and she looks up horrified. Two children are placed into the cage with her, two young girls. The woman rushes over, as best as she can, and grabs the two girls; hugging them with intense fervor.

"Oh my babies, my babies," she cries while rocking them back and forth.

"We'll worry about the rest tomorrow," says one technician to another. "Arthur screwed up again, so testing will have...," their voices fade as they exit.

Looking closer, Jeff sees that all of them have been treated roughly in some way. They not only look sedated, they look crushed. Some beaten, all defeated. They all have a look of hopelessness in their eyes. They all look as if they are being held in prison, not as willing subjects for a test. Jeff's heart goes out to them all. He walks around the wall to the security door to enter his I.D. card.

One thought keeps circling through his brain: "Why are volunteers being treated in this way?"

"NOT AUTHORIZED FOR ENTRANCE" flashes on the key card entry box.

"Not authorized? They're supposed to be my subjects," Jeff says aloud.

His emotions now turn to anger. He gathers up his stuff and wheels the cart down a corridor to his lab. After leaving his things in his office, he storms off. Jeff goes straight into David's office.

"WHAT'S GOING ON HERE?" he demands. "How come I can't get in to see MY subjects and why are they being treated like animals?" Jeff is almost shouting.

"Jeff, Jeff, Jeff," begins David, with a calming tone. "Please sit down."

"I don't wanna sit down, I want answers."

"Okay Jeff, but please calm down."

"Give me a reason to," Jeff retorts in a direct, abrupt voice.

"All right Jeff. Let me start with the reason you're not allowed to go in to see them."

"Okay," he says angrily.

"Please Jeff."

"I'm trying, but I don't like what I saw down there today. It was pathetic, degrading and just plain cruel. Now what's going on?"

"All right. First of all, we all know how ambitious and anxious you are. We also know how compassionate you are. We did not want to take the chance of you beginning your experiments before we had a chance to properly test and examine the subjects. Therefore, we restricted your access to them."

Jeff's face is starting to relax a little.

"I also didn't want you talking to them," David continues, "because it may have made you back out of this whole procedure. These people have been paid handsomely, and in advance I might add, for their services. If you back out of this, we lose all that money, and get no experiments done. I also know that you are a man of your word, so, if you promise not to go near the subjects until we, or rather I, give you the okay, I'll add your code to the door."

"Okay," he says sternly.

"Okay what?"

"Okay, I'll not go near them until I hear from you."

"Thanks Jeff."

David turns to his computer and calls up the security file. He proceeds to add Jeff's name to the list of people granted access to the holding cell.

"Here. I'll add your code in right now."

With the computer facing away from him, Jeff is unable to see what David is doing. David continues the process of entering Jeff's name into the system. He moves his cursor over to the two last fields. Before pressing enter to update the file, the fields appear as such:

LIMIT ACCESS TO ___ TIMES

(How many times can user enter/exit this room)

IS USER GRANTED EXIT AUTHORIZATION FROM

THIS ROOM (Choose one:)   > YES <
NO

"You can check it if you like, but only once, and don't go inside. Agreed?"

"Agreed," Jeff says reluctantly.

"Good. Thank you."

David then presses the number 2 on his keypad and clicks his mouse button. Jeff, of course, didn't see the final entry made into the system regarding his access to the cell area. David wants to make sure that if Jeff went inside, he wouldn't be able to get back out. Just before closing the file and putting it online, the two access fields take on a whole new appearance:

LIMIT ACCESS TO 2 TIMES

   (How many times can user enter/exit this room)

IS USER GRANTED EXIT AUTHORIZATION FROM

THIS ROOM (Choose one:)   YES   > NO <

"Now what about the way they're being treated," Jeff demands.

"You know, the only reason I'm letting you talk to me like this is because I like you and your work. Don't push it."

"When it comes to my involvement with something, I'll push it as far as I have to," Jeff says with a stern, cold stair, looking directly into David's eyes. There is a slight moment of intense silence before Jeff continues: "As far...as I have to."

"Okay Jeff, okay," David says, while motioning his hands for Jeff to calm down. "All right, it's okay," David is still motioning.

"What's going on?" he asks coldly.

"To be honest with you, we're not really sure."

Jeff pulls back in confused disbelief.

"When we gave them the sedative, several of them had bad reactions to it. They became violent, enraged. We had to move them from their suites down into the cages. They tore apart the rooms. We had to transfer them until we can figure out what is happening; why they are having such bad reactions to an otherwise stable sedative. As a matter of fact, one of the technicians received a broken arm because of the subjects reaction to the sedative. Broke his arm in three places."

"Just because of a sedative?"

"Yes Jeff, and we just cannot seem to figure out why."

"What did you give them?"

"As far as I know, it's the same thing we've

been using."

"We never had any problems with it before."

"I know.   I've got Arthur looking into the problem now."

"Oh, Arthur."

"Yes, I heard about your little, um, spat, shall we say? What happened?"

"Arthur said he gave me a list of each chemical used on each of the specimens, along with the dosage amount for each, but he actually never did."

"WHAT?" David is surprised.

"Didn't you get a memo?"

"No, I did not." David is very stern. "So what you're telling me is that we have not used our standard sedative. Is that correct?"

"I'm not telling you anything. I'm telling you what Arthur told me."

"I'll deal with him later. I don't know where he gets off testing one of his new chemical creations on specimens which are not designated as his; and, to top it all off, they didn't work." David sounds very disgusted.

"I don't know why you keep him around. You're hardly ever pleased with him, or his work."

"Well. We'll just keep him around and see what happens."

"About the Children..."

"Hold it," David says holding his hand up as if to say 'Stop.' "I know what you're going to ask. Yes we did get approval for the children. It was not at all easy, but we did. It's a deal worked out with the parents and with the children themselves. It seems there is a loop hole in the child labor laws which allows us to use children for this type of thing as long as they are not overworked, and as long as we have the parent's consent."

"You're amazing."

"Nope. Just careful. I do not want any surprises."

"Sorry for doubting you. I...I shoulda known better."

"It's okay, Jeff. That's one of the things I appreciate about you. You have the guts to question things. Okay, maybe you could question matters a bit less angrily, but hey." David smiles.

"Well, I've got a lot of work to do now. Gotta recalculate those doses."

"No no, NO," says David sternly. "We are not going to have you waste time trying to calculate an equation, to project a reaction, for a chemical which is already producing an unexpected result. We are going to wait until the subjects stabilize before continuing. Why don't you go ahead and take the rest of the day off...to clear your mind?"

"Oh, that would be great!"

"Fine then. You do it."

Turning to leave, Jeff stops and turns back.

"OH! One more thing."

"Why are they sedated?" David interrupts.

"Yeah."

"That was one of the conditions we had to agree to, in order to get the proper approval. The U.S.A. didn't want any undue anxiety put upon our test subjects. Our "volunteers" also felt the same way. They all know what is going to be done, and none of them wanted to be, shall we say, "awake" for it. Uncle Sam said they would approve our testing, if we maintain our subjects in a state of semi-consciousness, especially the children. You can say it is sort of an imposed kindness to our volunteers."

"Thanks Dave. I'll see you tomorrow."

"Good night, Jeff."

David watches as Jeff leaves his office, goes down the corridor, turns a corner and goes out of sight. David then places a call.

In another room, an office, a small blue light above the office door begins to flash. A hand pulls open a drawer and lifts the receiver of a blue phone with a blue flashing light.

"Yes sir, Mister Calvitch?"

"I need you to ransack nine of our 'volunteer' guest suites, and I need it done yesterday," he says coarsely.

"Yes sir, Mister Calvitch."

"And make it look like several, very extremely violent, people did it."

"Yes sir, Mister Calvitch."

"And this time...it had better look good."

The voice on the other end hesitates before responding.

"Yes sir, Mister Calvitch."

David puts down his phone and folds his hands on his desk. He is thinking; concerned.

Jeff had just come from his own office and is on his way out. About to leave, he decides to go back to the test room. He knows he should trust David, but he just wants to make sure. He goes to the cells where the volunteers are and walks to the security door. He slides his card in and pulls it out. A green light illuminates and the door makes a loud click. This means he now has access. Wanting to push the door open and go in, he remembers his promise to David. Jeff pushes the door enough to make sure it would indeed open. The light goes out and he lets go of the door, allowing it to lock. He heads up the stairs and again towards the exit.

Jeff settles into his car, starts it, and puts it into reverse. He is just about to leave when he puts his car back into park and turns it off. He feels bad for not trusting David, but he has to make sure. After all, these are real people he will be dealing with.

Getting out of his car, he goes back inside. He makes his way to the "Volunteers Quarters" section. There are twelve doors, six on each side of the hallway, facing each other. They are numbered 1001 through 1012. Eight of the doors have "House Keeping, Please Clean" signs hanging from the doorknobs. He hears noise coming from room 1011. He walks over to the first door and goes slowly inside. The room is a wreck. A total disaster. It looks like there were several people fighting in this room. He quickly leaves and checks another room. The same, a total mess. Quietly, he makes his way to room 1011. Slowly reaching out his hand, just about to touch the doorknob, the door flies open wildly. Jeff jumps back fast, as if he is being attacked by a vicious dog!

"Sorry, Mate. Didn't mean to start ya," says a husky man, holding one end of a torn up sofa, as he is coming out. He had swung the door open with his foot. "Watch ya fingers on the door coming out," he yells back, in an Australian accent, to the man on the other end of the couch.

They continue on toward the service elevator. The couch is completely ruined. The other gentleman nods to Jeff as he goes past.

Jeff goes into the room. Just like the others, it is a disgrace. He bends down and picks up a battered doll. He shakes his head "no."

"Arthur!" he mutters angrily, under his breath.

"I don't know what you're doin', but I sure wish you'd keep ya crazies out o' dee's 'er nice rooms. Save us a lot o' work ya know."

Jeff apologizes and makes his way out. He now feels even worse for not trusting David, but still, he had to be sure. This time, after finding his way to his car and getting in, he heads for home.

Chapter XII

"Where are we?"

A sleepy Virginia yawns as she pokes her head into the cab. She has been in the sleeper with Micah. It's now 11:45 p.m.

"Just entering Missouri." Mary is driving with Buddy asleep in the passenger's seat. "Why don't you go back to sleep? This way you can keep Buddy awake for me when he starts driving"

"I think I will." Virginia yawns again. "Just wake me if you stop off somewhere."

"Sure thing."

"Leave without a trace...," is faintly grinding from the radio.

Mary begins humming along as Virginia climbs back into the sleeper and dozes off. Mary always keeps the radio low.

Caleb and Jason are early to their posts. They are tossing a baseball around in the parking lot while waiting for the store to open. Mike pulls up and into the closest spot to the front door.

"Hey you kids!" he begins yelling. "Get outta here! This isn't a ball lot, it's a parking lot, now scram!"

"Yes sir," they both answer as they turn and run.

They expected Mike to react as he did and figured it would be a good cover. If the abductors did see them, hopefully they would think they were just a couple of guys tossing a baseball, not policemen. As the lot begins to fill, they each slip into their cars and wait.

"Look alive, Jason. I think we've got a customer," Caleb calls over the radio.

Sure enough, a station wagon is pulling into the spot. They didn't quite make the swing, so backed it out and re-parked. This time it was perfect. They pull in and bump the curb. Caleb sees a bright flash of light come out from under the car. The car then rolls back about three inches from the curb.

"Hey Jason, did you see anything?"

"Negitory. What did you have in mind?"

"Did you see a flash of light come from under the front of that car when they pulled in?"

"Nope."

"I did. It was really bright, but lasted for just a brief second."

"Maybe their bumper or hubcap caught the sun and flashed it back at ya."

"It's possible. Can you see them?"

"I have my eyes on them."

The family of four gets out and goes into the store. Caleb decides to examine the car. The flash of light didn't look like a reflection from the sun. As he approaches the front of the car he kneels down to check out the tire and the curb. Nothing looks abnormal.

"Find anything?" Jason asks. He had walked over after Caleb began to examine the car.

"No. It must've been the sun," he says as he takes a deep breath. "Smells like someone's been running a laser printer," Caleb says as he takes another deep breath.

"Or a copier machine," Jason adds while he breathes deeply.

They both look at each other perplexed then walk back to their cars.

Two and a half hours later, the family returns to their car with two carriages of groceries. The woman opens up and starts the car. She turns on the air conditioner and sits for a moment. She gets out and opens the tailgate, having some of the kids help her load the groceries.

"ALL YOUR COUNTRY FAVORITES ALL THE TIME...," is blaring out of the car. "KNTY RADIO 95.5..."

"TURN THAT THING DOWN IN THERE!" the mother yells, and immediately the radio goes soft. "What's wrong with you, you want to go deaf or something?" she begins yelling - and doesn't stop.

It takes them another ten minutes to load the groceries and she does not stop yelling for a second. The only thing that shuts her up, at least to the rest of the world, is when she finally closes the car door. As she drives away, Caleb and Jason can see she is still yelling.

"Good Grief," mumbles Caleb.

"Caleb."

"Yeah Jay?"

"I'm going inside to get something to drink. You want anything?"

"Please. I'll take whatever you have."

Jason leaves his car and starts for the store. As he goes inside a small Mazda convertible, with the top down, pulls into the spot. Caleb sits up attentively.

"WPXC 103 Your over the road...," can be heard emanating from the car. This is a very popular radio station.

Caleb sees the car drive in, and bump the curb. He sees that same flash of light. He immediately sees the beer truck which pulls in front of him, blocking his view. It is only in his way for five seconds. When it pulls past him his eyes open wide and he is left with a look of dread on his face.

"Jason, get out here quick!" he calls over the radio.

In the store, Jason dumps the munchies he has in his hands on a nearby shelf and darts for the door.

"I'm coming. Whatcha got?" he says into the radio, while running.

"Check for a balding guy with sun glasses and a red sweater around his neck on your way out. You should pass him coming in."

"10-4."

Caleb walks over to the car, gun drawn and

staying low. The car is still running, the radio still playing, the seat belts still fastened, and that same smell is in the air.

Jason comes running up.

"Nothing. No balding guys, no red sweaters," he says while catching his breath.

Jason looks over the car. He can feel his heart pounding. He sees each of the conditions Marshall had described to them. "Another one," he states.

"Marshall this is Caleb, you read me?"

No answer.

"Marshall this is Caleb. Do...you...read...me?"

Marshall is in a small diner at the telephone, with his radio at his table.

"Yo Sheriff!" calls one of the waitresses. "Your radio. Sounds urgent," she says holding up the radio and slightly waving it in the air.

"Marshall this is Caleb. Do...you...read...me?"

Marshall looks up and sees it is not the regular police radio. He hangs up the phone and doesn't even wait for his change. As he briskly walks back to his table, he thanks the waitress and takes the radio from her hand.

"This is Marshall, go ahead."

"Sheriff, you'd better get over here."

"Got another one?"

"Yes sir, but..."

"Go ahead."

"Sir, we didn't see anyone." Caleb now sounds concerned.

"You boys just stay put. I'm on my way." He gathers his stuff, takes one last gulp of coffee and heads out. "Jesse, put that on my tab, will you?"

"No problem sheriff."

Pulling away from the diner, he calls out on the radio, "Rich, Pops, you two out there?" Marshall wants them both at the scene since they were at the first one. "Suzie, come in."

"Go ahead."

"See if you can get in touch with Richard and Pops for me. Have them meet me at the Supermarket, pronto!"

"Yes sir, Sheriff."

Marshall is not far from the store, so it doesn't take him long to get there. He pulls up to the spot and finds the deputies strongly discussing what has just happened.

"How could he just vanish? You must have missed him going into the store."

"I didn't miss anyone going in, you missed him getting out of his car."

"All right fella's," Marshall interrupts. "Let's just settle down." He walks over to the two young men. "Tell me what happened."

"You said for one of us to stay here at all times, so Jason went inside to get us both a bite to eat and something to drink," Caleb begins.

Caleb and Jason would not let just one of them take the full blame for anything. When in a situation where both of them were responsible, they both took full responsibility, even if it was clearly only one of them at fault. This situation was a bit different though, since neither of them is at fault.

Caleb continues, "This car pulls into this spot. As soon as he pulls in, he hits the curb and I see a flash of light. Next thing I know that beer truck pulls in my view...," he says, pointing to the truck, now parked near the store, "...and this guy's gone."

"I came running out of the store as soon as Caleb called, looking for the guy, but didn't see hide nor hair of him," offers Jason.

"How long was the truck in your way?" asks Marshall.

"All of five, maybe six seconds. It didn't even

stop."

"You said you saw a flash of light?" asks Marshall.

"Yes, sir. It seemed to come from under the front of the car."

"Actually two," says Jason.

"Two?" Marshall turns to question Jason.

"Yes, two."

"Yeah, two," says Caleb. "There was a station wagon which parked just before this car did. I thought I saw a flash of light when she pulled in too, but dismissed it as a reflection."

They all walk over to the car. It is still running. Caleb and Jason touched nothing. They had been waiting for Marshall.

Marshall looks the car over and shakes his head. All the same conditions. He takes a deep breath and lets out a sigh while shaking his head. Marshall is taken aback as a surprised expression comes over his face. He thinks to himself, "There's that smell again." Before he can say anything, Pops comes driving up and screeches to a stop.

"Looks like we got another one Pops," Marshall says as Pops approaches them with his bag.

"Sir, I didn't see anybody. I didn't get out

when the truck drove in front of me because he wasn't there long enough," Caleb explains to Marshall.

"Five or six seconds doesn't seem long enough to me to grab somebody. Are you sure that's all the time that went by?"

"Sir? Are you implying something?"

"No son, I'm not. I'm just wondering if maybe that flash of light you saw was more than just a flash of light."

"What, like some kind of hypnosis or something?" Jason says in a tone of disbelief.

"It's possible," counters Marshall. "It's possible the abductor knocked Caleb out but didn't attack the first family because he saw you, Jason. Once you went inside, he hypnotized Caleb again, set the car up, abducted the man and then left. You didn't see any of the flashes of light, did you Jason?"

There is a brief, awkward, moment of silence.

"No. No sir I didn't," he says sadly. "Sorry Caleb, but I didn't see anything."

"Don't be sorry," assures Caleb. "If you didn't see it, you didn't see it."

"You two go check out that beer truck and let me know what you find."

"Yes sir."

Caleb and Jason walk off towards the truck.

"Marshall, would you come over here please?" Pops says, in a scared, shaking voice.

Marshall walks over to the passenger's side of the car and looks down.

"Will you please tell me what you see?"

"It's...that's impossible," Marshall says stunned. "That is just not possible."

"Sniff. Take a big whiff too," says Pops.

Marshall complies.

"Smell it?"

"Smells like someone's been running a copier or laser printer of some kind."

"Something's wrong here Marshall. Something's wrong."

"Print dust just can't do that," says Marshall again in disbelief.

"Well. It is."

"We'll be right back with your WPXC103 weather right after these..."

"Turn that thing off will you?"

Pops turns off the radio. This time the print dust not only appears to be being pulled to the center and front of the car, it IS being pulled to the center and front of the car. There is a layer of dust floating up from the seats, forming almost a funnel, and moving very slowly towards the radio. The two men stand there silent, looking down into the car and back at each other. Their silence is soon broken.

"That's it! I've had it!"

Marshall just grits his teeth and looks heavenward. He does not need this. Not now. Not anytime, but especially, not now.

"Had what, Mike?" Marshall asks in a stern, abrupt and very curt tone.

"You guys are causing a scene and now you have your deputies bothering my delivery drivers. I won't have it," says Mike, the store's manager.

"Mike, what would you have us do?"

"Just keep your cars out of sight, and stop hassling my people," he says snertly. "What's this, another abandoned car. I figured as much. You guys can't seem to catch anybody can you? Missing persons, abandoned cars. Then you try to blame it on me. Huh! Now whose fault is it? One of your own men can't even catch the bad guy in the act."

"Look Mike."

"No, you look," his voice beginning to squeak as its pitch gets higher and ever more nasal. "You get this car out of here and keep you and your men out of sight. You're ruining my business. I've already called Al's. Your boys already spilled it that another car was abandoned here." Mike turns quickly and walks away.

Mike doesn't want to give anybody a chance to counter what he just said. He doesn't want any explanations. This way he is the big man and he comes out on top - at least in his own mind.

"I'd really like to shoot that guy," says Marshall.

"Me too," agrees Pops.

Caleb and Jason find nothing unusual with the beer truck. The whole truck is so packed with bottles, cans and kegs there is no room for people in the back. They also check the cab, but find nothing.

Al's truck shows up and tows this latest victim's car. Marshall puts up the cones and police tape again. He doesn't want anyone parking in this spot.

Marshall, Pops, Caleb and Jason all go to the local diner to get some lunch and discuss what they have found so far. They need to see if they can get their facts put together to find a common denominator.

"Hey, here's Rich," says Jason.

Rich had just been down at the Supermarket.

He had gotten there several minutes after the other four had left.

"Hiya gentlemen," Rich says, taking a seat. He figured they'd be at this diner. It's their regular spot. "Hey Jesse, the usual please."

"You got it, Rich."

Rich turns to the other officers.

"So you caught the bad guy! Well I believe congratulations are in order. So, who was he and how did…"

"No we didn't catch him. What makes you think we did?" Marshall interrupts in a very serious, concerned tone, speaking more slowly than normal. He knows Mike, and is thinking Mike must have done something, or told Rich something.

"What makes me think that? You're kidding right?"

"No Rich. We are not."

"What makes me think that, is the red Chevy parked in the spot and all of you here, instead of over there on watch, that's what."

"I swear, this time I'll kill him," Marshall says bitterly, jumping to his feet while grabbing his hat.

"Jesse, hold all our orders. We'll be back later," Pops yells as he follows Marshall out.

The five of them reach the parking spot only to see a very sad and pitiful sight. Mike Toggle is crouched down on the ground balling his eyes out next to a blue Ford Areo Star. The van is running. Mike is on his knees, borderline hysterical.

"I thought you said it was a red Chevy?" Marshall questions Rich under his breath, turning his head slightly towards Richard, but never taking his eyes away from the sight in front of him.

"I did. It was a red Chevy two door," he answers slowly.

Pops, at once, grabs his bag and runs to the front of the car. It is locked so he has to get Rich's Slim-Jim to open it up. He immediately starts dusting for prints. He immediately smells that same familiar smell; that smell as if someone was just using a copier machine, or laser printer.

As the door pops open, the voices of a background chorus are heard singing from the radio:

"WPXC."

Then a song begins to play.

"Little child. Dry your cryin' eyes. How can I explain the fear you feel inside..."

"Marshall!" calls Pops. "We've got it again."

"Mike, what happened here?"

Crying out loud, Mike tries to explain: "Bright light, sucked inside." He lets out a yell. "Bright light, sucked in." He begins wailing again, uncontrollably.

"Rich, get him out of here."

Marshall walks over to the van. He can plainly see the outline of three people marked with the print dust. He can clearly see the dust floating towards the radio. This time it is moving faster than with the last car.

"I figure it's because we caught it sooner," says Pops.

"Yeah. Me too."

Caleb and Jason are helping Rich carry Mike off. They have to get him calmed down, if not, he will be no good to them. Marshall calls Suzie and has her place a call to Al's to send over a tow truck along with some wooden barricades.

He barricades the spot with wooden barricades this time. He wants to make sure everyone knows not to park here. Rich has come back; arriving just after Al's truck leaves and while Marshall is just finishing up his task.

"Why just some cars?" Rich asks, puzzled.

"I can't figure that one out either, but there's got to be a connection. Do we know whose car this is yet?"

"Mike's wife. He was so sure you didn't know what you were talking about that he took down your barricade and let people park here. After the red Chevy, he personally kept the spot open for his wife; according to him."

"Did he tell you anything else?"

"He tried. He never could get past the fact that he personally left this spot open for his wife, well, except for the part about a bright light and being sucked in. He kept getting hysterical at that point."

"Maybe tomorrow he'll be able to help us more," says Marshall. "Maybe tomorrow."

"What's our next step?"

"We have to sort this out. We've got to put our heads together, compare stories and facts, and see if we can come up with anything. I want you to meet us at the diner tomorrow morning. Be there at ten. For now, keep thinking about everything and see if you can make a connection."

"Good night, sheriff."

"Good night, Rich."

There is a puzzled and confused, emotion emanating from both of them. It has reached the point where it seems they are even confused about saying 'Good night.' This is undeniably the most abstract case either of them has ever been involved with. This is going to take time to figure out. More time, and probably more bodies, than anyone cared to spend.

"Come on man, it's closed!"

A group of teenage boys roll up to the store front on their skateboards. In the typical fashion of boys, they are making all the usual noise and trying all the latest tricks with their boards. To see them perform, is quite entertaining. It is well demonstrated that they practiced, and did so extensively. They are good.

"Too bad we don't have some kinda ramp!" says one of the young men.

"Let's build one."

"We ain't got no wood or nothin'."

"What about that wood?" one of them says while motioning to the lone barricade that seems to be out in the middle of nowhere, doing nothing.

"Yeah!"

In a wild frenzy, they retrieve the wood and set up a make shift ramp. This is new to most of them, but all are willing to try it. It isn't long before one of them loses control and gets hurt. This brings their acrobatic feats to a grinding halt.

"You guys take Billy home, we'll take care of this stuff," says one young man. This particular young man seems to be the one everyone else looks up to. Even if he didn't want to be, it is clear, he is their leader.

"Forget it man, let someone else clean it up," says another.

"Naw man. Let's take it so we can build a better ramp. One that won't fall apart on us."

"Yeah," offers someone else. "Then we can have a ramp whenever we want it and not have to worry about finding any wood."

The general response is all in favor of taking the wood. As the first group of boys are leaving the parking lot the second group catches up to them with Marshall's now dismantled barricade. They leave behind only a few small broken pieces which are of no use to them.

The air grows still as the night goes forward, reaching its darkest hour. To the rest of the world, it is just another evening approaching dawn. To those subjected to the strange happenings, and those trying to decipher such, the lot takes on a much more eerie feeling. As one looks back and forth across this parking lot, it gives the appearance of being deserted, empty, unused or at least, undisturbed. It is as if someone built this beautiful store and stocked its shelves, and hung banners in its windows, just to let it sit empty. The more you look upon it, the more eerie, yes, the more frightening it becomes. If ever there was a place that would give you the chills, this would be it. Not everyone knows it. Not everyone sees it this way. Marshall knows it. Rich sees it. Pops, Caleb and Jason can feel it. Something is wrong here. Something is just not normal.

Chapter XIII

Virginia is awakened by the sound of chains rattling and being pulled across metal. It is morning; seven thirty. She wakes next to Micah, with Mary next to him. Looking out from the sleeper, she can see Buddy is not in the truck. She catches sight of him at the back of the truck, unhooking a car from the trailer, through the mirror. They had arrived at Poplar Bluff. From here, she will have to make the rest of the journey on her own.

After climbing out of the truck she walks around back to Buddy.

"Good morning, Buddy," she says stretching and yawning.

"Mornin' Ginnie. Yer car's all set. It's over there," he points to her car parked a few feet away.

"No Buddy, you got down the wrong car. That's my car," she says, pointing to a Rolls-Royce on Buddy's truck.

"Uh, yeah. I don't think so."

The Rolls is Buddies next stop and it does stand out. It is the only exotic car on his trailer.

The morning is passing slowly. No one wants to be the first to say good-bye, but the time has come. After they finish breakfast they all linger in the diner. Slowly sipping their coffee and getting refills. They really aren't saying much; they're just enjoying each other's company.

"Well," Buddy says, as he picks up the bill.

Everyone knows what this means. He starts shuffling his utensils then gulps the last of his coffee and stands up.

"I'm sorry ladies, but we do have to get movin'."

They all know he is right. He has a load to deliver, and Virginia still has a long road in front of her. The whole scene seems to be moving in slow motion. Everyone is just dragging their feet, trying to avoid the inevitable and postpone their departure as long as possible. As they make their way out to the truck, Buddy gives Virginia a list of directions for getting to Georgia from here in Poplar Bluff. It is a direct, yet scenic route; the kind Virginia likes. She doesn't much care for the major expressways and interstates.

"Just take route 61 from here, you can get it just up the street, and stay on it 'till you get to Memphis, Tennessee. From there get on Route 64 and go all the way to Chattanooga. From there it's a straight shot to Atlanta on Route 41. Stay on this path and you should have no problems."

"Thanks Buddy. Thanks Mary."

Virginia takes the directions from Buddy and gives them both a heartfelt embrace. This lasts only a brief moment before Buddy has to break it up and get going. He does have a schedule to keep.

"You tell that old man of yours we said hi."

"Okay."

"Hey, we should be getting up that way in about four months. We'll look you guys up when we get there," he says climbing into the cab of the truck.

"Bye," yells Mary waving. She had already gotten behind the wheel and started the truck.

Virginia waves as Mary and Buddy drive off. Before getting into her car to leave, she decides to give Jeff a call. It is 9:45 a.m. now, so she feels he is probably up and getting ready for work.

"Hello." Jeff is eating breakfast.

"Hey babe."

"VIRGINIA!" Jeff says ecstatically. "It's so good to finally hear your voice again. I kept missing all your other calls, by just seconds, and the caller id kept coming up blank so I couldn't call you back."

"Oh, I'm sorry."

"So, how are you? Where are you? Is

everything going okay?" His concern is overtaking all other emotion in his voice.

"I'm doing great."

"And Micah?" Jeff interrupts.

"He's doing just great. In fact, he seems to really enjoy traveling."

"So where are you?"

"You won't believe this, but I'm on the Missouri, Arkansas, Tennessee borders."

"No way," Jeff says in disbelief. "To be there, you'd have had to drive all night, non-stop, without taking any breaks. Come on, really, where are you?"

"I knew you wouldn't believe me. I told Buddy you..."

"Buddy!" Jeff butts in, "Buddy SeBlue," he says with a trace of a chuckle and disbelief, mixed with amazement in his voice. "That old dog. How is he?"

"He's doing great. Bought himself a new truck, got married..."

The conversation continues in the same way as all conversations do with couples who miss each other. They both tell each other about their days without the other, get caught up on each other's lives, and of course, let each other know just how much they are missed.

They are finally able to break away from each other.

"Bye babe. I really miss you."

"I miss you too...so much."

"You drive carefully, and come back to me in one piece."

"I will. You too."

They give each other a kiss over the phone and Virginia makes her way to her car. She buckles Micah and herself in; starts the car; and with a tear in her eyes, she sighs. A big, heavy, lonely sigh. The sigh of a woman who misses, and wants to be with, her husband. Putting her car into gear, she heads for Highway 61, south.

With both hands on the cup, the cup to his lips, and his eyes firmly fixed straight ahead, Marshall waits for the others.

"Freshen that up for you Marshall?" Jesse is standing next to Marshall with a fresh pot of coffee in her hand.

There is no response. Marshall remains

motionless, occasionally blinking.

"Marshall?" she asks puzzled. "MARSHALL!" This time she gives him a nudge.

As if he is coming out of a trance, Marshall looks around then up at Jesse.

"Oh, um, please."

"Are you okay?"

"Yes, thank you. I've just got a lot on my mind. Oh, that's good thank you," he tells her as she fills his cup. "I've just got too much on my mind right now. Ever have one of those problems that seems to come from nowhere that you just couldn't make any kind of connection to allow you to move forward with it, to fix it?"

"Probably not the kind you've got, but I've had my share of confusin' problems. I know exactly what you mean. Kin I getcha anything else while you're waitin'?"

"Thanks, no. I'm fine for now." Marshall slips back into deep thought.

"Mornin' Jesse."

"Howdy Pops. What'll it be?"

"Sawmill, with two biscuits; two eggs, over medium; home fries; coffee, black no sugar."

"You got it."

"Marshall."

"Good morning, Pops." Marshall sounds tired.

"You sound like a man who's been up all night thinking."

"And thinking and thinking and thinking."

"Anything?"

"Nothing," he says disgustedly. "Not a blessed thing. Now this thing with Mike...I just don't know what to think of it."

"Went down to the junkyard this morning..."

"Here ya are," says Jesse handing Pops his coffee.

"Thank ya darlin'. Ripped out the console from the 'Vette and I pulled the dash out of Mike's wife's van too. You know, hopin' to find something, maybe some electronics or some type of air freshener, whatever, ANYTHING. Came up with a big fat goose egg. Nothing. Just normal car junk."

"I just don't get it, Pops. I just don't get it."

"Me neither. We need something else to go on. We've gotta be missing something and we gotta be missing something big. It's probably right under our noses and we just don't see it."

"Morning Jesse. Coffee please. Good morning gentleman."

"Morning Rich."

"Richard," says Pops with a nod.

"I stopped by the store on my way over. I think someone really liked your barricade. Thanks Jesse."

"Well, I was fond of it. Am I to presume 'was' is the operative word here?" questions Marshall.

"Yup. Someone took it down, dragged it to the front of the store, and broke several parts of it. I found the debris next to the curb by the front door."

Looking up quickly Pops asks: "Anyone parked there?"

"Yeah, there was a car in the spot. I waited for them to leave, then put down a couple of cones I had in my trunk to block the spot."

"Whoever it is didn't want them, I guess," Marshall says while turning to look out the window. "Caleb and Jason are here. Good, we'll be able to get started."

Jason and Caleb put in their orders and join Marshall, Pops and Rich at the table. They begin hashing through all the events, trying to find that one common denominator, that one piece of information to put the whole thing together. Every time they think they found a clear path, they soon discover it is a dead end. As their breakfasts arrive, they all begin to eat in quiet solitude. It is as if they are each at a separate table, eating alone. Together, they separately ponder over the situation.

"They say that I'm just wishful thinking..," Caleb begins singing quietly to himself.

"Hey, good song. Did you hear that on 103 on your way in?" Jason asks.

"Yeah, that station's great!" Caleb says excitedly. "They've been playin' great stuff all morning."

"Yeah, I heard. They've been spotlighting new bands all morning too."

"This is one of 'em. You should hear some of the other new stuff. It's great."

The boys are going back and forth about their 'Rock' music.

"You guys still listening to that noise?" asks Rich.

"NOISE?!?! You don't know what you're talking about," says Jason.

"Here we go," says Pops quietly.

"Yeah, he probably figures we should listen to the country music trash he listens to."

"Hey, it's not trash. It's good music. It's soothing and tells a story. It's the kind of music you live by." Rich is coming to country music's defense.

"Right. I'm sure I want the last song I hear to be a country song."

"You never know. You listen to enough country songs, you might learn something."

"Yeah, like what?"

"You might just learn how to deal with some bad hombre. Country music may someday save your life!"

"Yeah, right," Jason laughs.

"Yeah. Maybe that's what saved that witch of a mother and her three kids. She was listening to."

He turns to Jason and in unison they proclaim:

"KNTY   RADIO   95.5   ALL   YOUR COUNTRY FAVORITES ALL THE TIME"

Jason just laughs.

"See!" Caleb continues on, "If she had been listening to 103, like everyone else, she'd have been abducted." He briefly laughs again, but stops abruptly as the whole table falls quiet.

They all stare at each other, then back at him.

"What?" he questions the group.

Caleb briefly looks around, in a twitching fashion, at everyone staring at him.

"I'm sorry, I wasn't meaning to be disrespectful to those people."

"Did you notice anything like that?" Marshall asks.

"No. Well..," Caleb begins. He is thinking back to the past events. "The people in the wagon didn't get taken and they were listening to that country station. The guy with the red sweater...he was listening to 103 and he disappeared."

"Yeah, but the good looking chick was listening to 103 too, and she was okay," Jason inserts quickly.

"True, but there wasn't a flash of light under her car either, like with the wagon and the guy with the red sweater," counters Caleb.

"Mike's wife was listening to 103," Rich says very slowly and very softly.

The table again falls silent.

"Pops?" asks Marshall.

"Don't remember. It never occurred to me to check the radios."

"So was the 'Vette," Rich says softly, and a little faster than his previous comment. "I remember specifically, because of the song playing. It was 'Don't Give Up On Us, Baby' by David Soul. I remember because I hadn't heard that song in such a long time and it's stuck with me since."

"Kind of fitting, don't ya think. Don't give up on us...or rather them," Pops says while finishing up his breakfast. He likes to save that last piece of biscuit for the runny part of the egg yolk.

"If it's true, we may be on to something. You said you blocked off that spot again, right Rich?" asks Marshall.

"Yes." Richard nods.

"All right, it will hopefully be safe, for now. Rich, after breakfast, I want you to go down to Al's and check out all the cars there. You still have a copy of your list?"

"Let me see," he says while going through his pockets. Not finding it there, he checks his clipboard and finds it under some other papers. "Yes, I have it right here."

"Good. Make another column and let us know what station each car's radio is set at. This seems to be the only connection so far."

"That, and the flash of light," offers Caleb.

"And that it's only from that one spot," adds Jason.

"Right," says Marshall. "We have three good connections to work with."

All at the table agree. They remain a while longer as they finish up their breakfasts, talking over this case and the missing persons' cases. When they are ready to leave, Marshall instructs Caleb and Jason to return to the parking lot and keep an eye on that spot. They were to make sure no one uses it.

Chapter XIV

Jeff walks into the testing room with his service cart. Arthur is nowhere to be found so he proceeds to power up the equipment. Looking at a sole green light, Jeff pushes it with a satisfied smile. He is finally going to begin testing. The console illuminates and electric motors can be heard cycling up. Pushing a button marked 'Curtain' he looks up. The wall in front of the panel begins to open. He begins flipping more switches that cause light to emit from the separating curtains. The opening curtains begin to reveal a glass wall, 150 feet high. It is in fact an enormous glass water tank. It is twenty feet square and it towers 150 feet up. Flipping more switches, an eight foot square platform suspended by cables begins to lower. The platform floor is a grid, not solid. As the platform touches down, Jeff runs a test of the floor he is standing on. This entire floor raises and lowers the length of the outside of the water tank. This allows for observation of specimens in the tank, at any depth. As the floor raises, the platform cables automatically recoil with it. This keeps the platform in sync with the floor. Jeff reaches for the intercom.

"Yes, Jeff?" a voice responds.

"I'm just about ready to go here. What's the status on my SCUBA gear?"

"One moment, let me check."

By the time the voice comes back, the floor reaches the top of the water tank. Jeff begins to test a second platform which is suspended over the tank.

"I'm sorry Mr. Colt, but I can't find any request from you for any SCUBA equipment and the supply room can't seem to locate one either. Did you turn one in?"

Frustrated, Jeff rolls his eyes and head.

"A request? I was told all this would be readily available and at my disposal. I'm also supposed to have a staff of qualified helpers for this project. What are you talking about, 'a request'?"

"I don't know anything about any staff you're supposed to have. You may want to clear that with Mr. Calvitch."

"With whom am I speaking?"

"This is Betty, the receptionist."

"Betty? Out front?"

"Yes, at the switchboard."

"Why are you picking up this intercom?"

"It rang through to me."

Jeff looks up in wonder. This intercom is

supposed to ring through to the Lab Coordinator, not to the front desk.

"Okay, thank you Betty.   Sorry to have bothered you."

"Oh, no bother, Jeff. If there's anything I can do to help?"

"No. Thanks though. I'll have to go and see what's going on."

"Okay, bye."

"Bye."

Betty disconnects from Jeff and dials another number.

"Hello. This is Betty at the front desk. You asked me to call you if Mr. Colt requested anything. Yes sir.   He requested some SCUBA equipment. Thank you sir."

David Calvitch is busy in his office working on some papers. It is quiet in his room. You can hear the grandfather clock ticking away in the corner and the sound of David's pencil scratching on some paper. Except for his movement, the pendulum swinging on the clock, and the steam rising from his fresh coffee, the room is very still.

As it ratchets into the wall with a loud SLAM, the door to David's office flies open. David springs up in shock with a look of wild anxiety in his widely opened eyes. This takes him by the utmost surprise.

Quickly trotting towards David's desk, and babbling nervously, Arthur whines: "Wada we gonna do? Wada we gonna do?" Something has put a scare into him.

"What do you think you're doing bursting in here like that?" David says very sternly, almost to the point of speaking with downright rage.

"We gotta do something about Jeff. He's ready to start, and we don't have any subjects for him. I used them all again yesterday and they're not dried out yet."

"Calm down."

"What if he gets suspicious? What if he figures it out? We gotta do something." Arthur is nearly frantic.

Getting up, David grabs Arthur by the shirt and smacks him right across the face.

"Get a hold of yourself!" he shouts.

After doing so, David realizes he should have left his hand open. He looks down at his closed fist with a snap of his head, then springs it open. He looks at Arthur, back at his hand, back up at Arthur. Throwing Arthur away from himself, he throws his hands in the air and groans disgustedly.

"Get up."

On the floor and on all fours, Arthur cups his hand over his right jaw and coughs slightly.

"Get up I said." David is not happy, and it shows. "What are you talking about?"

Arthur slowly gets up, still holding his jaw.

"Jeff called for SCUBA stuff. I have been keeping tabs on him all day. He ran tests on the tank, the floor and the platforms. He's ready to get into the tank. What are we gonna do? If we put him off again, he's going to suspect something."

"You fool. You barge in here because of that? You forget the first rule to keep from being caught. Keep calm and cool. You really are a waste. Sometimes I think I should follow Jeff's advice and get rid of you, but I never renege on a deal. I had better see some progress real soon, or I may make an exception to that rule. As far as Jeff," he chuckles, "That's another area you need to improve in. Always get your people to trust you. That way they believe any excuse you give; and even if they don't believe you, they will still respect you. I will make-up something for Jeff."

"What if he catches on?"

"You don't worry about him. You just worry about you and your project."

"We promised him volunteers today. What happens when he finds out I didn't let them dry out? That I was working with them already?"

"Easy. I'll just tell him you went behind my back. When he asks why I don't just fire you, I'll tell him I'm putting you on a week suspension, without pay. That'll keep him off your trail. Besides, we got three more in last night. They arrived in the afternoon and were brought over after you left, so you see, we do have some 'clean' specimens for Jeff."

A look of relief sweeps over Arthur's face. His lip and jaw now beginning to swell.

"By the way. You slipped and hit your face on my desk when you came barging in here, didn't you?"

"Yes, sir," he answers meekly; in the same way an abused child answers.

"Now, how is YOUR testing coming?"

"Mr. Calvitch," a voice over the intercom interrupts. "Mr. Colt is here to see you. Should I send him in?" questions David's Secretary.

Turning away from the phone and back to Arthur he says, "We'll finish this later." He presses the intercom button. "One moment, Stacy." Focusing back on Arthur he continues: "And I want to hear good news. I want to hear about progress." David gets up from his chair as he is speaking. "You sit down over there while I talk to Jeff."

Arthur walks over and sits in one of the office chairs while David opens the door and greets Jeff. Excepting a seat, Jeff exchanges greetings with Arthur.

"Oh that," David begins. "He came running in here, slipped and smashed his face right into my desk. Poor guy."

Arthur just nods in agreement.

"What can I do for you?"

"What happened to the staff I was supposed to have at my disposal for this project? I called to get some SCUBA equipment and ended up reaching Betty at the front desk. I'm really excited about getting started, Dave. What's up?"

"Oh my!" David says surprised. You're ready, already?"

"Yes, I told you that yesterday."

"I know, but I didn't think you meant you were ready to start going into the tank. I'm awfully sorry, Jeff. I misunderstood you. I needed a few extra hands for several other projects and figured I could borrow yours, thinking you wouldn't be needing them until the beginning of next week. I'm really sorry about this, Jeff. I didn't want to go through the hassle of getting temporary help when I thought I had help available. You're really ready to start going into the tank?"

"Yes sir. I'm ready. I just need the SCUBA gear and at least one subject to put into the water. Is there any way you can get me any help today?"

"I think I can. NO! I WILL get you help! I

promised you a staff. The least I can do is get you at least one helper. I'll just take someone from one of the other projects."

"Great! Can I go get a volunteer as well?"

"How many do you need?"

"I'll take as many as I can get, but one will do just fine for now."

"Male, female, child, what?"

"One of each would be perfect, but with only one helper, I'd better stick with just one volunteer for now. I'll start out with a female."

"Perfect. We just got three more volunteers in last night after you left, a man, a woman and a young boy of about ten. I'll have them prep the woman for you and bring her over."

"Thanks, Dave," Jeff says excitedly as he stands up while shaking David's hand. "Thanks bunches!"

"No problem, Jeff, and I'm really sorry about my misunderstanding you."

"It's okay. Hey, look. We got around it didn't we?" he says as he is leaving. "Thanks again." Jeff closes the door behind him as he leaves the office.

"Okay. You get the woman who was brought in last night, and give her a good dose of our regular sedative," David says sternly to Arthur. "I want her out cold. Give Jeff a supply of it as well. We don't want her waking up while underwater."

"I don't know nuttin' 'bout no radios," a garbled, barely understandable and nervous voice states from behind a submarine sandwich. "If it ain't got one, it never had one."

Al is a sloppy man. Not just because he works in a junk yard; that would just cause him to be dirty during working hours. Al is clearly an unkempt man and doesn't care that he is. He is two steps shy of being proud of his slovenliness. Eating like a horse, though being skinny as a rail, most folks figure he has some kind of glandular problem. Pops is staring him down and Al is getting more nervous.

"Had no radios, ya say?"

"Nope," attempts to come from his mouth, as he stuffs another bite of his sandwich into it, not caring about all the fixings and oil dribbling down his shirt.

"And you're sure there was no radio in the 'Vette?"

"YUP!"

Pops snickers. "I'm going to take great pleasure in closing you down. I personally, along with

Marshall and Rich, saw the radio in that 'Vette."

Pops had gone to Al's along with Richard after breakfast. They wanted to inspect the radios for anything abnormal.

"Oh, the Corvette?!" Al exclaims, spilling food out of his mouth, then spitting on the floor. "I thought you were talking about the CHEvette. I was thinking Chevette, not Corvette. Yeah, I have the radio to the Corvette. I pulled it out because I didn't want it to get stolen before the owner had a chance to claim it. Nice radio. Not a factory model, no sir. It's a beaut."

"Funny how one's countenance can change," Pops thinks to himself.

"Let me check my records." Thumbing through some folders, he stops at one and, with his back to Pops, pulls a blank piece of paper from the file. "Ah, yes. Here it is." Stuffing the paper back into the folder he turns back to Pops. "I put that baby in my safe. I kin go get it for ya, if you want."

"Please. What about the others?"

"What others?"

"The Pick-up, the Trans Am and the Mustang. None of them have radios."

"Oh those. Those were also nice, so I was storing them here," he says, walking towards a closet door. "I have them locked up here, so they don't get stolen," he says as he is unlocking a door and opening it for Pops.

"Holy cow," is all Pops can mutter.

There, in the small room, is about 200 radios; all stacked up and piled everywhere.

"Where's the ones I'm looking for?"

"I'll have to cross reference them to these logs. That's gonna take me at least a couple a hours."

Al is holding up a stack of folders, that have a striking resemblance to his appearance. It is quite evident that Al's filing system is neither.

"Hey! How's about you going through this stuff while I go git that radio from my safe."

Reluctantly Pops agrees.

Al grabs his tool box and sets out for his car. Putting on clean coveralls, he gets into his spotless, shining 1957 T-bird. It baffles the imagination how someone so filthy can keep his car in showroom condition. Al lowers his radio and drives off, as he waves to Marshall who has just arrived.

"Good grief," sighs Marshall as he walks into the room to join Pops. "You have got to be kidding!"

Pops explains the situation and Marshall joins him in the search through the pile of folders. They must find the correct car, then match the radio pulled from it with one of the radios stacked in this room. A formidable task, indeed.

"Here's the 'Vette's radio." Al comes walking into the room. "Did ya find what you 'er lookin' for?" Al had been gone approximately 30 minutes.

"We found one of them, but would greatly appreciate your help in finding the other two," answers Marshall.

"Where's that safe of yours?" asks Pops.

"Whatcha mean?" retorts Al, uneasily.

"You said you had to go get that radio from your safe. You were only gone thirty minutes. This place out here is thirty minutes away from anything. You should have been gone at least an hour. Where's your safe?"

Holding out the radio Al stares blankly at Pops.

"Would you mind answering the man?" states Marshall.

Al continues to stare.

"There's no safe, is there, Al?" asks Marshall calmly.

"No sir."

"That's a nice radio. You pulled it from your car. Didn't you, Al?"

Scared and quivering, he nods in the affirmative.

"What do you think, Pops?"

"I think he's up to his old tricks again."

"Honest, Marshall, this is the first one I've taken. I swear, all the rest are still here. I haven't sold any before their time expired or nuthin' I swear, I'm clean. I just couldn't resist this one. I was going to give it back if the owners claimed their car, honest I was."

"All right, all right Al. Calm down and give us a hand finding these other radios. We'll let this one go," says Marshall.

Al has a history of bad business practices and selling peoples radios, before they get a chance to claim their cars, is one of them. He spent a year in the county jail for it and didn't want to go back. Since then, he sticks to the kind of lousy business he can't go to jail for. It's still shady, but no evidence is ever strong enough to stick.

"We may as well check this radio now since we have it here. Then Al can put it back into his 'safe'," says Pops with a glare aimed in Al's direction.

"Yeah. Okay, Al. We need to hook this thing up so we can see what the last station being listened to was. Thanks to you, we can't check the one from the 'Vette, but at least we have one to start off with."

Marshall knows Al listens to only Classical music. 103.3 doesn't play Classical music, so Marshall knows Al had changed the station. He also knows the odds of Al remembering which station the radio was previously set to would be enormous.

"You can't check it anyway. Those digitals have a memory that only works when hooked up to a battery. Once you pull the plug on 'em, you have to reset all the stations. They always go back to a factory set station if it loses power. If that's what you want the other radios for, you may as well forget it. I only pull digitals out of cars. The rest aren't worth enough to me to mess with."

"Well that's just great!" Marshall says disgustedly.

"We still have the other seven cars," offers Pops. "Rich is still down there pulling them out, and by the way," he pauses. "They are all on station 103.3."

"Okay Pops. You finish up here with Rich. I'm going to head down to the radio station. Maybe there is a link."

Marshall leaves abruptly and walks quickly to his car. Driving off, he radios for Jason to meet him at the WPXC studio. Caleb remains behind to watch over the parking space.

Chapter XV

"Mr. Colt?"

"Yes?"

"Mr. Colt, I'm Parker, Parker Villman. I've been assigned to work with you."

Parker is a big man. Six feet four inches tall and 350 pounds of pure muscle. Having been a bouncer and a hospital orderly, he found the muscle to be most useful in working with people.

"Great!" Jeff exclaims. "You like water?" Jeff motions to the water tank with a sharp jerk of his head.

Slowly looking up the length of the water tower, Parker's mouth drops open.

"Oh, yeah," he says as his eyes reach the top.

The quiet is disrupted with clanging and banging sounds as Arthur is wheeling a gurney in through the double doors. Several metal containers fly to the ground from a shelf Arthur collides with.

"Watch what you're doing," Arthur snaps at the woman helping him.

"You're the one driving this thing, you watch it!"

She plainly is not going to take any unwarranted abuse from him.

They continue bickering while bringing the gurney over to Jeff. Lying on the gurney is a full figured, big boned woman with long black hair. She lay so peaceful; not disturbed by the current goings on. She is asleep, and will remain that way, due to the sedative she was given. The gurney bumps to a stop as it runs into the platforms rails.

"Here's your body," Arthur flips as he turns and walks off.

"What a jerk," says Darla, the woman helping Arthur. She is holding an I.V. bag. She turns to Jeff. "How do you want to work this?" she asks, holding the I.V. bag up and pointing to it.

"What's the I.V. for?" asks Jeff.

"It's the sedative. Arthur suggested the best way to administer it was through an I.V. Will this cause any problems?" she asks confused.

"That I.V. bag won't hold up real well under water," says Parker. "Jeff, I'm going to grab all the SCUBA gear while you two sort this out. I'll be right back." Parker excuses himself and walks off towards a small corridor.

"Underwater?"

"You sound surprised. Didn't you know?"

"No. If I did, I wouldn't have let Arthur use an I.V. So now what?"

"No problem. I needed a way to extract blood from my volunteers while they were underwater anyway, so I'll just make sure this I.V. is secure in her arm and we'll dispense with the bag. Do you have any more of this sedative?" Jeff asks pointing to the I.V. bag.

"Yes," she says pulling a small vile out of her pocket. "Arthur said to leave it but I do not trust him, so I thought I would bring extra, just in case."

"Smart." Jeff smiles widely.

"Mr. Colt, what is this all about?"

"First of all, please call me Jeff. I'm conducting experiments to try to prevent the occurrence of the bends in divers, without them having to decompress. The first thing I want is to get samples of blood from bodies which have been breathing air while under water. I'm going to start with bodies having been down two atmospheres, sixty feet."

"Oh, so when they come up, you will extract the blood and run your tests on them."

"Almost. I can't wait for them to decompress before extracting the blood. If I wait for them to surface, they will have had to decompress, if not, they will get the bends. If they decompress, I won't get an exact picture of the condition of their blood as it was before decompression. I must extract a sample of blood while they are down under water, and have been for twenty five minutes. Once I get a blood sample, I can have the subject begin to surface. Of course they will have to stop to decompress, but I can get on with my testing while they do so."

"Sounds like you can use an extra hand," she says willingly.

"Like you wouldn't know."

"I'm not currently working on anything, may I join your team?"

"Yes!" Jeff says excitedly. He didn't catch on to what she was saying at first. "Oh, that would be great, thank you."

Parker returns with the SCUBA gear.

"I wasn't sure if either of you will be going in or not, but I brought extra, just in case," Parker says while setting down two extra sets of equipment.

Jeff begins to explain the procedures they will be using. Since he now has an extra hand, he will not be going into the tank at this time. Jeff flips another switch on the console in front of him, which starts an air pump. The diver's regulators and BC's will be attached to a long hose providing air, instead of being attached to tanks on their backs. This gives them much more mobility, as well as a continuous supply of air. As Darla and Parker are getting into their gear,

Jeff fits a regulator over the mouth of the woman on the table. It has to be sealed over her mouth and nose. Being unconscious, she will not be able to hold the regulator's mouth piece in place on her own.

Jeff is wheeling the gurney onto the movable platform where, suited up, Darla and Parker approach.

"All set?" he asks.

They answer positively and Jeff begins raising the floor.

"Here are three syringes with doses of the sedative in them. The current dose will wear off in about twenty five minutes, so give her the first needle in twenty. Each dose will last about an hour. You'll be at the sixty foot depth for forty five minutes. At that time, I'll need you to extract about a half pint of blood. After you get the blood, give her the second needle. Both of you keep an eye on this I.V. needle," Jeff says, holding up the woman's arm. "If it starts to bleed, you'll have to keep pressure on it until we can get you out of the water. I'll be able to talk to you via this microphone. That's why the head-gear, these are called diving hats, instead of just diving masks."

"How are we going to hear you underwater?" asks Parker.

"There is a speaker and microphone in each hat that you'll be wearing. Everything is hard-wired, so we should have excellent two-way communications. We'll be able to hear each other with no problem."

"Until the hat fills up with water and we drown?" States Parker inquisitively.

Darla looks up to Jeff concerned.

"No, no no," chuckles Jeff. "The air pressure will keep the water out. I forgot that you haven't been trained with this equipment. Don't worry, we'll go over everything before you go into the water. You won't know enough to be an expert, but you will be able to function."

"Yeah, good, 'cause functioning is a good thing to keep doing," quips Parker.

The floor stops at the sixty five foot mark on the tank. Parker and Darla step onto the platform with the gurney. Jeff follows them and proceeds to give them a briefing on the gear they are using, putting a lot of emphasis on safety.

"She's strapped down, but if for some strange reason she should wake up, give her a shot of the sedative. Parker, if she wakes up, she is going to be scared and may start to move her head violently. You have got to make sure she doesn't force the regulator off her head and inhale water." Handing a stethoscope and a blood pressure cuff to Darla, Jeff continues: "Keep an eye on her blood pressure. I'll be asking for readings several times during your forty five minute stay at sixty feet. I know this is the old fashioned way of doing it, but I can't find the electrodes for this rig, to do it electronically. Also, keep in mind that with all that water pressure, the cuff will react a lot differently than normal when you try to inflate it. Are we all set?"

"All set."

"Let's do it."

"Here we go," says Jeff as he flicks a switch to raise the platform. "Parker, here." Jeff hands him a syringe containing the same sedative Darla has. "Wrap this around your leg. I want you to have one also, just in case our volunteer comes loose and knocks Darla's needles out of her hands."

The platform raises to a height greater than the tank and swings over it. Jeff presses and holds another button which begins lowering the platform into the tank. Just as it gets into the water, he releases the button and flicks a switch directly over the same button.

"It's all yours, Parker. You'll control it from there."

"Got it."

Parker reaches over to the buttons located on the platform and presses the down arrow. The platform again begins to lower, this time into the water. Massaging the cheeks, and behind the jaw, as well as pulling on the ears of their volunteer, they descend down into the tank. As the platform descends, Parker sets a dial on the controls to read 60 and pushes the down arrow and a button marked AUTO. He begins to help Darla by moving the jaw of their subject up and down, as much as possible. It all seems to be working. As the platform stops at the sixty foot mark, there is no sign of blood coming from the woman's ears. They have succeeded in clearing the ears of the unconscious woman.

"Can you hear me in there?" Jeff asks into a microphone.

Both look out to Jeff and give him the "Okay" sign. Their testing is on its way. All looks well. Jeff releases a contented sigh and picks up his clipboard.

Struggling to get loose, the strapped down young man grits his teeth and pulls ever harder to break free from his bonds.

"Who are you people? What are you doing to me?" he yells angrily.

With a loud thump, a pneumatic device forces the equivalent of a ten pound weight from an equivalent height of five feet onto his shoulder and arm. The man wrenches in pain and lets out a groan. He isn't going to yell. He will not scream. He refuses to give these people the satisfaction.

"You just looking to see me scream? It ain't gonna happen! What do you people want from me?" he yells.

The technicians, wearing the form fitting black attire with the unique black hats are, busy working. The weight is withdrawn and repositioned. Another technician brings a needle, a large needle, over to the man on the table. With his eyes nearly bulging from his head, the man pulls frantically at the bonds holding him down on the table. He wenches as the piercing needle goes deep into his abdomen. As it is being pulled out, he drops to a relaxed, defeated position.

"Give it five minutes," a voice beckons into the room.

Backing from the table, one of the technicians walks to a dark tinted window and presents a "thumbs up." In a dark room behind the window sits two men dressed in fine suits, their faces barely visible. One being an older looking man; sitting with his elbows on the arms of his chair with his hands folded, except for his two index fingers which are on his lips and his two thumbs holding up his chin. The other man is nervous and fidgeting in his chair. This is his project, and he hasn't made any progress up to this point. He knows if this experiment doesn't show some progress, his project would be canceled. All are still for what seems to be forever to the young man strapped to the table. The longest five minutes for the nervous man behind the glass as well.

"Well! What now? You just gonna stand there?" The young man begins to struggle again. "Let me outta here!" He gives up trying again. He stops as abruptly as he started.

The five minutes are up. The young man on the table is looking at his arm. It is beginning to swell. He sees a large welt on it where the weight landed. A loud THUMP can be heard as the weight is forced onto his other arm and shoulder. This time, the pneumatic device is set to a force making it equivalent to having had a twenty pound weight dropped from a height of seven feet. A look of surprise washes over the man's face. As the technicians reset the device, he sees his arm is badly bruised.

"He didn't feel it," the younger man says to the older man behind the glass.

"We've gotten that far already, so it means nothing," is the older man's reply.

Barely able to move his head, the man on the table tries to move his arms. He is struggling. Gasping, he manages to move his fingers. Looking frustrated, he tries to move his feet. Using all the energy he can muster, he is finally able to move his toes. An eyebrow raises on the older gentlemen behind the glass.

Gasping, the young man's head falls back, his eyes roll and his mouth drops open.

"He's going into shock!" states one of the technicians.

The E.K.G. goes into one long tone. CPR is started and oxygen administered.

"CLEAR!"

"Clear."

They zap him and get his heart beating again, but not for long.

"Give him the antidote."

Another technician sticks a needle into his chest and administers the antidote.

"CLEAR!"

"Clear."

This time his heart starts beating and continues. The young man begins breathing on his own again as his vital signs steadily return to normal.

"Progress," says the older man. "I like that. It isn't much, mind you, but it is definitely, progress." The older man stands up. "Keep up the good work," he says as he is walking to the door.

"Thank you. Thank you, sir."

"Was that one of the new specimens we received?"

"Yes sir. I was going to use the first specimen we ever got, but there is still traces of the other chemicals in his body. I had to use a fresh subject."

"Understood?" he says, opening the door. "That leaves one new, fresh subject. Unless we get in more, leave that last one for Jeff."

"Yes sir, but..."

"No buts. You've been taking them long enough. Now, it's your turn to wait. If we don't get any more, you'll have to wait until the specimens you tainted get clean."

"The dissipation rate for those first chemicals will take another month to finally clean themselves out of the subjects bodies. What if we don't get more subjects in by then?"

"Don't worry, we will. I expect you'll be doing something to make your chemicals disperse more quickly with future advances. We don't want anyone to be able to find any traces of it, especially after we put it into production."

"I have been sir. The new chemicals, like the one you've just seen, have a much faster dispersion rate. I'm definitely moving forward. I am making a lot of progress with this difficult project."

"Yes, you are finally showing some progress. I like progress."

The older man walks out the door and turns on the light in the hallway. Looking back he says: "Keep up the progress. You may collect something monetarily yet. For now, I'm not going to renege on my promise and you get to keep your job."

"Thank you sir."

Stepping out of the shadow and into the

hallway, the older man walks away. The only sound remaining is the breath of relief exhaled from the now relaxing figure still sitting in the darkness.

A hand reaches down and opens a desk draw. Two phones sit next to each other: one blue, one white. The white one is chosen and the receiver lifted off the cradle. No numbers are dialed. The office is quite. Other than the sound of a loud clock, no noise or movement is heard.

"Sergeant Montgomery, please...Hello Marcus. How are you this fine day?...Oh, fine, just fine...She's doing great. Started knitting again, and yours?...No kidding?...That's wonderful. Hey Marcus, the reason I called is to give you some good news...No. No not yet, but he is making progress...Yeah...yeah...No, not for some time yet...He has got the pain deadening portion working, but it also stops everything else from working. We did have a small light of hope with this last test...After giving the drug, the subject was able to move his fingers and toes before going into shock...Yes, I thought you'd like that...It is wonderful. At least they don't go into convulsions anymore...Well, there's another thing I wanted to talk to you about...Yes, his attitude. Arthur is a bright boy, but he's got to learn to calm down...Thank you, Marc...No, no, no. I'm not going to throw him off the project. He's come too far with this thing. I just don't think he can handle this project and the Q-29 project

Jeff is working on...Not really, he's only assigned to the Q-29 project as a cover up to his real project...I was going to, but he went berserk with fear on me, saying he was going to get caught...Thank you, I'd appreciate that. I was thinking on reducing his share in the Q-29 project just to give him some relief. He refused. He seems to be under some kind of notion that there is going to be money made from the Q-29 project. Didn't you tell him Q-29 is just a cover up project and will never be marketed......Oh, really?......So we might be able to apply it to your needs as well, if it works?...Then there is a market potential for it as well?...Would you?...Thanks, I'd appreciate it a lot...Sounds great. Well, I'd better let you go. Don't want any tracers linking us up," he chuckles. "Thanks again Marcus. I'll tell Arthur you said hi and send your love...sure thing...Bye."

The hand-set is placed back onto the cradle; the draw is closed and locked. The room is again quite. The chair squeaks as the lone figure turns around and stares out at the picturesque scene beyond the window of his office.

"I just love this mountain," he says above the only other sound in the room: the ticking from the lone grandfather clock standing in the corner.

Chapter XVI

"I'm sorry miss, but you're not going to be able to get through this way. There's an overturned tanker truck up the road and there's no way around it."

"But I need to continue on Route 64 through to Chattanooga," says a worried Virginia.

"That's no problem," says the road worker who stopped her. "You can double back to Savannah and catch a number of roads east."

Feeling uneasy about traveling unknown roads, and not wanting to double back to Savannah, Tennessee, Virginia asks if she can wait there until the road is cleared.

"That's going to be at least three to four hours. Here, tell you what you do. You have a map?"

"No, I just have some directions given to me by a trucker friend." The map she had left home with flew out the window of her car, just after she left Poplar Bluff, Missouri.

"Hmmm. Okay, tell you what. I'm going to give you a direct route around this mess. It only involves two other roads and they're both easy to find.

Turn back here and go to route 13 south."

Writing down the directions, she says: "Okay."

"That'll take ya towards Collinwood. From route 13, you'll get on the Natchez Trace Parkway. Get on that going north. That will lead you directly back to route 64. When you get to route 64, take it east and you'll be right back where you want to be."

Thanking him, Virginia reluctantly turns her vehicle around and heads back west, looking for route 13. Just like the guy said, she has no problems in finding it. Turning south, she starts on her detour of route 64.

"Can I help you?" a voice responds over the intercom speaker outside the WPXC studios. It is just after five and the office is closed.

"This is sheriff Marshall Winston. I need to come in and talk to you."

"I'll be down in a minute, I'm just about to come out of commercial."

After a few minutes pass, the front door opens. Clad in blue jeans, a tee shirt and flip-flops stands a young woman with brown hair.

"Hi, sheriff. Come on in. What can I do for

you?"

"Do you have a few minutes to answer some questions?"

"Yeah, sure. Just follow me upstairs to the booth and we can talk in there." As they walk into the studio she continues, "Just have a seat on the other side of the desk and I'll be with you in a moment. Just let me set up enough music so we're not interrupted for a while."

"You don't look anything like I pictured you," says Jason. "You tend to sound like an air-head on the air."

"Jason!" scolds Marshall, "That is not very polite."

"No, you don't understand. She doesn't sound anything like this on the air. She sounds like, and excuse the expression, a dumb blonde!"

"You mean like this," she says adjusting the microphone while turning up the volume on the studio's monitors. "Just a 'sec." A song is just ending and she, is just beginning. "Wow! This is like, Storm Front, and I've got like a bunch of cops in here right now, and their like, sooo cute. So, like I'm just gonna play a bunch of these round silver things 'till they're gone. tee-hee. Oh, I do hope they frisk me..hee hee," She starts another Compact disc, "Okay boyz...I'm all yours! tee-hee. Wow!" Moving the microphone out of her way, she inserts several carts and pushes several buttons while she speaks. "Is that what you meant?"

"Yeah that's it," he says smiling.

Marshall is just stunned. He can't believe all that just came out of this beautiful and very intelligent girl.

"See what I was talking about, Marshall," Jason says, tapping Marshall on the arm. "I was not being rude."

"I owe you an apology," he says, turning away from Jason. "Storm Front, is it?"

"Well on the air, yes, but please, call me Linda."

"Linda. Pretty name," Marshall begins. "Linda, how long have you been working here?"

"About two years. I was here when the studio was in Florence, Alabama, before we moved it out here. Upper management decided they didn't want the studio so close to a dam, so they moved it out here. We still broadcast out of Florence, but we have broadcast capabilities from here as well. This antenna serves as a remote backup, just in case something should happen to the antenna in Florence."

"When did they make the move out here?"

"About a year ago."

"Has there been any changes to the equipment within the last couple of months or so?"

"No, not really. They did add what they called an antenna amplifier about a month and a half ago. I thought it was kind of strange, seeing how we don't use this tower. They said it was necessary to bring the tower up to specs, should the need ever arise to use it."

"Not that it's gonna do any good, but can we have a look at it?"

"Yeah, sure. Follow me."

"What time do you start your shift?"

"I come in about three. I have some paperwork to fill out, logs to fill in and I prepare my show before going on at six."

"It's not six yet," states Jason. "You on early?"

"Yeah. Bill, the guy on before me, had to leave early, so I'm finishing out his shift for him before I start mine."

Marshall is looking over the logs and notices Linda's initials signed on one of the logs at 5:37.

"Those are the FCC required logs. We have to log in our output power and other stuff. No one ever looks at them, but if we don't keep them, we can get fined, big time."

"You were in here about 5:30 yesterday. You see anything unusual, or out of the ordinary?"

"Well yes, as a matter of fact I did. I was

taking the readings over here when I noticed this new antenna amplifier all lit up. All five of these lights were lit, and really bright. I thought they were gonna burn out, they were so bright. It only lasted about a few seconds. I heard a low pitched, WUMP sound when they went out. Then it went back to looking like it does now, just the one light on. I left a note for day shift, but they never got back to me, so I don't know what was wrong with it, or what was done to fix it."

"Isn't that about the same time Mikes wife disappeared yesterday?" asks Jason.

"Yes. It was," says Marshall.

Virginia arrives in Collinwood. She wants to get more supplies for her trip. She feels comfortable now about where she is going. She saw signs on the Natchez Trace Parkway directing her to route 64. If she hadn't, she would never have gotten off the parkway. Waiting for the traffic light to change, she's about to go into the Supermarket.

"Yuk, I hate all these car commercials."

Virginia is sifting through the radio stations. She had found a country music station and was very happy with it, until all the car ads came on.

"Like, WOW! You're on 103.3, fer sure." The D.J.s voice is stepping all over the front of the next song but subsides just in time for the lead vocals:

"Momma told me yes she told me I'd meet girls like you..."

"Ooo. I like this song. But we like the way daddy sings it better, don't we boo-boo?" Virginia says to Micah, who has also recognized the tune.

"Daddy? Daddy?" says Micah.

"No, not Daddy, but you're right. Daddy does sing this song."

Jeff and a few of his friends get together once a week and work on songs. He would like to get a serious band together, but for now they just JAM. This is one of the songs they do together. Micah loves it when Jeff sits him on his lap and plays his guitar.

"Surrender. Surrender but don't give yourself away....," echoes on as Virginia proceeds forward.

An elderly woman puts her packages into her trunk and gets into her car in the Supermarket parking lot. She can barely see over the steering wheel.

Putting the car into gear, she attempts to back out this large Cadillac. Caleb watches as she maneuvers her car back and forth several times before leaving. What he doesn't see is the way she backs over the cones that are blocking the problem space. One of the cones gets hooked up under her tailpipe. The other just pops out of the way and behind another car as she runs it over and drags it.

"What in the world is that?" Caleb wonders aloud as he hears a scrapping sound.

Turning to look, he sees the lady dragging off one of his cones.

"Oh great!"

He gets out of his car and sees the other one has been dragged away from the spot. He walks over to retrieve it.

"Hey boo-boo, there's a spot. It's pretty close too. Let's get it before someone else does. Okay? Okay? All righty then," Virginia says playfully to Micah.

With his back turned as he picks up the cone, Virginia drives right into the spot and smacks the curb. Caleb hears a vehicle parking and quickly turns to stop them but is nearly blinded by a flash of light. He is close to the front passengers door when the light flashes. As he stares into the passengers compartment of the small car, he sees light emanating from the center console. It is coming from the radio. He is stunned, unable to move. The light seems to have frozen everyone in the car and, as if it has fingers, it moves into the back seat until the whole compartment is flooded with light. He begins to shudder and his mouth begins to gape open as he watches in complete horror. The two frozen bodies in front of him begin to warp and twist, as if he is looking at them through some kind of 'Fun House' mirror. They just keep twisting and bending and stretching. They stretch into the radio as if they are made of cloth; and someone pulled one lose thread from them into the radio. First the woman, then the little baby boy. After a thread from each of them is in the radio, it is as if the world is put into fast forward. The rest of their bodies look like they are just sucked into the radio. Caleb then sees a small spark shoot out of the car's antenna. Still shuddering, he drops to his knees, closes his mouth and tries to regain his composure.

A slight whining sound emits from the antenna amplifier as Marshall, Linda and Jason are talking.

"There it is again," interrupts a startled Linda as she quickly points at the device.

"There what is?" asks Marshall.

"Just watch it," she says pointing to the lights on the amplifier. "That's the sound it made, just before the lights flashed on it."

Staring at the amplifier, it does just what it did

yesterday, and every unnoticed time before. The lights grow so bright, they look as if they will burst. It only lasts about a few seconds, until they hear that low pitched WUMP she described. The room then becomes very still and very quiet.

"That's it. It did that yesterday too. I'm going to have to write another note to day shift to have them check this thing out."

Taking a deep breath and letting it out Marshall states: "I don't like this," as he turns to Jason.

"It's that same smell, isn't it?"

"Yup."

"Oh, that's nothing. Most electronic equipment will produce that, especially if it's using a lot of voltage. At least that's what I've been told," says Linda.

"Marshall? You out there?" a nearly quivering voice calls over the Police radio at Marshall's side. "This is Caleb. I've got some bad news. Marshall, you there?"

Satisfied with the blood sample obtained, Jeff lowers the floor back to its base position. He makes some final notes into his log and sorts the sample on his cart by separating the half pint into several smaller containers.

"Parker, Darla, when you finish decompressing, bandage up that woman's arm and bring her back to her room. I'm going to my lab to get started on these blood samples. We'll pick up again tomorrow morning around ten."

"No problem, Jeff. We'll be here," Parker answers.

As Jeff wheels his cart out of the room, he stops for a moment in front of the glass doors leading to the holding cells. He can hear Parker & Darla in conversation from within the tank, as they decompress, through the speaker monitor located on the control panel. He looks into the holding room with pity at the people on the other side of the glass.

"Arthur," he mutters shaking his head.

As he goes through the double doors leading out of the room, he sees two technicians walking in. He is hoping these two are going to offer some kind of assistance to the 'volunteers' who, through no fault of their own, have become prisoners.

Inserting their security cards, they go into the first room within the cell area.

"How come we're bringing them in from this unit and not the one upstairs?" one says to the other.

"The upstairs unit is malfunctioning. Some electrical problem or something. Ready?"

"Let me just clear this off first."

The first technician walks over to a chamber. The chamber has a steel floor and glass sides. There are many steel rods pointing towards the center of the chamber and towards each other. Attached to the glass walls are wires that lead to the steel rods. He picks up some refuse left inside the chamber.

"We're all clear."

The second technician flips a switch causing the chamber to glow and a glass, bi-fold door to swing shut.

"Flooding the chamber with negative ions." CLICK goes a switch as the technician states: "Now."

The steel rods began to produce electric bolts and static charges. The charges are jumping from rod to rod and arcing from rod to floor, floor to ceiling, ceiling to rod. This continues; causing the chamber to glow so brightly the entire cell area is flooded with light. The light goes dark in the blink of an eye. Inside the chamber can be seen little sparks jumping off the rods at will, but in no definite pattern.

"Negative ion level dropping, begin introducing positive ion charge."

Another switch is flipped. What appears to be a multicolored, thick, oily liquid begins pouring into the chamber from two of fifteen steel rods coming in through the ceiling. As if pouring into suspended, invisible containers, the liquid is forming shapes. The energy flow stops. Suspended in the chamber is a young woman and a small child.

"Calculate the seat position."

"Calculation complete. Seats projection ready. Proceed at will."

"Final phase of re-ionization sequence is commencing....now."

Several more buttons are pressed. A final burst of light explodes from the chamber. The shadows of the two figures can be seen dropping about an inch and landing onto padded seats.

"I hate using this machine. We've got to do everything by hand."

"Yea. The one upstairs is much better for this. It should be fixed within the hour. Let's get these two upstairs."

"Okay, but let's put them out first."

Looking startled and scared as the technicians walk toward the chamber, Virginia grabs Micah and holds him close. The last thing she sees before she goes out is the black suits, the black helmets and a bright light.

"Did you get 'em?" a voice calls out over the intercom.

"Yes, we did. Two of them. They both look

fine...no problems. We'll bring them upstairs."

"Hold off on that. Find a place for them down there. This set is going to Arthur."

The two technicians grab the now sleeping figures and put them into the cell with the other mother and her two little girls. As they open the cage door, the frightened mother grabs her two little girls and pulls them to her. As the door slams shut, she releases her girls and tries to help her new roommate.

Marshall had the store closed and the lot cleared, at least as best as a lot with several police cars, emergency vehicles and electrical generators providing flood lights can be. He formed a circle around the parked car with the other vehicles.

"Hey man, you okay?" Jason is trying to comfort Caleb.

"Yeah, I'm okay, but that was the freakiest thing I've ever seen. It's something to see stuff like that in the movies, but to see it in real life...It's just not normal."

Rolling the car back away from the curb, Marshall walks over to the curb and kicks it. A flash of light pales the overhead flood lights but does so for only a brief moment.

"I don't know if this will work, but we've got to give it a shot." Pops is strapping a dog he picked up at the kennel into the front passengers seat of a car.

"Okay I want those video cameras on and rolling," Marshall says, pointing to each of the camera operators. "I want to get pictures of this thing, whatever it is."

He walks over to Caleb who is sitting in a chair with a blanket over him, drinking hot chocolate.

"Okay now son. You're sure of what you saw?" Marshall says in a soothing voice. "If you say it, I don't doubt it. Just tell me you saw what you saw and we'll continue on with this."

"Yeah. I saw it Sheriff."

"All right. You think you can handle seeing it again?"

"I'll be okay," he assures Marshall.

Talking into his radio he calls out, "Linda, you there?"

"I'm here Sheriff. I'm watching."

"Okay boys, let it rip."

With the radio on 103.3, the car running and the dog strapped inside, they roll the car back into the space and into the curb. Caleb may have been ready to see it all happen, but most everybody else wasn't. As the light flashes and fills the car and the dog starts to warp, people begin to run and scream in a panic.

Several of the camera operators fall over startled and start running, dragging their camera's behind them. Marshall stands tall, like a pillar among them, a tower of strength. Standing with his hands poised on his hips, he feels himself tremble. He believed Caleb, but nothing could really have prepared him for what he is witnessing.

As quickly as it started it is over. People are still running back, trying to get safely away. Shouts of disbelief, anger and fear can still be heard.

"Sheriff?" Linda is calling for Marshall. "Sheriff, you there?"

"WUMP?" asks Marshall.

"WUMP." She pauses for a moment. "Do you want me to pull the plug on this thing?"

"No. No not yet. We may need it again."

Marshall's gut told him not to have it dismantled. At least not yet.

"Did we get any video tape?" Marshall asks as he looks around at all the broken, trashed video recorders.

From the many cameras, they did get three, from three different angles. These were going to take some time to review. This time, the car was not removed from the spot. No one is going to be allowed to park here. Not until this is over.

Chapter XVII

    Waking up, Virginia is frightened by the woman in front of her. She scurries into a corner with Micah. In their rush to leave the office, the technicians didn't allow Virginia to inhale enough sedative while she was in the chamber to keep her unconscious all night.

    "Where are we? Who are you?" she pleads.

    "Shhh. Shhh. They'll hear you. I'm trapped here just like you. I don't know where we are."

    "Did they do that to you?" Virginia points to the woman's bruised forehead.

    "Well, I was fighting them and bumped my head, so, technically they didn't do it to me. However, if they didn't bring me here this would never have happened, so, yes, I guess they did do this to me."

    "What do they want with us?"

    "I don't know. So far they haven't said a word to us. Just poked us and stuck needles in us. From the looks of a few of them," she points to the other cells behind theirs, "it looks like they been beat, or at least hurt real bad." She pauses slightly before continuing on. "I don't know. I hope you don't mind my saying this, but I'm glad I have some company." She breaks down and begins to cry.

"I'm just so scared," cries Virginia.

The two women huddle their children and try to comfort each other.

Rubbing his eyes and putting down his pencil, Jeff notices it's past eight o'clock. Scratching his head, he looks down at his watch one more time and decides it's time to go home. Before going, he looks over his next day's schedule.

"Oh, I forgot to turn off the heater in the tank," he says to himself while looking down at his charts.

He wants to get another sample but this time taken from a diver exposed to cold water at that same depth for the same period of time. He gets up to leave.

"Whada you stilla here, Jeffery?" the cleaning lady asks Jeff as he emerges from his office. "Howa many times I gotta tell ya, you should noa worka sa late. You shoulda be home witta you wife and little a' bombino."

"Yea. Thanks Maria. They're off to, Georgia, for the next three weeks; so you'll probably be seeing a lot more of me at night."

"Wella you justa donnna stay too late, eh! I gotta lotta worka ta do, ana ifa we starda da talkin' I'ma gonna be here all da nighta."

"Okay, okay," Jeff chuckles, "I'm going. I'm just going to turn the water heater off in the tank and I'll go home. Okay?"

"Okay. You justa drive nice a'. Theres a' too many craysee people outa there. Whena you talka to a to ya wife, say I says a hello, and donna forgeta to give that beautifulla little baby of yours a big kiss and a' hug from his aunti Maria." Maria loves children, and is every child's aunt.

"Okay Maria, will do. Good night."

"Gooda nighta, Jeff."

Jeff walks down the hallway with his suit coat over his shoulder.

"How we gonna get out of here?" asks Virginia hopefully.

"We? You're about the only one who can get out of here. The rest of us don't have a chance, at least not now."

"Why? You have just as much a chance as I do," Virginia says encouragingly.

"No. Whatever dope they've been stickin' us with has had some really bad side effects. I'm just now starting to be able to move my legs. I can't get up even enough to kneel on them yet. I feel them getting stronger, but it's still going to be a few days before I can do anything with them. Who knows, by then they might try stickin' us with something else."

Virginia is scared and her face shows it.

"Daddy! Daddy!" Micah shouts out excitedly.

Micah can hardly contain himself. He is pointing out away from the cells towards the console in front of the water tank; wriggling and squirming trying to get away from his mother.

"I know honey, I miss him too," Virginia says, giving him a hug. "I wish he were here right now too."

"Daddy! Daddy!" he says again, this time pushing away from his mother harder.

Glancing up Virginia begins to speak: "Micah that's not daddy," she says as she takes another quick glance up. "That's," her mouth begins to slightly quiver as her eyes glow with hope. "That's Jeff. JEFF!!" She begins yelling excitedly while pounding on the glass. "JEFF! JEFF!"

Jeff looks up and down over the console in front of him. He starts to flip switches, turning off the heater for the tank, and the filter motors. As they wind down, he can hear some noise coming from the area of the cells. He cocks his head to one side and exhales. He knows better than to look at those volunteers. He knows Arthur injected them with some strange chemical. He also knows the adverse effects it has been having on them. He shakes his head and presses another button. This one causes the whole console in front of him to go dark. Dark with the exception of one green button. He hangs his head and walks toward the double doors to leave.

"He doesn't hear me. HE DOESN'T HEAR ME!"

Virginia is now frantic. She starts pounding the glass as if she ias beating off a wild animal.

"JEFFFFFF! JEFFFFFF!" she screams in agony.

Micah begins crying and screaming. He is scared. He has never seen his mother like this.

"Hey everybody! This ladies husband is out there. He might be able to help us. Start screaming JEFF!"

The young woman in the cell is trying to enlist the help of the other prisoners.

"Here." She hands her wedding band to Virginia. "Beat this against the glass. It will make more noise."

Eight of the other victims in the cells are conscience enough to help and they begin yelling as loud as they can. Virginia is frantically beating the glass with the wedding ring given her as well as with her own.

Jeff stops in his tracks. He hears the loud clicking sound of the rings hitting the glass. He thought he heard his name being yelled but then thinks: "It couldn't have been." Standing there listening further, he realizes: "Yes, it is." It is a faint sound but it is definitely his name. "How can the volunteers know my name? What is that clicking sound?" He thinks to himself. He can bear it no more. He tenses up and storms out the door, without looking back. He can't. He knows he will not be able to look back and then not do something to help those people. Not knowing what chemicals were used on them, he knows there is nothing he can do to help. He cannot handle that. He has to leave.

Virginia slumpd down to her knees.

"Jeff.....Jeff....Jeff," she is crying. "I need you....Jeff....Help me please....."

"Ugggggg!" Jeff stops two steps beyond the door. He can't take it. He has to go help them, even if it is just a kind word to ease their pain and reassure them. He turns around and walks back.

"Quick, he's back! Call him again!" hollers out the wounded lady.

Virginia springs up and beats her fists on the glass again.

"JEFF....JEFF!

The tears are running uncontrollably down her face.

Jeff's mouth drops as he fights back the tears and darts over to the locked door. Slipping his card into the slot, the door opens with a loud click.

"Virginia!"

He rushes over to her arms and holds her with all his might while simultaneously picking up and hugging Micah.

"I missed you so much. What are you doing here? I thought you were almost in Tennessee?" Jeff is confused.

"I was. I don't know how I got here. Oh Jeff," she cries, "I thought you were just going to leave me in here!"

"I didn't know you were here, babe."

Virginia continues crying on Jeff's shoulder and holding him tight. The look of solace that veils Virginia's face is so warm it can melt snow. She feels safe and secure. She is in Jeff's arms.

"It's okay, babe. It's okay, Micah." He has both of them in his arms.

Jeff gives Virginia time to calm down and tell him what happened. It sounds like she is putting him on, with her story. She isn't. The young woman in the cell with them isn't saying a word; she remains silent as she doesn't yet know if she can trust Jeff.

"Babe, that sounds kind of farfetched. You pull into a shopping center then end up here? Come on. You just wanted to be with me, and thought this would be a neat way of doing it. All of these people here are volunteers."

Jeff is speaking as if he just uncovered her secret. He is feeling very flattered that his wife would go to all this trouble to be with him.

"I beg to differ with you," the woman in the cell speaks staunchly. "I am not some kind of volunteer. I too pulled into a parking lot and ended up here, where ever 'here' is."

"What are you talking about?" asks Jeff.

She tells him. Everyone else in the cell block, who is able, confirms her story. They are not volunteers. They are abductees. The last thing they all remember was being in their cars in the store parking lot before ending up here.

"We've gotta get out of here, NOW!"

Jeff now knows something is up, and it isn't good. If Arthur, and worst of all David, has been lying about this whole thing and going to such great lengths to cover it up, there was no telling what they would do next.

"We can't go," says the young woman on the floor. "Most of us in here can't even get up to go to the bathroom. We're not going to be able to just walk out of here."

"I want you to know babe, I had nothing to do with this. I had no idea all this was going on. I trusted David completely," Jeff reassures Virginia.

"I know Jeff. I know you would never be involved with something like this. Obviously, you can't just ask David to let everyone go. He'll make you his next victim. What are you gonna do?" she is starting to sound worried.

"Don't worry babe. I can't talk to David, but I can still come and go as I please. I'll just load everybody up one at a time and take them outside. We'll get out first. Get Micah and come on. Listen up everybody. I'll be back for you all. Just give me a chance to get help."

Walking to the door with a smile and determination in his eyes, he slips his card into the slot.

NOT AUTHORIZED FOR ACCESS

The bright red light illuminates Jeff's face. It keeps flashing. The door does not open.

"He let me in, but he couldn't take the chance of letting me out."

Jeff stands there, frozen in disbelief.

"Security! This is the lab. We have a code five coming from the holding cell. I repeat, code five coming from the holding cell."

"Roger, we copy. Notify Montgomery and Calvitch. We're on our way down."

"It looks so unreal."

"How is that possible?"

"I don't know boys, but it's real and it's possible and," says Marshall to Caleb and Jason, "it happened."

They all sit awe struck while watching the three videos play simultaneously. They are trying to see something, anything, that will let them know what has happened to the dog in the car.

"Yeah, but what happened?" asks Rich. "Did it go somewhere, or was it just vaporized or...or what?"

"That's what we have to find out. Do you think Mike's strong enough to look at this video?"

"Yeah. Pops went to go get him. How do you think he can help?"

"I just want to know if this is what happened to his wife, kid and that young man with them."

"His cousin," offers Jason.

"Yeah, is that who that is?"

"Yes, sir. His cousin's visiting from college. Mike's proud of him 'cause he's the quarterback over there."

While still being mesmerized by the images in front of them, Pops opens the door and walks in with Mike. Mike is still shaking from the event, and still has a look of shock on his face.

"Hi, Mike. Come in, please. Have a seat if you like."

Marshall greets him with a consoling attitude. Whatever their differences, Marshall feels that even Mike didn't deserve something like this.

"Are you okay?" he asks sympathetically.

"No," Mike answers in a short, abrupt, yet soft voice, while shaking his head back and forth in short even movements.

Marshall puts his hand on Mikes shoulder. "I'm sorry, Mike. I really am."

"No, Marshall. I'm sorry. I shouldn't have said the things I did. I should not have doubted you and I surely shouldn't have moved away your barricades." He starts to slightly shake, but quickly pulls himself together. "I'm going to do whatever you ask me. Any way that I can be of help, I will. I just want my wife and kid back," he says, now fighting off the tears.

"Okay, Mike. Thank you."

Marshall then explains what happened and how they got it on tape. Mike agrees to watch it and confirms this is exactly what he saw happen to his family. After seeing it, Mike feels a little relieved. He thought he was going crazy, seeing what he did. It was too unnatural for even him to believe, and he saw it happen. Pops escorts Mike back out of the room.

"I'm going to see him home, Marshall. I'll be back as soon as I can," Pops says, walking out the door.

"What did we gain from that?" asks Rich.

"Other than a confirmation that this is what's been happening, nothing," answers Marshall. "But, because of that, we've found a common thread and we know how to stop it."

"Disconnect the amplifier," adds Caleb.

"Yup!"

"Do you want Jason and me to dismantle it?"

"No, not yet. We still don't know what's happening. We'd better hold on to it."

"So, what's our next step?" asks Jason.

"Well, now we all go home and get some sleep. Tomorrow we find out exactly who installed that thing at the radio station, and under whose orders. You all go home and get some sleep. I'll wrap things up here. We'll meet at the diner at ten o'clock, sharp."

They all say their good-byes and leave for home. Marshall posts three officers to stand guard over the spot and all the equipment. He ordered the store to be kept closed, at least, for now.

Chapter XVIII

Grabbing Virginia's hand he starts looking around. Up overhead he sees, attached to the ceiling, what looks like a large cube scoreboard. This was installed to keep track of the specimens in the cells. It lists such information as: cell number, specimens per cell, last chemical injected into specimen, last time fed, food group I.D. and last entry code. This all provides a complete picture, at a glance, of each specimen in holding. It is also used in selecting the next specimen for more experiments, to be fed, or whatever else needs to be done.

"Come on. Up there." Jeff pulls Virginia over towards the scoreboard.

"I requested this thing for this project and was here when they put it in. It's attached directly to an air conditioning vent. It was running too hot, so we had to put it here. We can get out through the air duct."

"So anyone would be able to escape from here?" Virginia asks confused.

"Well, yes. This wasn't really designed to hold people. It was mainly designed to hold animals and also to keep people from getting in. This air vent will lead us outside via a door connected to the vents.

Although the door can only be opened from inside the air duct, it actually is a security breach because there is no security inside the ducts."

Jeff slides a bed underneath it and tries to reach the screw that will open a compartment into the scoreboard.

"I'm too short, come here."

Virginia gets up on his shoulders to try and turn the screw. She can feel the warm, nearly hot air blowing out from around the metal.

"I can't turn it."

"Wait." Jeff reaches into his pocket and pulls out a quarter. "Here."

Grabbing the quarter, she puts it into the screw slot and tries turning it again.

"It won't budge."

"Okay. Calm down. Push up on the panel, then try turning the screw."

Pushing up on the panel, she unsteadily inserts the quarter again into the slot and tries turning it. She lets out a groan and twists with all her might. Her fingers turn bright red as she exerts force on the quarter.

"MOVE, DOG GONNET! MOVE!" she squawks while twisting her wrist with every fiber of her being.

With a loud snap, the screw moves and the latch pops open.

"Hurry, climb up inside and I'll hand you Micah, but be careful going through. This thing gets really hot!"

Virginia reaches up and climbs through the scoreboard. She can feel the heat from the lights as she passes all the wiring. Only being about a foot deep, it doesn't take her long to feel the cool air coming from the vent beyond the scoreboard. She grabs the AC duct and feels it cold on her hand. Jeff gives a final push to her feet as she draws herself up into the duct work.

"I'm up."

"Here. Take Micah."

Jeff hands him up to Virginia who is crouching down to reach him.

"Got him," she says as she pulls him up and puts him down in the duct work. "Come on," she reaches down to grab Jeff's hand.

With both of them stretching as far as they can, they still cannot reach each other.

"Wait a minute." Looking down to the woman on the floor he says, "Would you please move this bed back, as best as you can, after I get up?"

"Yes, me and the girls will do it."

"Okay. Thanks. Virgie, move out of the way. I'm going to try to jump up here."

The opening is only two feet by two feet, but Jeff has no other choice. There is nothing else in the room to climb on. Positioning himself under the opening, he looks up; sizing up his entrance way. Bolting upwards, with the view of a support beam in his sights, he has misjudged and bashes his shoulder into the openings door panel, bending it slightly. Virginia lets out a scream as Jeff falls back onto the bed.

"I'm okay," he says clutching his shoulder. "I'm okay."

He staggers back to his feet and peers directly up into the opening again.

Looking down the hole, Virginia can see his shoulder is bleeding. Jeff again sizes up the opening and focuses on the area just around it, instead of the support brace further up. Again lunging upward, he springs off the bed as his hands and arms clear the opening.

"AHHHHHH!" Jeff yells as sparks fly from the inside of the scoreboard.

He immediately releases one of his hands and is hanging by the other one. He clutches his blistered hand to his mouth; trying to cool it off. He had reached in too far and grabbed onto several open ended connectors, thus shorting them out. Reaching in more carefully, he grabs the support bar and pulls himself up into the duct work with Virginia helping him in. As soon as the woman sees he is clearly going to make it up, she and her two children push the bed back to its original position in the room as best as they can. Jeff reaches down to close the panel. He doesn't want anyone to know they went in this way. Not closing easily, he has to lean farther down to use both hands. He manages to get it closed, but is not able to twist the screw completely from the inside. Pulling himself back up into the duct, he gives both his loved ones a warm reassuring hug by the light coming up from the inner workings of the scoreboard.

"It's not latched properly, but it should stay. We've gotta move."

"Where? We can't see where we're going."

"This is the only vent leading into this room. We just have to follow it until we come to another vent further down the line. Come on. We'll be all right."

Jeff begins to crawl into the blackness of the duct.

"Just hold on to me and Micah. We'll be okay."

Jeff begins scurrying quickly into the darkness.

"Jeff, slow down."

"We can't, babe. We gotta keep moving. If

they figure out we came up here, they'll beat us to the next vent."

The double doors crash open as several uniformed men rush in. Running over to the security door, they insert their card. The door clicks and the green light flashes, allowing the security guards passage. They bolt into the room and spread out.

"Check all these cells," barks the commander. "Find Colt!"

The men begin searching each cell. Overturning beds and shoving people around with no regard nor respect. After each room is checked they group back together at the door.

"He's not here, sir."

"He's here all right. He's gotta be," says Arthur, who just came sauntering into the room. "He's gotta be."

"Maybe the computer malfunctioned?"

"No. This was no malfunction. His name printed on the access log. He was in here."

Arthur begins to look around the room. He isn't satisfied that Jeff is not there. He knows Jeff has to be there somewhere. The scoreboard catches his eye and he begins walking to it.

"Arthur. Over here!" One of the guards calls out, from just outside the security door. "I think we solved our mystery."

"How's that?" Arthur questions, walking back to them.

"Look at this stuff," the guard says pointing down to some refuse and holding up a crushed fast food cup. "We found some wax, like the kind from this cup, on the door latch. It looks like he held the door open with this stuff and tried his card from the inside. Looks like he didn't much trust you."

Arthur accepts the cup from the guard.

"Looks that way," he says rubbing his hand over his mouth, nervously. "Don't let him out of here!"

With that, Arthur changes. He is no longer going to cower to anyone. From now on, he was taking charge. He would run the show. The world was going to have to kiss up to him.

"I want this place sealed off. I don't want anyone leaving this building. Call the front gate. I don't want anyone getting off these grounds," he says with an air of authority, instead of his usual consternation.

"Yes, sir."

"I want every inch of this building searched and I want it NOW!"

The guards all disperse. Arthur stands there, rubbing the back of his neck. He tosses the cup into the garbage can next to the door and turns to go. As the large door is silently swinging closed, he stops and turns back. He walks over to the computer console in front of him and reaches down to pick up the phone. He notices the display on this console:

14:27:16.014   08/13/94   TWO   ITEMS SUCCESSFULLY RECEIVED

"I guess they had to use this console for some of the specimens," he says softly to himself. He shrugs it off and dials the receptionist. "Betty, page me as soon as Mr. Calvitch arrives. Thank you." As he turns to put the receiver down, his eyes are pulled back to the screen.

14:27:16.014   08/13/94   TWO   ITEMS SUCCESSFULLY RECEIVED

"That's today's date and about two and a half hours ago," he says, looking at his watch.

Looking up at the tote board he notices the count has not gone up. It shows: 21 Total Specimens. Arthur didn't know the lab had just received a dog. In his mind, this count should have read 22, not 21. It indeed, has not been updated. Having used this computer console and receiving station, the tote board was not automatically updated. Whoever did the receiving down here didn't update the board. Arthur dials the other receiving station.

"Was this board updated down here for the two new items received?"

"It should read twenty-three, does it?" comes the reply over the phone.

"No, twenty-one."

"Okay, thanks. It was not updated. I'll do it now."

The numbers on the tote board change to read: 23 Total Specimens.

"Hey they're not all down there, though. I have one up here. It's only a dog. The owner must have gotten out, and the car rolled into the trigger. We'll be bringing him down shortly."

"Thanks."

Arthur puts down the phone and goes into the cells. He counts each person and comes up with 20.

"I'll bet Jeff took 'em and is saving them for

himself," he mutters disgustedly.

Looking out through the glass, he sees the platform resting on the base floor.

"EMMM!" he barks as he slams the phone down on the receiver. He turns and leaves.

The large security door closes and locks. The vibration causes the panel in the tote board to suddenly pop open. It swings back and forth for what seems an eternity to the woman in this cell. She grabs her daughters and shuffles over to the corner of the room. She is hoping Arthur doesn't see the swinging panel.

"Paging Mr. Montgomery, paging Mr. Montgomery. Arthur, please call the receptionist."

Arthur stops just short of the double doors leading out of the area and goes back into the holding cell area. Sliding his card into the slot, the door unlatches with a click. He walks inside and grabs the phone.

"This is Arthur," he says to the receptionist who then connects him to David Calvitch.

"Arthur. Calvitch. What's up?"

"Sir, Jeff was inside with the specimens."

"He what?"

"He came inside and, I believe, took two out with him. The computer log shows twenty-three specimens and there are only twenty-one accounted for. He's nowhere to be found. He tried to use his card to get out. I told you it was stupid not giving him exit authority to this door. He propped it open with a drink cup. I'm sure he suspects something now."

"Stupid, huh? Who do you think you're talking to? That door has a twenty-five second close alarm on it. If that door isn't latched within twenty five seconds from the time the green light goes off, an alarm is sounded. Did you check the time he went in? I did. That door latched, then he tried his card. Jeff is still in that room, now find him," David says sternly.

"He's nowhere in here to be found. It's not like there's any place for him to hide, especially with two other people."

Arthur glances up.

"Hold on a second."

He leans his head, then sets the phone down and walks over to the cell.

"You little sneak," he says to himself.

Arthur quickly turns and goes back to the phone.

"I've found him. He went up into the air vents, via the tote board."

"Good! I knew he didn't get out of that room by way of the door. Go on up after him. I'll call maintenance and have them turn on the lights."

Looking around, David realizes he has said too much there in the lobby. He decides to call security and maintenance from his office so he makes his way into the building.

Arthur takes the beds from several of the other cells and stacks them atop each other; he proceeds into the duct. It is dark. He can't go left. This is the last vent on this duct, so he knows there is only one way Jeff could have gone.

"I can see some light," says Jeff. "We must be approaching an office. Hopefully we can get out through there."

"Oh, I hope so!" Virginia says excitedly.

"Shhhh. We can't let anyone hear us."

They approach the vent slowly and quietly. It is way too small for any of them, except for Micah, to get through. As they look through the opening, Jeff thinks he hears some banging on the duct work.

"Did you hear that?" he asks.

"No. What did you hear?"

"It must have been nothing. Come on, let's go."

Going on a little further, they can see the duct work lead to a larger opening. Crawling up to it, they find themselves in a much larger network of ducts. These are two feet taller and wider than the two feet by two feet ductwork they have been crawling in.

"Jeff! What's hanging from the ceiling. Are they bats?" Virginia is even more scared.

Jeff swings at one of them and it doesn't move. He hits one with his hand, it doesn't budge.

"It's okay. Those are lights."

"In an air duct?"

"Larger ducts, like this one, especially when they're as long as this one, are sometimes equipped with lights. It makes maintenance easier. And if I'm remembering correctly, these ducts are also used as escape routes," his voice getting more elated. "We're on the right track!"

"YES!" Virginia says happily. "I just wish these lights were turned on."

As if someone hears her, her wish is granted. The lights come on and stretch out in two directions.

"Huh?" Micah says, staring at the lights.

"NO!" Jeff says disillusioned.

"What's wrong. Now we can see where we're going?"

"This means they know we're up here."

"Oh no."

"Oh oh," says Micah. "Dis, dis," he says pointing to the lights.

"JEEFFFFF!"

Virginia and Jeff stare sharply at each other.

"I know you're in there JEFF!" It is Arthur. "I'm coming after you. You may as well just come on back here and give up."

Scared, Micah starts crying.

"Come on, Jeff, we've gotta get out of here," Virginia says as she starts off into the duct.

Jeff starts after her but continues looking down at the duct work. They pass two sets of arrows pointing the opposite way they are going, then one set of arrows pointing in their direction. The next set of arrows is pointing back the other way.

"Wait!" Jeff shouts. "We might be going the wrong way. I don't know if we should be going that way or this way," he says motioning in each direction. He can't remember if he is to follow the double set of arrows or the single set.

"JEEFFFF! I'm coming for you!" Arthur is yelling and banging on the duct work.

"Jeff, come on. Which way?" Virginia pleads.

Micah begins screaming with fear because of all the noise Arthur is making.

"Which way?"

"I can't remember?" Jeff is getting frantic. He must remember. They have to get out.

"Should we double back, or keep going forward?"

"I don't know! I don't want to double back." Then it hits him. "That's it!"

"What's it?"

"Double back, single out?"

"What? What are you talking about?" Virginia interrupts, while trying to calm the baby.

"We gotta go the other way!"

"Are you sure?"

"Yes, it's our only hope. They know we're up here, so they'll be waiting at the exit point from this duct. We follow the single arrow to get out, but they'll be expecting us to do that. We gotta double back deeper into the building. It's our only chance. At least we might be able to put them off our trail by going back. That might buy us some time to figure a way out. Come on!"

Jeff grabs the baby, twists around and turns

back the way they came. When they approach the first duct they came out of, they can hear Arthur getting closer. Turning a corner, they stop to comfort Micah.

"Jeff we can't stop!" says Virginia.

"We have to," Jeff says, rocking the baby. "If we don't quiet Micah down, they'll know exactly where we are."

He continues rocking and soothing the baby as Virginia puts her arms around Micah.

"AAHHAA!" yells Arthur as he pokes his head into the lighted vent. "I know you're in here," he hollers. "I'm coming to get you, Colt," he says, checking the duct. "Double back, single out," he mutters to himself, before he darts off following the single arrows.

Jeff peeks around the corner and sees Arthur heading off in the other direction.

"Okay, let's go."

With the baby, now calm and in his arms, Jeff starts crawling again into the duct. They have traveled far and came upon another vent leading into an office.

"Okay, real quiet now."

Slowly and softly, they approach the vent. It is too small for any of them to go through because it is off a main duct and leads into an office. Peeking through the grate, Jeff can see a beautiful antique grandfather clock standing in the corner. Aghast, he thinks to himself: "This is David's office!" He hears a voice in the office.

"Come on, let's keep going," Virginia whispers while motioning Jeff to move forward.

"Wait," he motions. "This is David's office. Maybe we'll be able to hear him and find out what's going on."

"You've got the emergency outside duct covered?" David is speaking on the phone. "Good. He'll most likely come out through there. Keep me posted."

David puts down the phone. Jeff hears him unlock a desk drawer and pick up another phone.

"Montgomery, please....Thank you...Calvitch here. Listen, we've got a problem. Jeff is somewhere up in the duct work. Your boy is chasing him out. I know he suspects something, but I don't know how much he knows...right...We're gonna have to hold off testing those chemicals for you for a while. Your boy was getting close, but we can't afford to let this get out of...Exactly...Yes...Oh, Jeff is making progress, but I don't want him to find out his volunteers never really volunteered. I want to ship all these people out tomorrow...You do whatever you feel is in the best interest of national security. I'm putting them into your hands..."

"Dis?" Micah questions, pointing at the vent.

"Jeff!" shouts a very surprised David Calvitch, snapping his head back toward the vent above and behind him. "I'll get back to you," he says into the phone and hangs it up quickly. He grabs the phone on his desk.

"Come on, let's go," Jeff blurts out to Virginia.

They continue on into the vent.

"Security, Calvitch here. They're not heading out. They're making their way back into the building. They just passed my office. Send some people up there after them."

"Jeff, there's no more lights up ahead," states Virginia.

It is true. There is only another 20 feet of lighted ductwork. Beyond that, the duct becomes a little narrower and grows ever darker.

"I know, babe, but we've got to keep going."

"Where does it go?"

"I'm not sure, but if I remember right, it's our way out of this place."

"It's getting cold."

"They must have lowered the air. They're trying to freeze us out. Here, you hold Micah. If I remember correctly, there's a drop along this line somewhere."

"I'm just outside Mr. Calvitch's office now," a guard says into his two way radio. "I'm heading in their direction."

"I'm in and heading towards Calvitch's office from the other side," states another voice over the radio. "We should catch up to them and meet in the middle."

"WHOA!" Jeff says as his hands go down into a hole and he falls onto his chest. "Found it. I knew there was a drop here somewhere."

There is a very faint light coming into the duct from another office vent that is attached to this main duct. He can make out the image of four black holes in front of him. One going off to the left, one to the right, one going straight ahead and the fourth one dropping down directly in front of him.

"Be careful getting over this duct. We have to go straight to get out. I think."

Stretching over the hole, Jeff crawls forward into the duct. Virginia puts Micah onto the other side and slides herself to meet up with Jeff. They press on until they reach a dead end.

"There's nothing here," Jeff says exhausted. "We took a wrong turn. We've gotta go back."

"No," bemoans the saddened voice of his wife.

"I'm sorry, babe. I can't remember everything about these vents. It's coming back to me little by little."

"It's not your fault. We'll make it. You'll see."

She touches his calf and gives it a soft reassuring squeeze.

"I'm going to try to turn around so I can push you along."

Virginia backs up a little to give Jeff room. In the cramped area he rolls himself up into a ball to try and face the other way.

"I'm stuck!"

He makes it half way, but can't pull out of the ball he's rolled himself into.

"Give me your hand, I'll try and pull you."

"I'm at the four way now," the guard says into his radio. He then turns it down and listens. "I can hear them. They're directly in front of me. I'm going in after them."

"UUGGGGG!"

Virginia is pulling as Jeff continues to try twisting around. The duct begins to bulge and give way just enough for Jeff to be pulled straight. He lands on his belly and lays there for a second to catch his breath.

"JEEEEEFFFFF!" Virginia is screaming as she is being pulled backwards.

Jeff looks up and sees light. He sees Virginia being pulled backward. Micah begins crying and chases after his mother. Jeff quickly scurries off after them.

"I've got one of them. I'm at the four way. I need help," the guard calls out into his radio.

"I'm almost there," comes the other guards voice over the radio.

Jeff approaches Virginia and motions for her to be silent.

"He's got my leg, I can't come to you," she cries.

"How far are you from the junction?" the first guard speaks into his radio.

Before the other guard can answer, Jeff grabs Virginia's arm and gives it such a forceful tug she feels like he is going to pull her arm off. The guard holding onto her leg is jerked forward and thrown off balance.

"AAAAAAAHHHHHHHHH!" he screams as he bolts head first into the duct going straight down.

Losing his grip on the radio it flies over Virginia and hits Micah on the head. Micah begins crying again.

"Slide back to the other side of the hole," Jeff tells her.

The second guard continually calls for the first, but the first guard is on the move. He is sliding down the duct, only to crash through the air vent located at the bottom. With plaster flying everywhere, he lands in a vat of Styrofoam packing material with such force, it appears to be snowing in the mail room.

Listening closely, Jeff can hear the other guard coming from the vent at his right. Sliding back, Jeff hands Micah to Virginia and crawls around to the duct on her right. He continues into the vent to Virginia's right and proceeds forward.

"Come on Virginia," he calls out, clipping the guards radio to his belt.

"I wish he dropped his flashlight instead of that thing," she says as she puts Micah into the vent with Jeff and then scurries off after them.

"I'm at the four way junction, which way do I go?" comes over the radio.

"This is Calvitch. Keep to the right. Jeff's going to try to get out the back way. You'll have him cornered."

"Are you sure?"

"Of course I'm sure. Jeff knows this system and he knows the code for getting out. Single out, double back, it's not too tight, stick to the right."

"Yes, but..."

"JUST GET AFTER HIM AND STICK TO YOUR RIGHT!" David interrupts and yells angrily to the security guard.

Looking back and forth, and against his better judgment, the guard goes to his right. He is now heading back the way Jeff had originally come. Mister Calvitch is not thinking clearly. He neglected to find out which way this guard had come from and mistook him for the guard that went into the ducts via the entrance by his office.

"Yes!" says Jeff. "I had forgotten about that part."

"We're on the right track?" questions Virginia who is now hopeful again.

"Yeah, we're on our way."

Crawling onward, they begin to hear what sounds like large generators or electric motors. The sound is getting louder and louder as they go.

"VIRGINIA. I REMEMBER EVERYTHING

NOW!" Jeff has to yell so Virginia can hear him over the loud noise. "I CAN'T EXPLAIN. JUST DO EVERYTHING I DO!"

"OKAY."

Micah is crying, nearly screaming. The noise is frightening to him and now mommy and daddy are yelling at each other. He didn't know they had to yell to be heard. To him, they are just yelling at each other.

"Mr. Calvitch."

Looking around his office, David sees no one.

"Up here sir. In the vent. I took a right like you told me and wound up here."

David looks up and sees the guards fingers sticking out of the vent.

"Should I continue this way, sticking to the right, or go back and stick to the right?"

Hearing the voice more clearly now, David realizes this is the second guard who came from the other direction, not the one who came from the vent access attached to his office.

"Turn around and stick to your right. Please, be quick about it. There is a reward in it for you if you get them," David speaks more calmly, more humbly.

The guard quickly turns around and speedily crawls into the vent. This time, when he reaches the four way junction, he goes to the right. He is now in the same duct as Jeff.

"JEFF! JEFF!"

Virginia is trying to get Jeff's attention. Jeff can't hear her. The noise is just too loud.

Flickering light can be seen from the end of the vent. They continue to it. Upon reaching it, a siren goes off and a red light begins to flash. Virginia sees Jeff go down an opening head first, then swing around and pop his head up. He reaches for the baby and grabs hold of him.

"REMEMBER, DO EXACTLY WHAT I DO!" he screams.

"WHAT?"

He can see Virginia can't hear him so he repeats himself a few more times, although to no avail. With a look of desperation, he takes Micah and descends a metal ladder attached to a wall. Looking down he can see lasers shooting across his path at the bottom of the ladder. With Micah screaming wildly, he continues his descent. Waving at Virginia, he gets her attention. He is just about to go through the lasers. They are firing about an inch below the step he is on. When he sees Virginia looking at him, he motions for her to watch what he does. He slaps the ladder rung twice, then sticks his foot into the six inch space to the left of the ladder between the wall and the last laser and taps it. With each tap, he lifts a finger. After doing so, he climbs down with the lasers firing on him until he can no longer be seen.

JUMP OR TURN BACK! JUMP OR TURN BACK! JUMP OR TURN BACK...

The message starts booming through the ducts. The noise is at a level so loud, Virginia feels her ears are going to burst. Virginia reaches the ladder and starts down, following Jeff. Grabbing her ears, she stops, while still holding onto the ladder. She sees Jeff go down and then out of sight. She becomes more frightened then she has ever been. She starts back up the ladder, not knowing what to do. With lasers firing at the base of the ladder and all the noise, it is making her feel confused. Looking up, she feels dread in her heart. She sees the flickering of a flashlight. It is getting closer. Quickly she climbs down the ladder.

JUMP OR TURN BACK! JUMP OR TURN BACK! JUMP OR TURN BACK...

The message keeps ringing in her ears. She goes down almost to the bottom. Looking up, she can see the flashlight getting brighter twenty feet above her. She has to keep going.

"I'll never survive those lasers climbing down. I'd better jump like that voice is saying," she thinks to herself.

JUMP OR TURN BACK! JUMP OR TURN BACK! JUMP OR TURN BACK...

Letting go with one hand, and stretching one foot away the ladder, she holds on with only her finger tips; listlessly staring down at the lasers flashing in front of her in an almost hypnotic fashion. She hears the warning. It keeps telling her what to do.

JUMP OR TURN BACK! JUMP OR TURN BACK! JUMP OR TURN BACK...

Just about to let go, she remembers what Jeff told her earlier. 'I remember everything now. I can't explain, just do everything I do.' These words begin to echo through her mind, drowning out the existence of all the other noise around her. As she stands on the rung her husband was just on, she smiles. It is the kind of smile one makes when trying to smile through tears. She slaps the rung two times. She puts her foot between the laser and the wall, but not carefully enough. The laser burns the small heal of her shoe off. Scared, she quickly climbs up a few rungs. Breathing heavily, she descends again to that one rung just above the lasers. Slapping the rung twice again, she more carefully positions her foot between the end laser and the wall. She kicks it three times; lifting a finger with each kick. Jeff told her to do exactly as he did, so she wanted to make sure she did. After doing so, she descends cautiously into the lasers.

The flashlight comes over the edge. The guard sees only the flashing lasers. He sees nothing else down below. Quickly, he turns around and heads back; wanting to get away from the deafening noise.

Chapter XIX

"What are you thinking, sheriff?" asks Tommy, an officer who works the night shift.

Marshall just couldn't get to sleep and decided to come back to the lot. He is sitting in his car with his hands on the wheel, staring straight ahead at the well-lit parking place.

"I don't know what to think. I don't really know what's going on." Taking a deep breath, he continues: "I guess that's why I can't get any sleep. It really bugs me that I have no idea what happened to those people." He turns to Tommy. "I have no idea, and that scares me. I don't know if it's over or not."

The security patrol meets up in David's office.

"Well?" asks David hopefully.

The guard tells David how he ended up at a point where a voice was telling him to jump or turn back. He told how he shined his light down the hole and found nothing.

"Well then." David pauses. "It's been handled." He pauses again. "Truly a sad loss, but we can call this matter closed. Thank you gentlemen. Thank you for all your help."

"Can we call off the security alert?"

"Yes you may. The matter has been taken care of. If you happen to see Arthur, tell him: 'Laser city said hello.'"

"Laser city, said hello?"

"Yes, that's right. He'll understand. Now if you gentlemen will excuse me, I have a lot of work to do," David says while inviting the men to leave his office.

The security patrol leave David alone in his office. David just sits behind his desk, with his fingers crossed and his thumbs under his chin, thinking.

As Arthur finally crawls out of the duct work, one of the security guards informs him that laser city said hello.

"Well," he replies with a well pleased, satisfied smile. He then walks away with a cocky air about him, while brushing himself off.

"Do ya think it's aliens, sheriff?" Tommy is

twenty one, and a firm believer in U.F.O.'s. "You know lots of people claim to have been sucked up into flyin' saucers and taken to other planets. Whada you think?"

"I don't believe in flying saucers, Tommy. At least not yet."

"I got a fresh pot of coffee and some food from the diner over here. Can I get you a cup?"

Both men are stunned as a high pitch squeal emits from the parking lot light just in front of the trouble spot. As they turn to see what is going on, a flash of light stabs the ground from the fixture. It is a solid wall of light; brighter than all the flood lights provided by the generators surrounding the parking place. The light is so bright and intense, it looks like a solid wall is funneling down from the fixture atop the light pole. It lasts for a full four seconds. As quickly as it came on, it goes off. While shielding their eyes, they see what looks like the figure of a man drop out of nowhere onto the ground. It is a man, and he is holding a screaming baby. The man quickly backs up and looks up, while trying to calm the child.

"Come on, Virginia, come on," he is saying aloud. "I know you got my message. Come on!"

The man falls to his knees but continues looking up. A tear begins to roll down his face.

Marshall reaches for the handle to his car door. As soon as his hand touches it, the high pitch squeal pierces his ears again. He darts his head in the direction of the light pole. The man on the ground begins to smile hopefully. The blinding light blazes out of the fixture, causing the man to shield his eyes and the babies face. The light goes out. Marshall and Tommy watch as a woman drops out of nowhere and lands on the grass. Tommy's mouth is still in his lap.

"Virginia!" An excited Jeff jumps to his feet and falls on top of his wife. "I knew you got my signal, I just knew it. Micah, look. It's mommy!"

Jeff hands Micah to Virginia and the three of them begin laughing with ecstasy, clinging to each other.

"I'm sheriff Marshall Winston. I was wondering if I could have a word or two with the both of you?"

With that, their celebration is halted.

Arthur walks into David's office, wiping his hands. He throws a wadded up paper towel across the room into an ashtray, as if he is some great basketball hero. He catches the tail end of the conversation David is having on the phone.

"That's right, you won't need to come and dispose of our specimens...Yes, it is a real tragedy. Jeff was a good man...Okay then. I'll keep you up to date. Bye now."

David puts the phone down slowly with a look of depression in his eyes. He looks as if he just lost a close friend. He liked Jeff. He never intended, nor wanted, anything like this to happen.

Looking up at the nearly gleeful Arthur he grumbles, "Wipe that silly grin off your face."

"Why? Jeff is off the project. Now we can go on with mine."

"Jeff was a good man. This should never have happened. I just hope who ever finds his remains treats them with the respect they deserve. Do we know who the other two were that were with him?"

"Naa, just some chick and her kid."

"A little more respect here, please."

"Oh yeah, respect. Like the respect we've been giving to all of our 'volunteers.' Give me a break. They were just a couple of nobodies like all the rest of 'em back there."

"We will have to call Jeff's wife. I don't know if we have Jeff's mother's phone number on file. I'll have to check in the morning."

"Emmmmm," Arthur says with a look of sly mischief on his face. "I hear she's one cute chick-a-boo. She's gonna be real lonely and in need of someone to comfort her."

David just looks up in disgust.

"Poor girl. First her mother-in-law, then her husband and now your nonsense. Where did the Ion Pulse Transmitter send them?" David asks.

"The same town we've been picking them up from. I think in Tennessee somewhere."

"Well young man. It looks like you'll have to take over Jeff's work as well as your own. I was just speaking with your father and he already has several countries interested in buying into the product Jeff was working on."

"But..."

"It looks like we may make a killing with his product. I sure hope, for your sake, you were paying attention to what he was doing."

Arthur is left standing dumb-founded.

"Where are we?" asks Jeff.

"You're in Collinwood Tennessee."

Marshall hands Jeff a cup of coffee.

"This is where I was just before ending up back at your lab," Virginia says while taking a drink. "As a matter of fact, that's our car, still parked there."

Almost spilling his coffee, Marshall drops his arm bringing the cup away from his mouth.

"That's YOUR car over there?" he says confused.

"Yes. Actually, I need to see if Micah's diaper bag is still in there. He needs a change."

"That car right there," Marshall says, pointing to the car. "The Toyota parked inside all that bright orange tape?"

"Yes."

"Mr. Winston. That is our car," assures Jeff. "Are you okay?"

"Oh yeah. Oh yeah. I'm doing much better."

"Jeff, do you have your keys? I can't find mine."

"Yeah, here."

"Thanks."

Virginia walks over to the car.

After seeing her unlock the door and get their diaper bag, Marshall relaxes a little and breaks a hopeful smile.

"Tommy, get Caleb over here pronto!" Marshall yells over to Tommy. "Would you mind if I get someone who saw the last occupant of that vehicle over here to verify your story?"

"No, not at all," Virginia says, as she starts to change Micah.

"What's going on Mr. Winston?" asks Jeff.

"Please, call me Marshall."

Marshall proceeds to explain everything that has been happening here the last few days. He explains how they had 20 people missing, Jeff's wife and baby made it 22 and adding the dog, brings the total to 23. He explains how the dog was sucked in through the radio and how Caleb, one of his officers, saw the same thing happen to Jeff's wife and kid; and how the manager of the store saw his own wife, kid and cousin get sucked into the radio. He tells Jeff how it only happens when the car's radio is tuned into one particular radio station: 103.3.

"We didn't know what was happening to them. Of course, we were thinking the worse. If you are who you say you are, I'm going to start feeling a whole lot better knowing that the other 20 people might still be alive too."

"So he did get it to work?" muses Jeff.

"Get what to work?" asks Marshall inquisitively.

"Let me explain. I work in a scientific laboratory which focuses on the application of previously learned knowledge from research and directing that knowledge into new products. My current project was that of applying knowledge of Nitrogen and breathing air under pressure, you know, like SCUBA diving, to invent a device which could prevent the bends, without decompressing. David Calvitch, the big cheese over there, had long been working on a way to use air ionization to transmit radio signals. According to his theory, he should also be able to use ions to transmit solid materials via radio signals. The way his system was designed to work, he would fill a chamber with a charge of radiation. This would in effect take a snapshot of the solid matter within the chamber by counting atoms and calculating their placement. Once completed, the chamber would be flooded with negative ion particles. The matter, now positively charged because of the radiation blast, would bond with the negative ions, causing the solid to become millions of separate particles. These particles could then be beamed through an antenna and received at another location, anywhere. Sort of like bouncing a laser light off a mirror or a satellite dish. The receiving station does it all again but this time to bring the matter back. The receiving station floods a chamber with negative ions as well. When the matter was transmitted back, the negative ions would attract the positive ions from the matter, causing them to break free and then bond with the negative ions causing a neutrally charged atom again. The image of the matter would remain as particles until another blast of radiation caused the particles to bond back together. This was his theory. Whether this is how he's doing it or not, I don't know, but it looks like he 'is' doing it."

"That would explain the fresh air smell accompanied with each instance. All those Ion's charging the air would act just like an ion air freshener."

"Exactly."

"But a car radio is a receiver, not a transmitter."

"He must have discovered a way to reverse the polarity of the receiver so it would act as a transmitter instead. Sort of like, getting it to go into reverse."

"So why only one station?"

"This way he wouldn't have to run an algorithm to determine which station the car's tuner was set to, but that's only a guess."

"Yes, but following that, how did you get here? There is no chamber to contain the ions here. That's just a light pole standing in the middle of an empty parking lot."

"They must have learned how to intensify the ion content to where it doesn't need to be kept in a chamber."

"Okay, but why here? Why didn't you come out in some house or office or something?"

"That I don't know. I expected to come out at the base of a mountain."

"You didn't know we were going to come back here?" asks a surprised Virginia who is holding their now sleeping baby.

"No. I had no idea."

"You said you remembered everything?"

"True, but this is new. I didn't even know he had this whole thing working. I was involved with the installation of the duct work we were in. I knew about the chamber with the lasers under the last visible ladder rung. When we put that system in, it was meant to be used for an emergency escape route in case we were held by terrorists or guerrillas or spies. That last part, with the lasers, is a safeguard in case they followed us in. There is a black panel about five feet above the lasers. To disengage the lasers, we all have been informed to press our security badges to the plate, then look directly into it. This will make sure we were the good guys, not the bad guys, then it would inactivate the cutting lasers and just send out beams of light. Once the light is broken, by a body passing through, it resets the cutting lasers. As soon as a person completely goes through, the beams of light will reach a reflector setting off the switch which again activates the cutting laser. If anyone tries to jump, thinking they will be able to get through the lasers, they will set off another set of lasers which will instantly cut them in two."

A look of shock overtakes Virginia.

"The bottom lasers would then burn most of

the rest of their body."

"I'm sure glad I didn't jump," says Virginia.

"You almost did?" asks Jeff, surprised.

Virginia just nods her head.

"I'm sure glad you didn't either."

"It was that voice that kept saying jump or turn back. It made me believe that the only way out was to jump and that would get me out safely."

"Then it works. It was put in like that, purposefully, to throw off any terrorists or intruders. Once under the lasers, it was only supposed to be another ten foot climb down to a floor leading to a door which was cut in the side of the mountain. I went down the ten feet and was just about to step down off the ladder when doors above and below me closed, a bright light flashed and I landed here."

"Okay, but what was with the tapping and slapping the rung and lifting your fingers?" asks Virginia.

"I didn't trust the system from the day we put it in, so, I put what is called a 'back door' into the security system. The system would detect two slaps to the ladder rung, then three taps to the area just to the left of the last laser beam and the wall. This would then shut down the cutting lasers and fire only the beams of light. The only reason I lifted my fingers was to show you how many times to tap your foot."

"Oh," she laughs, "'Cause I lifted my fingers with each tap, just like you did. I didn't want to take any chances, so I did exactly what you did."

The three of them begin to chuckle.

"What about everyone else, are they all right?" asks Marshall in a concerned tone of voice.

"The last we heard, they plan on disposing of them. We have got to get back there."

"What are you doing with those people and why all of a sudden do you want to help them?" asks Marshall, distastefully.

"Mr. Winston, sir. I promise you I had no idea this was going on. I was told they were all volunteers and that all the appropriate paper work was in place. I did not know they were being abducted."

"It's true, Mr. Winston. Jeff almost left me in one of the cells. I was trying to get his attention and when I finally did, he wanted to know what I was doing there. He said if I wanted to be in one of his experiments I should have just asked him."

"Honest, sheriff. I still don't know what they're doing with those other people."

"I do," Virginia says sadly.

She explains how the mother with the two little girls told her everything that has been going on. How they are trying to develop a pain numbing drug which will allow the user to feel no pain, yet still be able to keep all their mental and physical faculties.

"The lady overheard something about the drug having guerrilla, war, terrorist and sports applications. Being able to keep fighting, no matter what kind of pain the body was in. She also overheard them saying something like 'Wait until we start cutting off body parts' or something like that. They plan to test the drug very thoroughly."

"So no matter what, those people are going to be," Jeff stops abruptly.

"Dead. I believe that's the word you're looking for," says Marshall. "This all sounds very fascinating, and very made up. Except for the part of you dropping out of a street light, I'm finding the whole thing extremely hard to swallow."

"Marshall, you wanted to see me," Caleb calls out as he approaches them.

"Yeah, over here,"

"Heya Marshall, it's kinda...THAT'S HER!" he shouts, interrupting himself. "That's the girl I saw get sucked into her radio."

He continues shouting pointing to Virginia walking around her. Stunned, he continues looking up and down at her. He never thought he would see her again, at least not alive.

"And that's the kid I saw. How did you get

here? How did you get into the radio? How..."

"Okay, calm down Caleb and we'll fill you in later," Marshall interjects.

"It's U.F.O.'s I tell ya," says Tommy. "And these three are probably aliens," he says pulling his gun, shakily.

"For crying out loud, put that thing away before you hurt yourself. If they are aliens, and can beam in and out through radios and street lights, don't you think they would have something to make our guns ineffective?" Marshall turns back to address Jeff. "Sorry about that. Tommy here's been reading way too many U.F.O. magazines."

"It's okay, no harm done."

"Okay Jeff. You've got my attention and now, like it or not, I have to believe your story. It's the only lead I've got and the only sort of logical explanation for what's been going on. Our next step is obviously to get those other people to safety. I'll radio for some help and we can head on over there. I can have a search warrant drawn up in no time. Where is your lab? Over in Florence, Alabama? We can be there in a couple of hours and call for some local help to meet us there. I'm sure the local police will be there in no time."

"Florence, Alabama? No. Bridgeport, Washington. Washington state. What made you think it was in Alabama?" asks Jeff.

Marshall goes on to explain about the radio station and the amplifier they saw there. Marshall can't believe it was all the way across the country in Washington state.

"It is going to be hard enough to get anyone else to believe this story as it is, but now, to tell them a local radio station is beaming people clear across the country," Marshall says as he shakes his head. "Okay, Jeff. We need a plan. You're the only one who knows that place, at least better than anyone of us could hope to. We've got to go back and get those people out." Turning to Tommy, he says, "Hey Tom. Get Jason, Pops and Rich out here for me, will ya?"

Looking up, Marshall offers Caleb a seat.

"As soon as everybody gets here, Jeff and I will fill all of you in on what's been happening, and what we're going to do. The 'what we're going to do' part still has to be figured out, but I want to wait until everyone is here."

Looking through binoculars, two men watch as Sergeant Marcus Montgomery puts down the receiver of his phone.

"Got it," says one of them, pushing the stop button on a tape recorder.

"Yes, but did we get the trace?" asks the

second.

They both turn to a third man sitting next to some equipment, holding one side of his headphones to one ear. He puts down the headphones and slumps over in disappointment. He turns to the other gentlemen and just shakes his head back and forth.

"Shoot!"

"Did we at least get any closer?"

"Nope. They keep changing their pattern with each phone call. They've got their signal bouncing off so many satellites, and being transferred from so many phones, we can't get close. They don't want to get caught, so they are keeping their conversations fairly short."

"They'll slip up sooner or later."

"Yeah, I mean, come on. They were talking a lot longer this time then they ever have. You tellin' us we didn't get any closer?"

"Oh, no. We have narrowed it down. This call did that for us. We have now eliminated the rest of the world and figure they are calling from somewhere in the United States," he says in a 'matter of fact' way.

"Let's just bust him for conspiring to sell unauthorized technology to a foreign country. Being that country is Iraq, we should have no problem."

"But then we only get him. That won't prevent

the sale from taking place, nor will it put the manufactures out of business. We've got to get all of them; or we may as well just pack it in now."

"He's right."

"I know. I'm just getting anxious. I don't want anything to get out of our country that could bite us on the back of the neck later on."

"Relax, man. We'll get 'em."

Chapter XX

"Another thing," David continues speaking. "It looks like we will be getting that extra funding for your project. Your father received payment for an anticipated shipment of your drug from some terrorist group in Iraq. It's just a matter of him cleaning up the money and getting it to us." David turns to the computer on his desk and calls up a spreadsheet file. "We're over budget already and our creditors want their money. Now," David begins to speak more sternly, "have, YOU, been bragging about your project to anyone?"

Arthur swallows hard.

"Your father and I have to cut off communications for a while. He believes they might be on to him. That's also going to prevent our money from getting here as quickly as we need it. You're a bright boy, but you're not careful. With all your brains, you still don't think," David says getting up and walking out from behind his desk. "I'm going to shut down the Ion Transmitter for now. You'll have to make do with the specimens you have. If they're getting close to us, we don't need anything else to attract additional attention to ourselves." David presses his hands on Arthur's shoulders. "Do not breathe another word about ANY of these projects again. Understood?"

Arthur nervously shakes his head yes.

"Good."

David releases his hands from Arthur's shoulders and walks to a closet. Reaching in, he swiftly grabs his coat.

"I'm going to stop off upstairs and shut down that Ion transmitter before I leave so we won't have to worry about it." Exiting his office, he stops at the threshold and turns back. "I'll see you in the morning Arthur, and remember," he positions his finger over his lips as if to say 'shhhh.' "Not another word to anyone." He turns and walks off, leaving Arthur standing alone in the office.

"This is Montgomery...You had better be on a blue phone boy!"

"Don't worry, I am." Arthur is now in his own office talking to Sergeant Montgomery.

"Okay then. What can I do for you, son?"

"Dad, I want to shut down the Ion Particle Transmitter, but I can't remember the code. What is it?"

"To shut it down? There isn't any code required to shut it down, only to bring it up."

"That's what I thought, but when I tried to shut it down, it asked for a security code. I'm imagining they are the same and that's why I called you."

"When was this put in? David never told me anything about this."

"I have a feeling it was put in tonight."

"Oh? Why's that?"

"David and I were arguing about it. I told him we should shut the thing down for a few days, until the heat on you cools off, at least a little. I told him I was going to shut it down just before I left for home. He told me I would do no such thing! He said, and I'm quoting dad, so please don't get mad at me. He said, 'Shut it down nothing. If your stupid father can't use the gray matter between his ears so as to keep the heat off, then it's his own problem! We've got buyers and no product, and we can't produce product without subjects to test and develop it on.' I tried to reason with him, Pop, but he wouldn't listen. He just stormed out of his office and yelled 'Good night' back at me. I thought he was going to the restroom before leaving because he didn't walk towards the front. I guess he came up here and put a pass code on this thing. I don't know what to do, Dad. I'm afraid for you. That's why I chanced calling you."

"Right. You're worried about me. More like your own neck," his father voices back in a tone of intolerance. "If he put a password on for shutting it down, he most likely changed the one for bringing it up as well."

"Ohh, I didn't think of that." Arthur pauses for a moment. "So, what should I do?"

"I don't know. Here. You got a pencil and paper?"

"Yeah, go ahead."

"Try this number anyway. Hopefully he was so miffed with you that he wasn't thinking clearly enough to change it. Try 5X903327-Q29 and see if it works. We've gotta go. We've been on this line too long already. I hope you get the code to work. Bye now."

"Bye," says Arthur, as his cocky, devious smile brims through. "So, I guess I'm not so stupid after all, now am I, Calvitch?" he says in an undertone as he begins to snicker piously and contentedly.

"Good evening Mr. Calvitch. What brings you up here, especially this late at night?" asks the control operator.

The Ion Particle Transmitter/Receiver station always has an operator present. This station is completely automated but an operator is posted on duty twenty four hours a day, just in case something unexpected happens.

"Good evening. I've come up here to bring you some good news. I'm letting you go home early tonight, with pay."

"Whoa! You serious?"

"Yes, very much so. I want to close this station down for a few days, because of security and safety reasons, so there will be no need for you to man your post. As a matter of fact, you can take the next two weeks off, with pay of course. This should give us enough time to make sure we're meeting the Federal Safety Commission's regulations. If there's one thing I can't stand, it's to see someone get hurt from an avoidable problem," David reassures the control operator.

"I tell you, Mr. Calvitch. I speak for, probably, everyone here when I say we really appreciate the way you take care of all us employees. If there were more employers like you, there would be a lot less people trying to steal from their bosses."

"Please," he says, turning his head with an assumed embarrassment. "I only want to do good by my people. The way I figure it, without all you workers, I wouldn't have a business." David smiles and nods to the worker as he invites the man to leave.

"Well, thank you very much. Boy is my wife going to be pleasantly surprised!" he is gathering his things. "Did you want me to shut it down for you?"

"Nooo, noo, no. Thank you. I'll take care of it. Besides, we put in a new code which is required to bring it down and only I know what it is. It was put in as a safety feature. This way nobody accidentally shuts it down right in the middle of receiving a transmission. That would not only be messy but it would really be hard on whoever accidentally shut it down."

"Is that why they had to receive a couple of people downstairs, at the other computer, so you could activate the code?"

"Yes," answers a surprised David. "How did you know about that?"

"Hey, I'm here all night with very little to do and I get bored. To keep myself busy, I sometimes read the logs. This machine was logged as being down today and a manual adjustment was made to the specimen count. I just put two and two together and figured that was why."

"Very good. You'll go places. I'm going to remember you."

With the worker now gone, David can shut down the station. On the computer console, the following dialogue ensues:

SYSTEM: READY TO RECEIVE INPUT

system shutdown

SYSTEM: 'SYSTEM' COMMAND

```
UNRECOGNIZED PLEASE TRY AGAIN

SYSTEM: READY TO RECEIVE INPUT
```

"Oh, what is that command to get in?" David mutters to himself. He reaches back for his wallet and pulls a small slip of paper from a hidden compartment therein. "Ah, yes. That's what it is." He glances back up at the screen, and tries it again.

```
SYSTEM: READY TO RECEIVE INPUT

system shutdown

SYSTEM: 'SYSTEM' COMMAND
UNRECOGNIZED PLEASE TRY AGAIN
SYSTEM: READY TO RECEIVE INPUT

access

COMMAND ACCEPTED
PLEASE ENTER SYSTEM TO ACCESS OR
'HELP' FOR LIST

ACCESS READY:

help

PLEASE ENTER ONE OF THE FOLLOWING
SYSTEMS TO ACCESS:

SYSTEM      USER        TERMINAL
DIAGNOSTICS SHUTDOWN    STARTUP
FILE
```

ACCESS READY:

shutdown

LEAVING 'ACCESS' SYSTEM....
ACCESSING 'SHUTDOWN' SYSTEM....

'SHUTDOWN' SUCCESSFULLY ACCESSED.

ENTER YOUR NEXT COMMAND OR 'HELP'
FOR A LIST OF OPTIONS
SHUTDOWN: READY TO RECEIVE INPUT

shutdown full system

SHUTDOWN: 'SHUTDOWN' COMMAND
UNRECOGNIZED PLEASE TRY AGAIN

SHUTDOWN: READY TO RECEIVE INPUT

help

SHUTDOWN: DISPLAYING HELP
INFORMATION:

        FULL   SUB   PARTIAL   LIST

FOR SPECIFIC HELP, ENTER 'HELP
function'

SHUTDOWN: READY TO RECEIVE INPUT

full

SHUTDOWN: FULL SYSTEM SHUTDOWN
REQUESTED

```
************************************
*                                *
*WARNING WARNING  WARNING  WARNING*
*                                *
************************************
```

YOU ARE ABOUT TO SHUTDOWN THE ENTIRE
STATION, INCLUDING THE TRANSMITTING
AND RECEIVING PORTIONS.   ANY
TRANSMISSIONS CURRENTLY IN PROCESS
WILL BE LOST!!

ARE YOU SURE THIS IS WHAT YOU WANT
TO DO?

ANSWER 'YES, I AM SURE' TO CONTINUE,
ANYTHING ELSE TO CANCEL SHUTDOWN

SHUTDOWN: READY TO RECEIVE INPUT

yes, i am sure

SHUTDOWN: FULL SYSTEM SHUTDOWN
CONTINUING...

ENTER THE AUTHORIZATION CODE TO
PERFORM THIS TYPE OF SHUTDOWN

```
SHUTDOWN:  READY TO RECEIVE INPUT


5X903327-D29


SHUTDOWN:  AUTHORIZATION
GRANTED....FULL SYSTEM SHUTDOWN
CONTINUING

SHUTDOWN:   ***************
            **  WARNING   **
            ***************
            SHUTDOWN CODE DIFFERENT

YOU WILL NOT BE ABLE TO
BRING THE SYSTEM BACK
UP WITH THIS CODE!!!

ARE YOU SURE YOU WANT TO BRING THE
SYSTEM DOWN WITH THIS CODE?

ANSWER 'YES, I AM SURE' TO CONTINUE,
ANYTHING ELSE TO CANCEL SHUTDOWN


SHUTDOWN FULL SYSTEM:   READY TO
RECEIVE INPUT

yes, i am sure

SHUTDOWN: FULL SYSTEM SHUTDOWN
COMMENCING
```

```
SHUTDOWN: PROCESSING REMOTE
RADIATION TRIGGER #1....
SHUTDOWN: REMOTE RADIATION
TRIGGOR/TRANSMITTER #1.....
SHUTDOWN: REMOTE ION
GENERATOR/TRANSMITTER #1 COMPLETE.

SHUTDOWN: PROCESSING REMOTE
GENERATOR/TRANSMITTER #1...
SHUTDOWN: REMOTE ION
GENERATOR/TRANSMITTER #1 COMPLETE.
SHUTDOWN: PROCESSING REMOTE ION
BOOSTER/AMPLIFIER #1...
SHUTDOWN: REMOTE ION
BOOSTER/AMPLIFIER #1 COMPLETE.
SHUTDOWN: *************
           *** NOTE ****
           *************
           REMOTE SYSTEM #1 NEVER
      ACTIVE

SHUTDOWN: PROCESSING REMOTE
RADIATION TRIGGER #2....
SHUTDOWN: REMOTE RADIATION TRIGGER
#2 COMPLETE.

SHUTDOWN: PROCESSING REMOTE
GENERATOR/TRANSMITTER #2...
SHUTDOWN: REMOTE ION
GENERATOR/TRANSMITTER #2 COMPLETE.
SHUTDOWN: PROCESSING REMOTE ION
BOOSTER/AMPLIFIER #2...
SHUTDOWN: REMOTE ION
BOOSTER/AMPLIFIER #2 COMPLETE.
```

```
SHUTDOWN: PROCESSING REMOTE
RADIATION TRIGGER #3.......
SHUTDOWN: REMOTE ION
GENERATOR/TRANSMITTER #3 COMPLETE.

SHUTDOWN: PROCESSING REMOTE ION
BOOSTER/AMPLIFIER #3...
SHUTDOWN: REMOTE ION
BOOSTER/AMPLIFIER #3  SHUTDOWN
COMPLETE.
SHUTDOWN:   * * * * * * * * * * * * *
            * * * NOTE * * * *
            * * * * * * * * * * * * *
            REMOTE SYSTEM #3 NEVER
            ACTIVE

SHUTDOWN: PROCESSING SUB
SYSTEM.............
SHUTDOWN: SUB SYSTEM SHUTDOWN
PROCESSING COMPLETE

SHUTDOWN: PROCESSING MAIN
PROCESSOR...................
SHUTDOWN: MAIN PROCESSOR SHUTDOWN
PROCESSING COMPLETE

THE ION PARTICLE
TRANSMITTER/RECEIVER STATION AND ALL
REMOTE STATIONS SHUTDOWN IS NOW
COMPLETE.  ALL STATIONS AND
TRIGGERS, LOCAL AND REMOTE ARE NOW
INOPERATIVE
```

```
SHUTDOWN: READY TO RECEIVE INPUT

access

COMMAND ACCEPTED
PLEASE ENTER SYSTEM TO ACCESS OR
'HELP' FOR LIST
ACCESS READY:

system

LEAVING 'ACCESS' SYSTEM....

ACCESSING 'SYSTEM' SYSTEM....

'SYSTEM' SUCCESSFULLY ACCESSED.
ENTER YOUR NEXT COMMAND OR 'HELP'
FOR A LIST OF OPTIONS

SYSTEM:  READY TO RECEIVE INPUT
```

"Now I feel a whole lot better," he says as he clears the computer's screen and gets up to leave.

Stepping out of the room, David closes and locks the door. He pauses a moment.

"Maybe I should change those codes so they're the same," he thinks to himself. "No. I'll leave it this way."

David turns and heads for the front door, to go home.

Chapter XXI

"Siberia? What do you mean, Siberia?" asks Joshua, the senior officer in charge of this operation. He has been trying to catch Montgomery 'in the act' for a couple of years.

"Just what I said, Siberia," answers James, as he presses stop on the tape recorder and puts down his headphones again.

"He's putting a piece of paper into his briefcase," states Manny, the third in this team assigned to work with Joshua. Manny had not taken his eyes off of Sergeant Montgomery. "I can't make out what's on the paper," he says, adjusting his binoculars, "but it's the same piece of paper he was reading when he gave that code over the phone. It appears to be some kind of instructions or directions."

"Most likely instructions for shutting down the Ion, whatever, they were talking about. So, how did we end up in Siberia? We were somewhere here in the United States?"

"I don't know; but according to this trace, they are in Siberia. I've radioed in and H.Q. is going to check it out."

"Man, this is tough! I can't believe how far off we are? It felt like we were getting so close!"

Far off is putting it mildly. David's labs have developed a 'Phreaking' box they like to call: 'Get Lost.' When attached to a phone line and activated, it sends any telephone line tracing equipment on a wild goose chase, making it follow a ghost path that is generated by the device. The ghost path fools the tracing equipment into thinking it found the location of the phone, when, in actuality, it found nothing.

The three men, clad in green fatigues, wait, watch and listen. Hoping for something to tip them off. Hoping for the one clue to set them into motion. The one clue to tie everything all together. The one clue to send Sergeant Marcus Montgomery to a new place he can call 'home.'

"All right everyone, listen up," begins Marshall. Pops, Jason and Richard have arrived. "Everyone, this is Jeff, Virginia and little Micah Colt. They just dropped in from Washington and I'm talking the state, not our capitol. Jeff is going to fill you all in on what's going on, then we've got to come up with a way to make it all stop. Jeff. The floor's all yours." Marshall invitingly motions Jeff to step up and speak to everyone present.

Jeff begins to explain to the newly arrived officers everything he had explained to Sheriff

Winston. A lot of things now make sense to them. They can comprehend the situation more fully, having had their horizons expanded. Jeff goes on to explain the scope of the project he is working on and the scope of the project Arthur is working on. He was able to figure out the magnitude of Arthur's project with all the information Virginia had given, along with everything he had seen and heard at the lab and while in the duct work.

Marshall then went on to implicate the wide range use for each of these two projects, especially if used in warfare and or counter intelligence.

"If it's such a great weapon, why don't we just call the army, or something, and have them invade the place and take over. I'm sure they could find some way of justifying it, you know, like national security or some other such pretentious cause," says Jason.

"No good. It would have been a great idea, but I think the military is already involved."

"How's that?" asks Pops.

"I overheard David Calvitch talking to Arthur Montgomery's father, Marcus."

"Montgomery?" questions Marshall in disbelief.

"Yeah, why? You know him?"

"Yes, I know him," he says distastefully.

"Great! Maybe you could get in touch with him and get him to call this whole thing off. This has gone too far already, and it's not about to stop."

"Well. I know 'of' him, would be a more appropriate statement."

"Oh," says a disappointed Jeff.

"Last time I heard, Montgomery was serving time for conspiring to sell military secrets to some foreign country. He was never convicted though. They couldn't get anything to stick on him so he was release and acquitted." Marshall is staring off into space, thinking. "I still say he was guilty but there has never been any proof."

"Lot of money to be made selling technology to foreign countries," adds Pops. "If he was guilty the first time, he ain't gonna pass up something like this."

"But, he's a Sergeant. Who they gonna believe, me or him?" asks Jeff.

"Way I figure it," Pops says, taking a drink, "he's probably had a tail ever since the last ordeal. If he's in on it, the army more than likely knows about it and it wouldn't be all that hard to figure out." He raises his eyebrow and nods with a grin.

"What do you have in mind, Pops?" asks Rich.

"Yeah. What's going on in that head of yours?" Marshall asks with a gleam in his eye.

"Shut down my project, will you? I don't think so," Arthur is mumbling to himself as he picks the lock to the Ion transmitter/receiver room. "I can't wait for those useless people to dry out. I need new ones every day. I can't wait another month for them." The door pushes open with a pop. "Heh, heh heh, heh," he is again snickering. "I knew that locksmith course would come in handy someday," he says as he walks into the room. "Now, let's see if the old man changed the password."

Arthur proceeds to bring up the system. When it asks him to enter the password, he feels his heart miss a beat. If he doesn't get it right on the first try, he will be sealed in this room until security comes and releases him. He wants to keep the door ajar, but knows the system cannot be activated unless the rooms security door is latched. He types in the code:

5X903327-Q29

He holds his hand over the 'ENTER' button and feels himself begin to sweat. He can't get this wrong. He can't stop chasing himself around in circles in his mind.

"What will Calvitch and my father do if they found out what I am trying to do? They'll blame me for everything. I'll do time and they will pin this whole thing on me! They'll blame me for Jeff's death," he thinks as he is making himself frantic.

With sweat dripping down his cheeks, his quivering hand slowly moves closer to the enter key. He turns his head back and pulls away quickly. He relaxes a little and is able to breathe again. He turns to walk away but can't seem to tear himself from the console. He peers intensely at the screen. There it is; the password all keyed in and the cursor just blinking at him; almost taunting him to press the 'ENTER' key. He sits back down in front of the keyboard. His trembling hand now reaches out for the 'ENTER' key again. He begins hyperventilating as he moves his hand over to the key. Taking a deep breath, he lashes his hand out at the keyboard smacking the button. The chamber in front of him floods with light causing Arthur to panic. Darting his head back and forth, he looks to see if he has been sealed in. He bolts to the door and frantically tries to push it open. It doesn't move. The doorknob won't turn. Banging the door back and forth, he feels the room closing in on him.

"NOOOOOOOOO!"

He begins banging on the door. He tries to break the glass with his elbow. It won't break. It won't even crack. It's bullet proof. It won't budge.

"NOOO!" he screams again pushing the door.

The light goes off in the chamber and the room returns to its normal luminance. Nearly whimpering, Arthur crouches down at the door.

"No."

"BLIP"

Arthur's eyes pop open. That small, singular beep from the computer was its way of mocking him. He can't get out, and he just knew the computer had to have the last laugh.

"I guess I'm not so smart after all, Mr. Calvitch. Looks like you have won yet another round," he says aloud to himself in a sad defeated tone.

The lone occupant releases the doorknob and sits on the floor with his legs stretched out. No longer feeling in control, the exhausted Arthur closes his eyes, only to collapse into sleep.

Having to wait until morning to initiate Pops plan, the officers have regrouped at the store front. They ran a phone line out into the parking lot, to enable them to make a direct phone call to Washington. With the information Jeff has given them, and the information and leads Marshall and Pops have on Marcus, they are able to find Marcus' office number.

"Sergeant Montgomery, please?" Pops initiates the conversation.

"He hasn't come in yet. May I ask whose calling?"

"Sure!"

"Okay. Who is this, please?"

"This is Pops, who else would it be?"

"Oh, I'm sorry Mr. Montgomery, I didn't recognize your voice. He usually isn't in this early. He doesn't normally show up until eight o'clock...Oh, wait," says a perplexed receptionist. "He just walked by the soda machine. I'll patch you through now. He should reach his office in a couple of seconds, so, hold on and he will be right with you."

Pops just cocks his head to one side and smiles.

"It seems to be working, she's putting me through," he says, cupping his hand over the receiver. "She thinks I'm Montgomery's father."

"We've got one coming through," says James, grabbing everyone's attention.

"Okay, we're all set. Maybe we can get something from this one. Get the trace going."

"I don't think we'll get anything from his office line. Aren't we only supposed to trace calls on that other line?" asks Manny.

"If he thinks we're on to him, he may stop using that phone and use his office phone. He might count on us not listening in to his regular office calls. You know, the old hiding in plain sight, trick."

"He's walking to the phone now. Make sure the tape is rolling," instructs Manny.

"We're rolling, and tracing. We should have the location in about forty five seconds."

These three men have been watching Montgomery's office for six days. They have been sleeping in shifts during the night, with all of them alert and awake during regular office hours. Their two years of trailing Marcus Montgomery has culminated into these last six days of direct, intense observation.

"Remember, Pops, you have to keep him on the phone for at least a minute to get a trace."

"Don't you worry. I think I can keep him on the line for at least that."

"Montgomery here.   With whom am I speaking?"

"This is Pops. Who else were you expecting?"

"Pops?" Marcus replies, shaking his head. "I'm afraid you have the wrong number."

"Listen, you told me to call you at this number,

bright and early, so here I am."

"Sir, I'm quite sure I don't know who you are nor what you're talking about." Marcus always spoke with a snobbish air about him, especially when talking to strangers.

"Wait a minute. Let me check this out again," Pops says, while rustling some paper into the telephone. "Let me make sure I got this number right."

"Sir, I'm very busy. I'm sure you've dialed it wrong, so good day."

"If you hang up on me you young snot I'm just going to keep calling back until you confirm or deny the phone number I'm dialing. Now you just keep yer pants on and let me get this here number."

The other officers are quite amused with Pops' performance. Going on like he is, they are sure he'd be able to keep Marcus on the line for at least a minute.

"Lemmy see. Did I call, for goodness sake, I can't hardly read my own writin'. Is this, okay, let's see. Is this 206-555-8523?"

"No, sir, it is not. Now would you please hang up and leave me alone?"

"We got the trace," yelps James.

"Where's this one at, London square?" quips Manny.

"No.   This time it's from a little town, in Tennessee."

Rich is signaling Pops to let him know they need 15 more seconds to allow enough time to get a trace. They are unaware of the new tracing equipment which works faster than the equipment they are familiar with.

"Well you don't have to be such a..."

"I'm hanging up now," interrupts Marcus.

"Q29," whispers Jeff, who is listening in, via an extension.

"Q29!" comes blurting out of the phone's receiver as Marcus is putting it down. He freezes for a second, then regains his composure. Within the blink of an eye, he forces the receiver down onto the telephone base.   A   morbid   fear   overtakes   his expression.

"Was it long enough?" asks Pops.

"It should have been," answers Rich.

"Okay, he hesitated before hanging up the phone. That means he must have heard you say Q29. That means we got his attention," says Jeff.

"That'll at least put a scare into him," says Marshall. "Okay Pops, what's next?"

"Just hang on for a few minutes. If his line was tapped, this place will be crawling with feds and possibly the military in no time."

The three men in the surveillance vehicle all look up at each other.

"Did you hear that?" questions Manny.

He replays the tape and sure enough, there it is. Whoever was on the other end of the phone shouted: "Q29."

"It must have been a code of some kind. The whole thing must have been an act."

"Yeah, but meaning what?"

"Hey guys," says James, holding up a piece of paper. On it is written:

5X903327-Q29

"Notice anything?" he quips, pointing to the last three digits.

"Get a message to H.Q. Tell them we just might have a connection," instructs Joshua.

"Okay. We got his attention. It's evident he's involved with something by the way he hung up the phone," states Marshall. "So what's our next step?"

"I think we should get those innocent people out of there before anything else happens to them," says Jeff.

"You're right. You'll need some help. Take Rich, Jason and Caleb back with you and get those people out of there. You're going to have to keep them up there with you until we can transport them back here. We may be getting some visitors soon, so you won't be able to send them back the way you and your family got here."

"Marshall. How we gonna get to Washington?" asks Jason.

"The same way Jeff's wife did."

"I was afraid you were going to say that," he sighs.

"It's really our only way," states Jeff. "If we

drive, or even fly, it will take too long. We've got to get them out as soon as we can, especially if the military is involved."

They are all as one with this decision. It really is the only way. After talking to Virginia, they figured out they would need some type of gas mask. Virginia told them she remembered falling asleep almost immediately upon entering the chamber.

Clad in their gas masks, they enter Colt's car and start it up. With the radio tuned to 103.3, Rich backs the car away from the curb.

"We're ready, Jeff. We gotta go," Rich yells from the car.

Jeff and Virginia are saying good bye, again. She doesn't want Jeff to go, but knows he has to. He gives her one final embrace and ducks into the car. Donning his mask, he turns to Rich and gives him the thumbs up. Rich turns to Caleb and Jason in the back seat. Caleb gives the thumbs up. Jason a sideways thumb, then a thumb up, then a sideways thumb. He shakes his head side to side then takes a deep breath and gives a positive, determined thumbs up. Rich adds his thumbs up to the rest, then turns to face forward and puts the car into gear. Pulling forward slowly, Rich bumps the car into the curb.

Shielding her eyes from the light, Virginia can't prevent the tears from running down her face. She watches as the figures swiftly disappear into the radio. Startled by the flicker of a spark shooting from the car antenna, she feels the warm embrace of Marshall Winston putting his arm around her.

"They'll be okay. I know they'll make it." Marshall is very reassuring.

The silence is broken by the sound of a helicopter looming in overhead, followed by several military vehicles driving into the parking lot.

"Yup! He was being watched," says Pops. "Here comes the cavalry."

Pops, Marshall, Tommy and Virginia just wait as the vehicles approach. Not expecting to see several police vehicles and flood lights along with the press, the army approaches cautiously.

"Come on over, it's all right," Pops declares through a bullhorn. He had anticipated their arrival and retrieved it out of his car, just before they got there.

Finding a place to land, the chopper sets down about 50 yards away from the scene. As the M.P.'s exit their vehicles, their commander exits the helicopter and walks over to the group.

"Good morning. I'm Sheriff Winston, this is one of my deputies, Pops. We've been expecting you."

"G'mornin'. I'm Captain John Litchfield, U.S. Army. What's going on here?"

Marshall explains how they knew about Marcus Montgomery. He saays they received some information from an insider in the lab.

"The insider didn't want to get too involved, so he called our little town in Tennessee to have us handle it," says Marshall.

He also explained how people were being abducted from this town and, according to the insider, were being brought to the lab.

"You know where and who Montgomery is dealing with?" asks the Captain.

"We know what he's up to. We don't know who he is dealing with as far as who he wants to sell his chemicals and inventions to," is Marshall's reply.

"Great. Where is their base of operations?"

"Now, hold on a minute. We've got our men on the inside trying to get those abducted people out. We have to wait until we hear from them first before we do anything. If you send your people in there now, you could have a hostage situation on your hands and that won't help anybody." Marshall looks down at his watch. It is ten fifteen in the morning. "Come on. Let's go get a bite to eat and some coffee at the diner, and I'll fill you in on everything. You can send your men home, because their base is nowhere near here."

"Why should I trust you?"

"Number one, you have no reason not to.

Number two, I'm the only lead you've got right now, and number three, I want this guy nailed just as badly as you do. I don't take kindly to people who like to steal other people. Especially when they use them for guinea pigs."

The captain just nods then dispatches some of his men to leave.

"You know, we don't just want Montgomery. We also want the chemicals and that new underwater device his suppliers are working on and we want everyone involved on the projects."

"Well that's up to you. But know this: I trust our informant. I know he had nothing to do with all this..."

"That will be up to us to decide," interrupts the captain. "I don't have any idea of all the people involved. H.Q. has been keeping tabs on all the phone conversations to Montgomery, as you figured out. If there is reason to suspect others who might be involved with this, we will have to bring them in for questioning. I'm gonna trust you, for now, but you will have to tell me where the lab is."

"Of course Captain, of course. In due time."

"So where's that diner you mentioned."

Chapter XXII

Arthur is awakened by a sudden, bright, flash of light. Startled, he realizes something is coming in over the Ion Pulse Transmitter. He rushes over to the console and is greeted by the following display:

```
STARTUP: REMOTE ION
BOOSTER/AMPLIFIER #2 STARTUP
        COMPLETE.
STARTUP: BYPASSING REMOTE RADIATION
TRIGGER #3....
STARTUP: BYPASSING REMOTE
GENERATOR/TRANSMITTER #3.....
STARTUP: BYPASSING REMOTE ION
BOOSTER/AMPLIFIER #3....
STARTUP: ***********
        *** NOTE ***
        ***********
        REMOTE SYSTEM #3 NOT
    ACTIVATED
STARTUP: PROCESSING SUB
SYSTEM............
STARTUP: SUB SYSTEM STARTUP
PROCESSING COMPLETE
STARTUP: PROCESSING MAIN
PROCESSOR.....................
STARTUP: MAIN PROCESSOR STARTUP
```

```
PROCESSING COMPLETE

THE ION PARTICLE
TRANSMITTER/RECEIVER STATION AND ALL
REMOTE STATIONS STARTUP IS NOW
COMPLETE.  ALL STATIONS AND
TRIGGERS, LOCAL AND REMOTE ARE NOW
IN OPERATION.

STARTUP:   READY TO RECEIVE INPUT


MESSAGE FROM SYSTEM: RECEIVING
TRANSMISSION FROM REMOTE
                          STATION #2
```

"Then I'm not sealed in!" he says excitedly, while he watches as sparks arc within the chamber. He sighs. "I'm not sealed in." He then becomes alert to what he is saying and bolts to the door. "I'm NOT sealed in."

Racing to the door, he reaches down and grabs the doorknob. It doesn't turn. He starts to panic. Calming himself, he looks down and notices the lock on the doorknob. Twisting the lock with his hand, the doorknob becomes free and turns as well. Opening this type of doorknob from the outside with a key, or picking the lock as he did, does not release the locking mechanism; it merely allows the doorknob to turn. In his panic the night before, he couldn't think enough to turn the lock. His mind kept telling him the door had already been unlocked when he broke in. Pulling the door open, he steps outside, dusts himself off, and adjusts his tie.

"I guess I'm really not so stupid after all," he says aloud. "I guess we'll have to call this one a draw, now won't we Mr Calvitch?" he says sarcastically as he walks away.

Although excited about receiving more specimens, he cannot allow himself to be seen in this area. If seen, he will be suspected of reactivating the machine. Having more suspicion heaped upon him is the last thing he wants.

As the sparks subside, four fluid-looking streams begin pouring into the chamber. As the process is completing, four bodies are seen suspended in air. Four seats spring out from the back and sides of the chamber. One last burst of light, and the bodies drop into the chairs and are automatically strapped in. The sound of a gas being released into the chamber overtakes the still silence. Two minutes later, the walls of the chamber lift and the chairs begin to move.

Rich looks around and down and notices an emergency release button on the side of his arm rest. Pressing it, his straps spring loose. He had anticipated something like this because of what Virginia had told them. Just before the car hit the curb, he raised his hands up over his head. When the straps went over the arms of the chairs, his arms were not strapped down. Reaching over, he un-straps the other three.

"Where will this take us?" Rich asks Jeff.

"I'm not sure, but I think it will take us to the cells downstairs."

As they are traveling, the chairs lay back to a full reclining position. Initially falling back with the chair, Rich springs back up. Looking down at the seat he sees small holes with plastic covers over them. With a snap, the covers slide back.

"GET UP, QUICK!" he hollers.

Caleb, Jason and Jeff quickly stand up in their seats and watch as needles come up through the holes and shoot forth a liquid.

"Oh, right in the keester. That would've smarted something fierce," Jason says, watching as the needles retract.

"What do you think it is?" asks Caleb.

"Probably another knockout drug," says Jeff.

As they move on, they can feel the chairs beginning a descent. The conveyer is indeed taking them down into the lab, to the lower floors. Entering the holding area, Jeff recognizes where they are and can see the light coming from the water tank. They enter the room and are rolled off the chairs onto the floor. The chairs then continue on and up into the ceiling, where they will return to the receiving room to await their next victims.

"Well, it looks like we're here," says Jason.

"Yes, but where is here?" Caleb adds as he looks around the room.

"Here comes our next ride," states Richard, pointing to a robot fork lift heading their way. He turns to Jeff pointing at the machine and asks: "Do we ride, or what?"

"We ride. This thing is expecting four bodies. If it doesn't get four it may set off an alarm, and we don't want that," Jeff tells the group.

"Here I go," says Rich as the device picks him up. "Bye." He waves leisurely, grinning while laying back.

Caleb looks to Jeff and says, "Why don't you follow that thing and see if you notice any way out of here? After it takes me, I'll come back and let it take me again. That way you can get busy and it will still get its four bodies."

"Good idea. I will," he answers.

The robot comes back and picks up Caleb. When it turns to leave, Jeff gets up and follows it. The robot is in a hallway behind each of the cells. When it comes to the appropriate cell, it unlatches the solid door to the cell, deposits the body, leaves and closes the door. This is a perfect way to get all the people out of the cells. The only other problem is finding a way out of this corridor. Jeff lets Caleb out so he can run back and get picked up again by the robot. Once four bodies are picked up, Jeff follows the robot back into the corridor. It comes to a large room where several of these robots are located. It is a storage and repair area for the robots. These robots serve several functions throughout the building, from delivering mail to bringing food to employees. Looking around the white room, Jeff can see several work benches and spare parts stacked all around. He also finds the way out. Walking over to one of four doors that lead into this room, Jeff tries to open it. Looking down, he sees the access box that requires an I.D. card to be inserted. Security is needed to leave this room to prevent anyone from walking out with robot parts, machinery or tools. Jeff was never in this room. He didn't know if he was ever given any access to it. He tries his card.

NOT AUTHORIZED FOR ACCESS

The words flash in red letters from the box. Just to be sure, he tries the other three doors as well. He gets the same response. Picking up several flashlights from the work benches, he hurries back into the hallway behind the cells.

"Okay gentlemen, I have a way out," he says to the officers. "But it's not going to be easy."

Jeff explains how they will have to crawl into the duct work via the first cell.

"Get everybody from the other cells and bring them to the front cell, but don't put them in yet. Keep them outside. We'll bring them in one at a time, just in case we get caught."

As Caleb, Richard and Jason began pulling people out of the cells, Jeff goes back inside and fixes the beds to make it look like someone is still there. Opening the back door to the first cell, Jeff crawls in.

"It's him mommy. He came back for us!" whispers an excited little girl into her mother's ear. "Mommy he came back."

Looking up, the woman grabs her two children and pulls them close.

"Did you come back for us?"

"Yes, I did. It's not going to be easy though. Can you walk?"

"Barely," she says sadly.

"Can you Crawl?"

"That I can do," she answers hopefully.

"Great. Then you're all set." Jeff smiles at her.

Looking out, he can see the water tank. "All those years down the tubes," he thinks. Looking up, he can see the panel still open which leads through the tote board and into the ductwork.

"Here's what you do. We're going to lift you up into the duct. You crawl until you see overhead lights. Here." He hands them a flashlight. "The overhead lights may not be on, but you just keep crawling until you see lights hanging down from the top of the duct. When you get there, stop and wait for the rest of us. And remember, be extremely quiet. This is very important. No noise."

Jeff explains to the entire group what they will be doing. He stresses the importance of being quiet and the importance of following his directions closely.

"Jeff, Marshall said to," begins Richard.

"I know. I know," Jeff blurts in. "We have no choice. Of these twenty people, only nine are in any kind of capable condition and five of them are children."

"Marshall, I have a feeling Jeff isn't going to take your advice," Pops says after Captain Litchfield excuses himself to the restroom. "I don't see how he can. If those people are being abused as badly as they say, he'll never be able to get them to any safe distance quick enough to avoid getting caught. What are you planning to do about it?" Pops asks, intentionally being very vague.

Pops has a feeling the captain may have left a bug at the table and went to the restroom with the purpose of getting some information through it.

"I'm going to tell them where they are, but

only after I've given Jeff enough time." Picking up the captains hat, Marshall begins speaking to it. "Did you hear that Captain. You can come out of the restroom now. I'm not going to give you any information until the time is right; then I'm going to tell you where to find Montgomery's supplier."

The restroom door opens and Captain Litchfield returns to the table.

"So you boys talk about anything interesting while I was gone?" he asks presumptuously.

"Don't insult our intelligence, captain," says Pops. "We know you, or at least someone in your truck outside, heard our conversation."

"Look, let's get to the point. Time is wasting. You have to tell me their whereabouts now."

"Like I said," Marshall looks down at his watch, "after I've given them enough time, I'll let you know."

"Can you give me an estimate?" asks the captain.

"In another thirty minutes, I'll tell you where the lab is."

Jeff quickly draws diagrams of the duct work

and what they will be facing; he gives a copy to everyone – even the children. It is just a simple line drawing showing where the duct breaks off into four other vents, with one of them dropping straight down.

"Remember, keep going to the right." Bending down, he gathers the children to him. "It's going to get very, very loud in there, and it will sound very, very scary. I don't want you to be afraid, because it's just a bunch of noise trying to scare you, but don't you let it. Okay?"

They all shake their heads and tell Jeff it's okay.

"Okay, Caleb. You're first. When you get to the end, you will have to carry two of the children down the ladder. Remember, eye level rung, slap twice, left foot between the laser and wall, tap three times, then proceed down." Turning to the group, he continues, "Listen up. The five of you who can, are going to have to carry another person. Between you five, and us four, we should be able to get everybody through. Everybody ready?"

"YEAH!" is the collective response.

"Then let's go. And remember, NO noise. None at all if possible."

Climbing up into the vent, with the aid of a second bed which was taken from one of the other cells, Caleb gets up through the opening of the tote board.

"What time do you have, Rich?" asks Jeff.

"Eight thirty Washington time. Why?"

"Everybody's gonna be getting into work soon. We've got to hurry."

"Jeff, I have an idea to get the army out of Tennessee," says Jason. "Let's just call Pops from here and let the army trace the call back."

"It's a great idea," answers Jeff. "It'll work just fine. Once all of you get up into the vent, I'll give you about fifteen minutes to get to the end, then I'll place the call. Jason, when you get up in there, pass the word on to Caleb. Tell him not to begin his decent until nine o'clock sharp." Looking over to Richard he continues, "That should be enough time for all of you to be close to position."

"Good morning Mr. Calvitch," says the security guard at the front gate. "How are you doing this fine morning."

And a fine morning it is. There is a crispness in the air and the weather is cool. The sun is bright and warm against your face and there is not a cloud in the sky.

"I'm doing just fine, Anthony. How about yourself?"

"I'm just great. Say, what happened here last night? Did you ever catch Jeff? I know we had this whole place shutdown tight and he didn't come out through here."

"Umm, Jeff, yes." David breathes a heavy sigh. "Jeff, yes we did take care of that and you're right. He didn't get out through here." David's expression turns to sadness.

"I'm sorry, sir. I didn't mean to bring you down."

"No, it's all right. I just...well. I should be getting inside. I'll talk to you tomorrow, Anthony. You have a good day."

"You do the same, Mr. Calvitch. You do the same," he says as he opens the gate and allows David to drive through.

Chapter XXIII

"Well! It's eleven o'clock. Where is the lab?" questions Captain Litchfield sternly.

"You're not going to believe me, but it's in Washington state," answers Marshall. "A town called Bridge something."

"Bridgeport," offers Pops.

"Yeah, Bridgeport. Bridgeport, Washington."

"My patience is getting very thin, Mr. Winston. I don't like playing games."

"And neither do I, Mr. Litchfield; so I suggest you get your boys over there and get my people back."

They are interrupted by a voice over the radio.

"Excuse me," Marshall says, picking up his radio. "Go ahead."

"This is Tommy, over here at the store."

"Yes."

"This phone is ringing over here. Should I pick it up?"

Pops' and Marshall's eyes meet as they stare at each other. It is only for a moment, but it is a solid stare.

"Well, Mr. Winston? If you're not playing games, let the boy answer it; or do you realize that if you do, we'll trace the call?"

Turning to John, Marshall looks at him sharply, then his whole facial expression brightens.

"Now why didn't I think of that? If it is him, this will be perfect." Picking up his radio again he says, "Tommy, pick it up, quick, and leave your radio button in so we can hear you."

"No need," says John as he pulls a radio from his pocket.

"Forget the radio part Tom, just answer that phone," says Marshall.

"Hello?"

"Hi. This is Jeff. Is Marshall there?"

"He's not here, but I can relay a message by radio."

"Okay, good. I just wanted to let him know that we are on our way. We can't get out the original way we planned, but we do have an alternative. Could you ask him if he thinks it advisable to use it?"

"Marshall, this is Tommy. Jeff is on the phone

and he wants to know if you think it would be okay if they use an alternate way out."

"I read you Tom. Just to let you know, I can hear both sides of the conversation. This line is tapped and being traced."

"10-4."

"Tell Jeff that he has got to get those people out of there and that he will have to use whatever means he has at his disposal."

"10-4. I'll tell him now."

As the conversation continues, an M.P. walks into the restaurant. "We've got it, Captain. It's over in Bridgeport, Washington, just like he said."

Turning off his little radio, Captain John Litchfield gets up to leave.

"Thank you, Sheriff. Sorry I doubted you. Good day gentlemen. I will be back in touch."

Captain Litchfield leaves and, on his way out, orders all his men to leave. He immediately has headquarters dispatch men from Washington over to the location the phone trace indicated.

"Let's get back to the store. Those people are going to need some help when they get here. Jesse, check please," Marshall says while gathering his things.

Rich is the last to go up. After doing so, he realizes Jeff will have to move the beds back from under the opening to avoid being caught. Taking off his belt, he calls for the belt from the man in front of him and hooks them together. Strapping the belts onto one of the braces holding the tote board in place, Rich lets the other end hang down into the cell.

"Okay, thanks. Tell Marshall we'll be seeing him soon," Jeff realizes enough time has elapsed for the call to be traced.

He puts the phone down on the workbench and goes back into the hallway behind the cells. He reaches the first cell and goes in. The door latches behind him. Jeff pauses and stares at the door for a moment, knowing that he will not be able to go back that way anymore. The only way out now is up into the ducts. Walking over to the tote board, he reaches for the belts hanging from within. He is startled by the site of the double doors that lead into the cell area as they fling open. He ducks back out of sight.

"Good morning, Mr. Calvitch," says Betty the receptionist. Her bright smile warms David's heart a little and his countenance begins to rise.

"Good morning, Betty. Your smile is always a welcome sight for me. You never fail to bring me into a good mood."

"Thank you sir."

"I saw Arthur's car in the lot, so would you do me the favor of paging him and telling him to meet me in my office, pronto?"

"Sure thing, hold on." She dials a number into the phone.

Jeff is hiding as best as he can under one of the beds in the cell. He feels tense as he sees a man putting his I.D. card into the slot of the main door. With a click, it begins to open.

"Paging Mr. Montgomery, paging Mr. Montgomery. Arthur, please report to Mr. Calvitch's office, pronto. Please report to Mr. Calvitch's office immediately."

"UGH. What's that old man want now."

Jeff hears only the fading footsteps as the figure turns to leave. The sound is punctuated with the low thump and click of the large security door tightly closing.

"Thanks Betty. You really are a sweetheart."

"Thank you Mr. Calvitch. Here are your messages."

"Thanks Betty. I'll see you later," he says, accepting his messages and walking off into the building.

"Caleb, I'm getting scared!" says one of the little girls.

"Me too!" pouts the other.

"It's okay. It's really okay to be scared. Just remember, nothing is going to hurt you here. It's just going to get really, really loud," Caleb says, trying to comfort the two young girls. "Don't forget, all brave people get scared. They just won't let it stop them."

They are sliding further into the duct and nearing the exit chamber. The noise level continues increasing, growing ever louder.

"Man, Jeff wasn't kidding when he said it was going to get loud," Caleb thinks to himself.

The bodies stretch out into the duct work. Those who can, are pushing along those who cannot move under their own power.

"Can you hold onto the feet of the lady in front of you?" Jason asks one of the nearly paralyzed men.

"I think I can, just barely."

"Okay, you hold on to her feet as she crosses the hole and that will stretch you across. Got it?"

"Okay, let's give it a shot."

Gripping the feet of the lady in front of him the man slowly slides over the hole.

"Okay hold on!" yells Jason, as quietly as possible. "Wait! Hold on!"

"Whoa!" yells the man as his head falls into the hole followed by his limp arms and hands. His head bangs into the duct work, sending a thundering rumble through-out the vent. "Help me! Don't let me go!"

"Don't worry, I've got you."

After sliding the man back into the vent, Jason turns the man on his side and slides up alongside him. Jason makes himself into a human bridge to get the man over the gaping hole beneath them. Safely on the other side, they all continue on into the duct.

The children begin crying now as the sound has become defining. Caleb is the first to reach the ladder and climbs onto it. Prying the children away from their mother, Caleb begins his decent.

"Don't listen to that voice," he thinks. "Just do what Jeff said."

JUMP OR TURN BACK! JUMP OR TURN BACK! JUMP OR TURN BACK...

The phrase is echoing through the tunnel. Reaching the lasers, the children are trying to climb back up to their mother. Caleb quickly slaps the rung twice and kicks the wall three times and grabs hold of the girls and starts down the ladder. Once through the lasers and down another ten feet, doors close above him and below him.

"I guess I'm next," the girl's mother mutters.

Grabbing the top rung, she pulls herself over the ledge. Her body swings out into the tunnel and slams back up against the ladder. Having only a limited use of her legs, she lowers herself down using her hands. Reaching the rung, she slaps it twice and pulls herself up enough to free her feet from the rung just above the lasers. Letting her leg dangle, she twists her body, causing her leg to swing. Grunting with each swing and kick, she counts to three, then proceeds down. Going through the now harmless beams of light, she proceeds down about 10 more feet. Just about to reach the bottom step, she is startled by doors above and below closing around her.

Not seeing her children, nor the officer, she grows frightened. With a bright flash of light, she too is gone.

"There's the light!" Marshall says excitedly. "He got the message."

Tommy is watching as a light, so powerful it pales the sunshine, emerges from the light pole. He sees, what looks like, three figures suspended in mid-air suddenly fall to the ground. It is Caleb with two children. Tommy dashes over to help them as Caleb gets up and moves himself and the children to the side. The light flashes again, and there is their mother. They are all coming through.

Jeff watches as he sees the double doors swing closed. He comes out from under the bed and reaches for the belt again, watching the door. As he pulls himself off the floor, the doors burst open one more time. Dropping to the floor, he bolts across the room and back under the bed. With a click, he hears the security door open. From his vantage point, he is able to see and hear two people working. They appear to be doing some programming at the terminal, just outside his cell. Remembering the belt hanging down, Jeff grows concerned of his being spotted.

"Okay gentlemen, let's go get him. I just received word from a Captain Litchfield's office. They've confirmed and targeted the location of Montgomery's connection. Let's go get him," Joshua repeats, with an elated smile.

"Yes, I'd love to....Sure, I can meet you at the country club in about an hour."

Marcus Montgomery's office door slowly opens. Marcus finds himself looking directly into the eyes of several M.P.'s.

"Let me get back to you on this...Yes, I've gotta go now." Putting down the phone he inquires: "Can I help you and, what is the meaning of entering an officer's office unannounced?"

"Sergeant Marcus Montgomery?"

"Yes?"

"You are hereby placed under arrest," Joshua states, snapping open an official arrest warrant and smiling proudly from ear to ear. "We have already picked up your friend, David Calvitch, and he didn't have too many nice things to say about you."

"Calvitch, I don't know any Calvitch," he retorts as two M.P.'s walk over and began putting him in handcuffs. "I'm telling you, you've got the wrong guy. I don't know any Calvitch," he persists.

"Oh, well, that's okay, 'cause he knows you. He told us all about your deal with Iraq."

Marcus suddenly stops squirming.

"He told us about the forty million you're getting for this deal. He said he wasn't going to say a word, if you would have just split the profits 50-50."

"I was splitting it 50-50, that greedy, no good two-timer was trying to milk more than that out of me. He wanted me to use part of my money to pay for the production costs as well, and it wasn't forty million, it was only twenty million."

Marcus is running off at the mouth.

"Well, if you tell us your side of the story, we might be able to cut you a deal. If not, we'll just have to take his word for it."

Not realizing he is being set up, Marcus agrees to make a statement. Trying to get himself in the clear, he gives up everything he knows about David Calvitch's operation, and, how they were going to make their fortunes.

"I guess David's 'Get Lost' device don't work that well after all," snaps Marcus.

"What 'Get Lost' device?"

This is great for the prosecution. They are getting all the information they need, plus learning about technology which could be confiscated for use by the U.S. government. This kind of technology would be a great asset for law enforcement; but possibly deadly, if it ended up in the wrong hands, as it was perilously close to doing.

"Arthur, thanks for coming up so quickly. I know how eager you are to get to work on your projects; but I wanted to clear the air a little between us before you went on." David is being concerned. "I just don't want anything to hamper our friendship."

"More like hamper your profits."

Arthur is being very cavalier.

"Look. I'm trying to smooth things out between us and patch things up. I don't need any of your off the cuff remarks."

"Mr. Calvitch. Security is on line two for you. He said it's urgent," reports a voice through the intercom in David's office.

"Hold on while I get this." David reaches for the phone. "Calvitch here. What's going on?"

"I don't know, but I think we have bad trouble. The guard at the front gate just spotted several army helicopters coming this way and at least six army trucks coming up the road."

There is silence.

"Mr. Calvitch? Are you there?"

"Yes, I'm here."

"I've also got some security violations coming from the robotics center. Someone must have gotten locked inside. They tried their card but, of course, it wouldn't let them out."

"Who was it?"

"Let me see. It was," David can hear the security officer rustling papers in the background. "Here it is. It was Jeff Colt."

David's eyes grow happy for a moment. He is glad Jeff wasn't killed; however, his joy quickly turns to solace.

"Sir, you're not going to like this. The army just went through the front gate and I mean literately through the front gate."

"Sound the alarm. I want everyone out of this building, NOW!" David turns to Arthur. "The army is here. It looks like your father turned us in."

A loud pulsating alarm irritatingly signals. Everyone quickly gets up and begins to leave the building.

As the trucks and troops approach, they find there is not going to be a fight. They approach the, 70 or so, workers making their way to the green outside the front door.

Chapter XXIV

"Where's Jeff?" exclaims Virginia. "Where's Jeff?"

It has been 15 minutes since Richard arrived. He was the last one in line to go through the transmitter.

"Don't worry. He was right behind us. I'm sure he's just taking care of a few lose ends. Don't worry. He'll be all right," assures Richard.

Jeff hears the alarm and sees this as his chance to get out. The two people inside the cell area make their way out of the building. Jeff grabs the belt and begins pulling himself up into the tote board. Just about to grab the second belt, the first one gives way. Jeff comes crashing down onto the floor, hitting his head hard. He lay there unconscious, unaware of the noise and commotion going on around him. Opening his eyes, he sees the room, blurry and spinning. He can't move. He closes his eyes and again falls back into unconsciousness.

"We've gotta get out of here, come on!" Arthur

shouts; jumping excitedly.

He beckons David to follow. David does not.

"You go. I'm going to stay right here."

Arthur knows something is up.

"Then I'm staying here with you."

"Oh, all right," David says with disgust. "Let me get this data secure first, then I'll take you with me."

David turns to the computer on his desk and begins opening files. He opens a program called security, then opens a file called 'Special' which is in the security file. He enters the password for this screen and it gives him a list of names. The screen title is:

```
EMERGENCY     DUCT     LASER     CUTOFF
AUTHORIZED USERS
```

David mouse's down to the name Arthur Montgomery and presses delete. After confirming the name deletion, David updates the file and brings it online. Opening to a list of files, he selects several to be backed up to a removable disk, then deletes them after they're backed up.

"Come on, we haven't got all day. They're coming in," Arthur quips frantically.

"They're not coming in. Those outside doors

should be sealed down by now. The only way in now is to blast."

David is right. Several employees had to dive under the closing steel door. It is like a fortress. What David does not realize is that this commanding officer is not afraid to use fire power. The whole building trembles as an ear shattering explosion sears through it.

"They're blasting! THEY'RE BLASTING! We've got to get out of here!" yells Arthur.

"No, not just yet. I've got another thing or two to set here."

David knows they will get in. It is just a matter of time.

BOOOM!

Another ear splitting blast sounds through the hallways of the now nearly vacant building.

"Okay. I've got the information on disk."

David goes to his closet and pulls out a small radio controlled plane and puts the disk inside. Pulling the grandfather clock out from the corner of his office, a small chute is exposed. He drops the glider into the chute. Looking out through his window, he can see the glider sail down the mountain and out of sight.

BOOOM!

This time, the blast is louder than all the previous blasts. It echoes through the halls faster and more intensely than all the rest. They know the army got through, or at least, managed to put a large hole into the steel door. It is now just a matter of moments before the soldiers file in.

"Quick, we can get out through the duct work," says David.

"What and get caught at the base of the mountain? You're nuts!" retorts Arthur.

"Don't be foolish. Remember, I have an Ion Pulse Transmitter set up down there. We can use it to get clear of this state and set-up our alibis. Now come on."

The two men hurry out of David's office.

"Where are you going?" asks Arthur. "The escape duct is this way."

"We have to go upstairs first and startup the transmitter."

"Forget it. I'm not taking the chance. I'm

going through the duct and coming out at the base of the mountain," says Arthur, knowing full well he had started the transmitter the night before.

"You fool!" snaps David. "They'll find you in the mountain. They'll send out search dogs after you!"

"You're the fool. That transmitter will send you right to Tennessee where Jeff's remains were sent. Plus we'll never get back down here in time to get into the ducts before the Army gets here. Now who's the fool?"

BAAAAM!

Another blast rips through the building. Arthur runs off into the direction of the holding cells to go up into the duct work, not knowing of the entrance near David's office. David runs upstairs to the Ion Pulse Transmitter to start it. On his way, he realizes he might not make it back to the duct. He realizes he just might get caught. Stopping at a desk, he accesses his files from this remote computer. He accesses a program called 'DOOMSDAY.' He enters the password and receives the following dialog:

COMMENCING WITH DOOMSDAY DESTRUCTION

As he continues on to the Ion Pulse Transmitter room, all the functioning robots from the robotic center instantaneously come to life. Of the twelve that exist, only eight are in working order. These split up into groups of two and go to each of the four doors leading out of the center. Facing the doors, as if in some kind of showdown, they each began firing lasers. The shots are not fired in some hap-hazard way. They specifically target the hinges and locks. Once melted through, the robots ram the doors, knocking them over, allowing them to traverse through. Part of David Calvitch's business is legitimate. He isn't worried about those legitimate projects being found. No time would be wasted on destroying the information on those projects. As the robots make their way out of the center, they go into four different directions. Two make their way to David's office, two go into Arthur's office, two into Jeff's office and two depart beyond the cells and stand in front of the water tank.

David finally reaches the Ion transmitter room. Desperately trying to open the door, he can hear the soldiers approaching. Upon opening the door, he rushes into the room, slams the door shut behind him and runs behind the console; only to be greeted by a message showing four specimens were received this morning at five minutes past eight o'clock.

"Why that dirty double crosser," he says slowly.

"FREEZE! GET YOUR HANDS IN THE

AIR."

Looking out beyond the window in the door, David sees several soldiers. He knows the glass is bullet proof, but he also knows there is no way it will survive a blast from the missile launcher staring him in the face.

Discreetly opening the door, he calmly states, "Gentlemen. There are laser equipped robots heading this way. They will shoot to kill anyone they see in their path, so may I suggest we just quickly leave."

Facing into David's office, the robots are firing on everything in sight. Nothing is left in one piece. Everything in the room has been reduced to small chips and pieces. These two robots then face each other and engage their lasers on each other, causing one another to explode into balls of fire, setting the room aflame.

Bursting through the double doors, Arthur runs into the cell holding area. He can see two robots poised in front of the 150 foot tall glass water tank. Looking at their front light panel one of four indicators is lit. Arthur knows this means one set of robots has completed its task. Once three of those lights are lit, this fourth set of robots will begin their task. Just before looking away, he sees a second set of lights begin to glow.

Shoving his card into the slot, he enters the cell area and heads to the first cell. Unlocking the door, he sees Jeff's body lying on the floor. He pauses for a moment, then hurries inside. Grabbing beds from the other cells, he makes a scaffold and stations himself to climb into the tote board.

"I don't know what you did with my specimens, but if they went out this way, I'll find them." He begins to climb the beds. "You loved your project so much, you chump. I guess it's only fitting I let you die with it," he laughs out loud. "I spit on your grave."

Arthur sprays spit into Jeff's face several times and dashes up into the duct work, laughing. Moving as quickly as he can, he hurries off into the dark.

Two robots emerge from Jeff's office. Nothing in the room can be identified. Everything is completely destroyed. Jeff's office is closest to the transmitter. It is the function of these two robots to finish off the transmitter after demolishing Jeff's office.

Arthur enters the loud tunnel and begins down the ladder. Reaching the dark panel on the wall he presses his I.D. badge to it, then looks directly into it. With the deadening sound of 'JUMP OR TURN BACK' pounding his ears, he slowly puts his foot into the path of the lasers. They instantly burn the tip of his shoe. With a stunned look on his face, he quickly rushes back up the ladder; realizing David removed his code from this exit. He will not be able to get out this way. He knows he has got to get out of there before the robots destroy the water tank. These ducts will become flooded and he will be trapped.

Jeff's eyes pop open. The cold spray from Arthur's spit was just enough to startle his body into semi-consciousness. He slowly lifts himself up to a standing position, wiping the spit off his face. Clutching his head, he falls to the floor. Struggling, he manages to stumble over to the eye wash sink and floods his head with water. Feeling stronger, he looks back over to the task in front of him. He must get into the duct and out of this place. As he staggers back, he can see the stacked beds under the tote board. He know right then that someone else has gone out this way. It doesn't matter, at least not now. He just has to get back to Tennessee.

"Here they come gentlemen. May I suggest we duck into this office until they get past us?" says David to the soldiers who are escorting him out.

"What are you talking about?" quips one of them as a bolt comes firing out from the front of one robot, knocking the gun out of his hand. Startled, he yells: "HIT THE DECK!"

The soldiers scatter, darting into the closest

offices they can find. The robots go by them without further incident. The robots must complete their mission.

"You two, take him outside. You two come with me and bring that missile launcher," the commander barks out his orders.

"Let me warn you gentlemen. There is going to be a flood down here, so you had better get out soon!"

"Get him out of here!"

The soldiers follow the robots as they go toward the Ion transmission room. Stationing themselves and taking aim, the robots prepare to fire.

"Stop them things. I don't want that computer destroyed."

Aiming and firing, the soldier with the missile launcher fires at the first of the two robots. The blast shatters them both and sends the soldiers back. The doors and walls blow over and scatter into the small computer room, destroying the glass Ion chamber. Flying at the table where the computers console sits, the door lands and becomes a shield for it, protecting it from the falling debris. Now that they are destroyed, the robots are no longer sending a signal back to the robots in front of the water tank.

Climbing the beds, Jeff watches as a third set of lights illuminate on the two robots standing in front of the water tower.

"I got to get out of here!" he stutters while taking a deep breath.

Jeff then climbs the make-shift scaffold and pulls himself up into the duct work.

Aiming their lasers at nearly the same spot, the robots begin firing. The cool water behind the glass helps delay the inevitable.

Jeff pulls himself along as quickly as he can with a renewed vitality. Approaching the spot with the lighted duct work, Jeff sees Arthur pass by in front of him. Arthur is going back the other way. He is going to have to exit at the base of the mountain. Jeff waits a few seconds after Arthur passes before going on. He wants to wait longer, but knows there is no time.

As the two robots continue firing on the water tank, the glass begins to turn white. Then it happens. A small flow of water shoots straight out of a hole about a half inch in diameter, knocking one of the robots clear across the room. It only takes a second after that for the pressure to cause that small hole to shatter the entire structure. It is an incredible sight to witness. A giant wall of water, one hundred fifty feet high, comes dropping down in one fell swoop, showing no mercy for anything in its path. The glass walls of the holding cells are smashed to pieces. As the glass shards from the 150 foot wall go sailing, they are embedding themselves into the steel structure holding the floor. The steel girders of the floor crane began to bend and warp. The double doors are blown off their hinges as the water begins to flood into the building. Relentlessly surging forward, the massive flood of water continues on its path of destruction.

Jeff is moving as fast as he can. He hears the water coming up into the vents. Arthur lets out a scream as he picks up his pace, scurrying towards the exit door of the duct. They both feel the pressure as the wind begins to kick up in the ductwork. Jeff makes it to the ladder and goes down as fast as he is able. The water starts pouring down over his head. Exhausted, Jeff slaps the rung, as best as he can, twice, and kicks his foot into the six inch space. He starts down and the laser burns a hole in his shoe. He tries it again. It still doesn't work. The water is pouring down and hitting the rung. Jeff realizes the water hitting the rung is disrupting the sequence of the two slaps and three kicks.

Arthur is crawling faster than ever. He feels water touch his feet. Looking back for a brief second and before he can even let out a yell, a wall of water envelopes him. He tries to withstand it, but to no avail. It carries him off. He is close to the exit. He saw it just before being engulfed by the water.

Jeff has to find his way out. More water is coming down. He can hear the rage of the flood getting closer. He has to block the water from hitting that one specific rung. Climbing up a little, he protects the rung with his body and slaps it twice. The water comes down so fiercely it knocks him from the ladder. Jeff catches himself just before hitting the lasers. His hand never leaving the ladder. He frantically kicks the spot three times. Putting his foot barely into the lights, it doesn't burn. He proceeds down. Going through the beams of light, he enters the next room. He climbs down quickly. About to reach the last rung, a wall of water floods the tunnel, entombing him. Almost unconscious, he looks up and sees the door close above him. Just before the bright flash of light overtakes him, he can see the door that is underneath him has already closed; sealing him in.

With intense speed, Arthur sees the exit door rushing in upon him. The water slams him into the door with such force it brakes his arm and three ribs. Arthur feels the pain and hears his bones crack. The door bursts open and spews Arthur out onto the side of the mountain.

From the sky, a chopper spots Arthur flowing down the mountain with the river of water. They see a window in the side of the mountain get blown out, followed by a flood of water. From the air can be seen several rivers bleeding out of the sides of the mountain. These rivers carried with them debris from all areas and offices located on the lower floors.

Inside, the water rises up to the Ion transmitter room and flows in. The console displays the following message, as water begins infiltrating the room:

```
MESSAGE FROM SYSTEM:
            TRANSMISSION IN PROCESS
```

As the water begins to rise in the room, electronics begin to short circuit and sparks begin to fly. Another message starts scrolling across the screen, never to be seen. A surge of water douses the room and everything goes black.

Chapter XXV

"David Calvitch. I hereby place you under arrest, for conspiracy to sell unauthorized technology to foreign countries. We have your friend Montgomery and he already spilled his guts. You can either have your turn, or we'll just have to take his story as gold!"

"I have nothing to say to you."

"Suite yourself. Take him away boys. I want a team out here to wipe up this mess. This place is dirtying up this beautiful mountain. Chopper one, did you get him?"

"Yes, sir. We just picked him up out of a tree. He's got some broken ribs, but he's gonna live."

"10-4. Okay everybody, shows over. It's time to file for unemployment. Chaskin, get your men in here now. I don't want this cleanup to take forever. Make sure you try to save any of the technology you can."

"He should have been here by now," says a

very saddened Virginia. "He should have been here by now."

"He's gonna make it. Even if he doesn't come here, he'll be picked up by the army," says Rich, trying to console her.

With that, the light flashes down from the light pole. This time it is brighter than it has ever been. The light fixture is humming and crackling. As the beam of light goes out, the top of the pole can be seen glowing. This receiver was never designed to handle this much information and it can't dissipate the heat quickly enough. Everyone watches as they see the shape of a man suspended in the air, suspended in what looks like water, begin to form. With another flash of light, the top of the light pole blows off and shoots up into the air like a rocket. Water and mud fly everywhere as a ten foot column of water crashes onto the ground. There lay a soaking, hurting, Jeff Colt. Unable to contain herself, Virginia rushes to his side.

"Okay, Pops, send a team over to that radio station and dismantle that amplifier. I'm going to get a team over here to tear up this spot and pull out what ever device is under that curb. Jeff, you all right?"

"Yes. I'm fine now," he says coughing. "I don't think you'll have to worry about that device any longer."

"Why's that?" asks Pops.

"Calvitch destroyed all the technology. He set up a type of self-destruct system for the entire lab, just in case he was ever caught. That's where all this water came from. This was the final blow to the laboratory."

"Well, just to be sure, I'm going to have all that stuff dismantled anyway," says Marshall with a tone of disbelief.

"I don't believe it....Captain, Sir, did you see that?" asks a perplexed soldier, peering through his binoculars, from his vantage point atop a hill facing the rear of the store. "Captain, Sir, did you see that?" he asks again.

As the Captain faces the scene, another soldier walks up from behind.

"Captain, Sir. I've just received word from Special Agent Joshua Schaffer. He says Mr. Calvitch and both of the Montgomerys are in custody."

"Thank you, private," comes the reply from the motionless, staring figure.

"He also said to tell you it appears the lab has been destroyed. He doesn't think they will be able to get anything much from it."

"Thank you again, private. If there is nothing else, you are dismissed." He continues staring.

"That was the wildest thing I've ever seen.

Did you see it Captain, Sir?"

Having decided in his own mind that the world is just not ready for this kind of technology, Captain John Litchfield decides that no one saw anything.

"No. I did not see anything."

"Sir, it was..."

"I did not see anything, and neither did you, private. Do I make myself clear?"

"Yes, sir."

"What you just saw, never happened. It was just an illusion. You will tell no one."

The trial went swiftly. Because of the nature of the crime and all the evidence stacked up against them, David Calvitch, Marcus Montgomery and Arthur Montgomery were found guilty of selling, and conspiring to sell, unauthorized technology to a foreign country. They were each given twenty five year sentences for their treason in a state prison with no chance of parole.

There were no charges of kidnapping brought against them as all the victims were rescued and wanted to stay as far away from the proceedings as possible.

The employees were all found 'not guilty' but were put on probation. They are not allowed to work in their chosen field for a minimum of five years and are not allowed to work for, as partners for nor as employees of, the same firm for a minimum of three years.

"Mr. Calvitch, you have a visitor," calls a guard to David who is reclining in his cell.

"Me? Well isn't that a pleasant surprise."

As the guard accompanies David to the visitors room he tells him he has ten minutes. Walking into the room, David's eyes open wide and begin to dance. He cannot contain the smile that tries to hold back his tears of joy.

"It's so good to see you, David," says a female voice from beyond the partition separating the two.

"It's wonderful to see you."

"I brought you a present. The guard will be bringing it over just as soon as he checks it out. I put fresh batteries in it for you."

"Oh, how sweet of you." Gazing into her eyes he softly says: "I do miss you so."

"I know. I feel it too."

"Here you go," a harsh voice hands David a small brown paper bag.

"Thank you," he says without removing his eyes from the figure in front of him.

Peering into the bag, he stares puzzled at its contents. Curiously, he looks up to the woman in front of him.

"I found your airplane."

Hearing that, David smiles widely as he pulls the contents out of the bag. A small black box with a cord hanging out of it.

"I've had people working on it for some time now, so it won't be too much longer," the sweet elderly voice says. "I can't wait to be with you again, so don't forget to keep it turned on. Those batteries won't be strong enough, so make sure you plug it in. Remember: Always keep your radio tuned to 103.3"

Clicking the radio on, David and Elizabeth softly hear one of their favorite songs:

"I hope I will see you tomorrow...I hope you will see me today ....I hope to be the one to see you when the morning sun....rises up and caresses your face...I hope you will be here tomorrow...Then I'll hope to have another day...And when that day is gone I'll pray to have another one...Up until my dying day..."

"I love you Mrs. Calvitch," says David, as he smiles lovingly again, holding up his radio. "I really, really do."

The End.........maybe

<u>Works Cited</u>

99 Bottles Of Bear – Music & Lyrics by: Unknown, as made popular by: everyone!

Don't Give Up On Us Baby – Music & Lyrics by: Tony Macaulay, as made popular by: David Soul

Don't Take The Girl – Music & Lyrics by: Craig Martin & Larry W. Johnson, as made popular by: Tim McGraw

I Hope – Music & Lyrics by: David R. Mohr, as made popular by: David R. Mohr

Leave Without A Trace – Music & Lyrics by: David Pirner, as made popular by: Soul Asylum

Something – Music & Lyrics by: George Harrison, as made popular by: The Beatles

Surrender – Music & Lyrics by: Rick Nielsen, as made popular by: Cheap Trick

Third Time Lucky – Music & Lyrics by: Dave Peverett, as made popular by: Foghat

When The Children Cry – Music & Lyrics by: Vito Bratta & Mike Tramp, as made popular by: White Lion

Wishful Thinking – Music & Lyrics by: David R. Mohr, as made popular by: David R. Mohr

About The Author

- A Little About Me -

I've been a creative person for as long as I can remember. I still think of the first song I ever wrote - it was about a red robin. One day, I'll remember enough of it to write it down again, just for posterity.

My first introduction into music was when I remember hearing the radio and the DJ's. I just knew: "That's what I want to do!" I began drum lessons when in 3rd grade, but finances prohibited my continuing them and definitely prohibited getting any kind of "real" drum kit. I settled for a recorder and learned a little about music with it.

Years went by and I never had, nor made, the opportunity to pursue my real desire. Finally at about 20, I hooked up with a few guys and the band "Don't Walk was formed. As time went by, we got really good! We played some parties, some picnics and the like, but mostly jammed on the weekend and every other spare minute we could find. After a few years, we worked on a few originals, but never were able to complete them. As the old song goes...."Those wedding bells are breaking up that old gang of mine." We actually got down on our very primitive equipment a few cover songs. Unfortunately the recordings really don't do "Don't Walk" justice, but it's all I've got from a time gone past. You can visit my web page to hear the recordings.

- What I've Done -

♪ Performed as Disk Jockey on WZTA 94.9's Amateur Hour.
♪ Broadcast as an on-air personality for WKPX with my own 4 hr show on Saturday morning's.
♪ Run board for live stage performances and public appearances.
♪ Appear as Master-of-Ceremonies for weddings.
♪ Perform as Disk Jockey at weddings, parties, functions, etc.
♪ Host Karaoke shows.
♪ Perform as lead singer in local bands.

♪ Guest performer for bands at various venues.
♪ Written numerous songs in Country, Rock, Pop, AC, Dance, Metal, Rock genres
♪ Written novels & screen plays
♪ Self-taught guitar player

- Where I Am - Where I'm Going -

From these beginnings, the seeds of creativity had been sown and have begun to flower. After Don't Walk disbanded, I continued on with my music and creativity. I've worked with a number of musicians over the years on various projects and have performed at many live events. I have written numerous songs that are just now emerging into the public eye; hopefully to be performed by everyone at one time or another. I am currently working on other novels, along with other writing projects. If you need some copy or other creative material, please feel free to call. All original production work on my pages are for hire. Drop me a note for details. My goals are set, and the course has been laid out. My intent is to be able to provide songs for use in all facets and genres of music; and for my stories to be read and made into movies for the big and small screens. Please visit my pages often, as they will continually be updated with new material, content and noteworthy items.

The Mohr intimate story...

David Robert Mohr was born in New Haven Connecticut in July of 1962. Being interested in music and stage from a very young age, David has performed on stage and with bands first starting in 4th grade where he had the lead role in the play: The Crab That Played With The Sea. David assisted the teacher in creating and arranging several of the songs used in the play.

David wrote his first song in the 3rd grade about a robin. The inspiration for the song came after hearing a song from a then famous film. His love moved more toward the musical side of the entertainment world from that point on. He joined a drum group being offered by the local Fire department while living in East Haven, but was unable to continue any of the lessons due to financial set-backs. David continued to teach himself the drums, using anything he could find, including phone books and oatmeal containers.

Continuing to cultivate his love for music, David continued delving deeper into songs; analyzing their lyrics, melodies, backing vocals, harmonies & instrumentation. Learning dozens of songs and following the charts, he found he was able to pick new songs that would be hits.

As life would have it, many years passed before he was able to connect with the right people. Forming a band called "Don't Walk" David was the lead singer and drummer. The band went on to cover many songs by many artists; paving the way for development of his talent. As years passed, David found himself in and out of a few bands looking for the right combination. During this time, he found himself doing more and more writing, but not being able to put his songs to music. Not finding help with the musicians surrounding him, David decided it was time to branch off on his own and learn an instrument other than the percussive ones while continuing to improve his voice.

During a personal tragedy, David found himself out in Texas for a short time where he re-connected with an old band mate. They started another band where David was again the drummer and lead singer. After much convincing, encouragement & the gift of a guitar (and a promise to learn to play it) from that ole band mate, David left the drum kit and set out to learn the guitar; thus making it possible for him to put music to the lyrics he has been creating.

In addition to writing novels, short stories, scripts for commercials, songs, poems and compositions, David also writes, directs, produces and stars in music videos he creates for his songs. David also lends his voice where possible in book reading and audio publications. David continues to showcase his talent throughout the cities in which he lives and travels. He can always be found with a song in his heart and a tune echoing through his lips.

David has performed as a DJ on WZTA & WKPX in Fort Lauderdale, has performed at festivals & venues ranging in size from 2 to 2000 persons.

David maintains internet presence with several different pages and social networks. You can stop by his main artist page at: www.singingdave.com where you'll find some of his original music, original Novels & short stories and more information & links to the many facets of David's creative life.

www.ingramcontent.com/pod-product-compliance
Lightning Source LLC
Chambersburg PA
CBHW062010170626
46813CB00001B/107